Murder at St. Alfanus

by
Todd Vogts

Strategic Book Group

Strategic Book Group
P.O. Box 333
Durham, CT 06422
www.StrategicBookClub.com

ISBN: 978-1-60976-611-5

Book Design: Arlinda Van, Dedicated Business Solutions, Inc.

Dedication

This book is dedicated to my mother, Karen, who instilled within me the love of reading. Also to my father, Steve, who showed me the joy of golf, and to my brother, Troy, who always made sure I never won a round against him.

Acknowledgments

I wouldn't have been able to complete this novel without the help of an amazing group of family and friends. When I first told them I had written the manuscript and had found a publisher, they were almost more excited than I was, if that's even possible. I am grateful for each and every one of them. I want to give special thanks to my friends Jerod Horchem and Travis Schafer. These two helped me proof the novel and get it ready enough to even attempt to send it to a publisher. They both told me when something sounded dumb or just didn't work. They also put up with me bouncing ideas off of them at all hours of the day.

Of course, I also thank everyone who has purchased this book and helped me realize the dream of being a published author. Thank you. It truly means a lot to me.

Yours,

Todd Vogts

PART ONE

Chapter One

A warm breeze was blowing across the course, rustling the leaves of the trees lining either side of the fairway. It was No. 8, a par 5 and 476-yard hole, and it was the longest and straightest hole on the eighteen-hole course that made up the eastern edge of St. Alfanus College.

St. Alfanus was a private, Catholic college located about two miles south and west of Hooks, Texas, which is in Bowie County in the northeast corner of the state.

Tyler Fox surveyed the fairway and looked down at his ball sitting on his tee. It was June 2. The summer sun was beating down on the course, and Tyler's light T-shirt was damp with sweat. He was playing his second round of golf that day. He had finished his first just before lunch. He took a short break for a bite to eat and hit the course again. He had to keep practicing. He was playing golf on a scholarship for St. Alfanus, and the coaches had high expectations for him to win the National Association of Intercollegiate Athletics national championship in the coming spring.

Tyler squared his body up to the ball, bringing the over-sized head of his steel-shafted driver just behind the ball. He took a deep breath.

It was his swing that got him noticed and earned him the scholarship that covered the majority of the $50,000 per year tuition.

His swing was relaxed yet powerful and since he was left handed, relatively rare in the eyes of the scouts. He easily pulled the club face backward away from the ball as he shifted his weight to his back leg. The club head arched over his head as his hips cocked, ready for the second half of the swing. As the club reached the peak of its journey, Tyler straightened his right elbow and swung his hips forward. The club's shaft arched downward, and he shifted his weight to his front leg.

Upon impact with the ball, Tyler brought the club head through the area of impact and allowed the club to wrap around his front shoulder until the club came to rest across his back.

Tyler's eyes, squinting against the bright sun, followed the flight of the ball. It sailed effortlessly down the center of the fairway. When it hit the lush, green grass, it bounced three times before rolling. Tyler estimated he hit it nearly 280 yards.

He bent over and plucked the tee from the grass and placed it behind his ear. He walked over where his golf bag stood perched on its stand. Tyler shoved his driver in and removed his Kansas City Royals baseball cap. He wiped his brow on his forearm before pulling the hat back down over his buzz-cut brown hair. He picked the golf bag up and slung the straps over his shoulder.

Tyler began to walk off the tee box and down the fairway toward his ball when he noticed a glimmer of light out of the corner of his eye. He stopped and turned, facing the source of the light.

There stood a guy of medium height and a stocky build. He had shaggy, curly blond hair spilling out over the top of a red Nike visor. Clutched in one of his hands was a camera with a long lens. The guy was smiling as he waved and walked toward Tyler.

Much like Tyler, the guy had a deep tan, and his teeth were perfectly straight and brilliantly white. His smile was disarming, and his blue eyes made Tyler feel at ease. So Tyler lowered his golf bag from his shoulder and sat it on the ground at his feet.

"Tyler Fox. A five-foot-eight sophomore from Goessel, Kansas. You're here on a golf scholarship and are expected to bring a championship home to our beloved St. Alfanus," the guy said with a drawl that could only mean he was a true Texan.

Tyler cocked an eyebrow and tilted his head back. "Who are you?"

The guy let go of the camera and let the device hang from the strap around his neck. He stepped closer to Tyler and extended a hand.

"My name is Charlie Harrison," the guy said.

"Hello, Charlie," Tyler said, shaking his hand. "So why do you know so much about me? And what's with the camera?"

Charlie smiled. "I'm the editor-in-chief of the campus newspaper, the *Clarion*, and I'm working on a profile of our star golfer."

Tyler nodded and looked around. "Where is he?"

"So you're modest," Charlie commented as he chuckled. "You are the star, and after your quiet yet successful season last year, I hear you are the top pick to win the national championship this year."

"That's what people say, but I try not to listen to all the hype. I don't want to try and live up to the expectations of everyone. I just want to play golf and do well."

Charlie flashed another grin as he pulled a narrow reporter's notebook from his back pocket and fished a pencil from behind his ear and underneath his mop of hair. He began to scribble.

"What are you writing down?" Tyler asked.

Charlie looked up. "That quote. I liked it. I think I'll use it in the story about you. It really shows how down to earth you are."

Tyler shook his head. "Wait. This is an interview?"

"Sure," Charlie said with a shrug. "I got pictures of you practicing, and now I have to talk to you. That's how this whole journalism thing works, but you know that. You've taken a few journalism classes here."

"How do you know that?" Tyler asked.

"First, I am an English major like you, and I have elected to minor in journalism. Therefore, I know the teachers, so they are willing to talk to me about what students are in their classes if I need a little background on an article subject. Secondly, I'm a fifth-year senior. I have developed a few connections over the years. I can get access to almost anything," Charlie said smugly.

Tyler shook his head and looked down at the grass.

"Don't worry, though. None of the teachers had anything bad to say about you. They said you are an exceptional student. Someone who might do well in the journalism world."

Tyler looked back up at Charlie. "Oh really?"

"Yeah," Charlie said, nodding his head. "Which actually brings me to the other reason I am here. See, I'm not just doing a story on you. I also want to recruit you. To work for the *Clarion*. I could use a reporter, especially over the summer. Even though school is out, we still produce the weekly edition, and a lot of my reporters have left for the break."

"I don't know," Tyler said. "I really need to practice. I don't know if I'll have time."

Charlie waved a hand at Tyler. "Don't worry about that. There will be plenty of time. Besides, it's not like you need that much practice. You're an incredible golfer, hence the hype and the story I'm working on."

"I've never written for a paper before," Tyler said, twirling his putter in his golf bag.

"Stick with me," he said, putting a hand on Tyler's shoulder. "I'll teach you the ropes. Maybe the two of us can finally win a Texas Intercollegiate Press Association award. I've been trying since I got here. I would love to get one of those and have that plaque hanging on the office wall."

Tyler looked at Charlie.

Charlie smiled again. "You're right. You need time to think about it. Tell you what, why don't you meet me at the clubhouse after you finish your round. I will interview you for my story, and then we can talk about working at the *Clarion*. If you want."

Tyler nodded. "Okay. That sounds all right."

"Great!" Charlie said. "See you after bit."

With that, Charlie turned around and walked away. He crossed the fairway to the cart path and began a casual stroll toward the course's clubhouse.

Tyler watched him go.

"That was weird," Tyler said to himself.

He picked up his golf bag and once again slung the straps over his shoulder before continuing his journey to his ball.

He found the white, dimpled sphere sitting dead center in the fairway, less than two hundred yards from the pin.

Tyler fished his 8-iron out of his bag and took a swing. The ball flew toward the green, hit and skipped over, coming to a rest in a sand trap.

"Crap," Tyler said to himself.

Tyler Fox never overshot a green from this close. His mind was clearly occupied, and his game didn't improve.

By the time Tyler got to the short par-three No. 14, he worried he might not even finish with an even par, especially since fourteen was the most treacherous hole on the course. It was tucked down at the far south end of the course. It was heavily wooded and doglegged sharp to the left. Even though it was so short, the green couldn't be seen from the tee box.

Some golfers liked to try and go over the trees and drop the ball onto the green from above, but that carried its own risk. There was a pond hidden behind the green, and it swallowed any golf ball that came near it.

Tyler teed up and swung. He sliced. The ball sailed into the trees. Tyler didn't need to hear it splash. He knew the water had it.

Tyler slammed the club head on the ground. He never sliced. His game was going down the tubes, and it was Charlie Harrison's fault.

It wasn't the reporter coming up to interview him that bothered Tyler. He had talked with reporters before. Though he didn't like to admit it, he was a good golfer, and newspapers had shown interest in him before. When he won the state golf championships for the Goessel High School team, he was all over the papers in the area, and he was okay with it.

No, what had Tyler's mind on things other than his golf game was the offer Charlie had made. He hadn't ever told anyone, but he decided to major in English because in the back of his mind he had always thought he would like to work for a newspaper.

His grandfather had done just that. Alfred Sterling had worked at *The Canton Pilot* when Tyler was a youngster. Tyler fondly remembered going to visit his Grandpa Al in nearby Canton and smelling the newsprint and ink that stained his hands and clothes. He wasn't a press operator. He was a reporter, but the *Pilot* was a team effort. Everyone helped with everything, and Grandpa Al enjoyed helping with the delivery, which always left him smudged while he proudly dropped each new issue into the news racks.

Tyler decided to give up his round of golf. He carried his golf bag over to a bench near the No. 14 green and sat down. He pulled a bottle of water out of a pouch in his bag and took a long drink.

He looked around at the most secluded part of the course. The trees closed in around him, and it felt like more than just a golf course. It was his future. Tyler didn't know if he would be able to make the PGA tour, and he wasn't sure what he could do with an English degree. Even though he was only entering his sophomore year, he felt his future pressing in on him.

Maybe he was being melodramatic, but ever since he was a freshman in high school the only tough decision he had had to make was which club to use. Perhaps his sudden anxiety over a simple job offer was warranted. He actually had a decision to make.

Tyler put his bottle of water back in his bag and cut across the course toward the No. 18 tee box. He decided to play the final hole up to the clubhouse in order to ward off any unwanted questions about his game.

He teed off and played out the hole. He got a double bogey, but he barely noticed. He just wanted to get inside and talk to Charlie.

Tyler found the newspaper editor sitting at a table in the corner. He had a bag of popcorn laying on the tabletop so the buttery puffs spilled out for easy access. He was idly tossing handfuls into his mouth as he stared up at a television showing the Golf Channel.

Tyler sat his bag on a rack near the entrance and made his way over to Charlie. Tyler was coming up behind him, but as soon as he got close, Charlie said, "Hello."

"That was quick," he said, without turning around.

Tyler went around to the other side of the table and pulled out a chair. He sat down so he was facing Charlie. "How did you know I was coming? I didn't make a noise, and you weren't even looking at me."

Charlie smiled coolly and tossed more popcorn into his mouth. "I'm that good."

Shaking his head, Tyler protested, "No way. You expect me to believe you are some sort of psychic or something?"

"No," Charlie said. "I expect you to believe I'm observant."

He pointed one buttery finger toward the wall behind Tyler. Tyler craned his neck to look. A mirror was partially protruding from behind a display of golf balls for sale.

Tyler faced Charlie once again. "Nice."

Charlie flashed a grin. "See. Being observant is an important part of being a journalist. You've got to keep your head on a swivel and see things others overlook. That's how you get the story. Or the photo. See, no one else would have known you were practicing today unless they happened by. Not me, though. I noticed you practicing here yesterday around this time as I was walking across campus, and I figured it was a daily occurrence for a pro like you. My observations paid off."

"I guess so," Tyler said with a shrug, indifferent to Charlie's spiel. "So shall we get on with the interview?"

Charlie leaned forward and wiped his hands on a napkin. He fished his pencil from behind his ear and pulled his narrow reporter's notebook from the back pocket of his tan cargo shorts.

"You're absolutely right," he said. "Enough of my yammering on. Let's talk about you."

And so the interview began. Charlie asked Tyler everything from about growing up in rural Kansas, to being so far from home, to his goals in life and his expectations for the coming golf season. Tyler answered every question with honesty and candor. He considered himself a pretty open person, so he wasn't inclined to hold back as long as someone asked. It wasn't very often he voluntarily gave up such information, but he didn't mind sharing when prompted.

The interview lasted for the better part of half an hour, and when it was over Charlie pushed back from the table with a wide smile.

"That was great, Ty," he said.

Tyler winced at his named being shortened. It wasn't that he didn't like it. It was just that no one had ever done it before. He had to admit, though, he kind of liked the way it sounded. He decided not to protest.

"You are so easy to talk to," Charlie continued. "The interview just came naturally. It's going to be a great story."

Tyler smiled slightly. "That's good to hear. I thought it went well too."

Charlie leaned forward once again. "You know, someone as easy to talk to as you should really be in a position to do some of the question asking."

Tyler looked at Charlie. It hadn't taken him long to bring up the job offer again. Tyler sat back in his chair. He still hadn't decided what he was going to do, although he felt closer to an answer than he had after Charlie mentioned it the first time on the course.

Sensing Tyler was still teetering on the edge of the decision, Charlie jumped up. "How about a beer? This is a Catholic joint, and every good golfer enjoys a cold brew. Whatcha say?"

"I can't," Tyler said, shaking his head. "I'm only 19."

"So? I'm buying. You're just drinking."

Tyler protested again. "Thanks but no. I don't drink."

This stopped Charlie dead in his tracks, and his eyes went wide. "You mean to tell me that you, a country kid who is attending a Catholic school in Texas, don't drink? Well now I've heard everything."

Unable to help himself, Tyler smiled, and Charlie returned the grin.

"Then I'll have a beer, and you can have a Coke. Still my treat."

"Sounds good," Tyler said as Charlie ambled over to the counter and came back with the beverages.

After taking a few sips from their drinks of choice, Charlie looked Tyler directly in his brown eyes. "Listen, Ty, I'm going to cut the crap. I need your help. You've got the abilities to do this, and I only have a damned columnist hired for the summer. Do you know how helpful a columnist is in trying to fill a paper? Not very. My photographer and I can't do it all by ourselves, and our ad director always seems to sell enough ads to make a relatively thick paper, which means we need the content. So will you help me out? Will you be a reporter for the *Clarion*?"

"I don't know," Tyler said. "I've never done it before. I'm not sure I could do a good job, and if things are so tight, I'm worried my schedule with practice and whatnot might be more of a hindrance than a help."

Charlie was shaking his head furiously even before Tyler finished. "No. No. No. You can do this. The scheduling won't be an issue, and I will be your mentor. I will teach you everything I can. You're good at golf. I'm good at newspapering."

A slight smile tugged at the corners of Tyler's mouth. "You called me modest earlier. From the sounds of it, I'm surprised you know the meaning of the word."

"So you got jokes?" Charlie said wryly.

Tyler shrugged.

"Think of working for the *Clarion* as doing me a personal favor."

"I don't know you well enough to owe you anything."

Charlie flopped backward in his seat. "You're killing me, Ty. Throw me a friggin' bone here. I'm asking you as nicely as I possibly can."

Tyler smiled openly and tipped his chair back on its two back legs with his arms crossed over his chest. "What's in it for me?"

Charlie shook his head, and though he was fighting it, he was smiling. "Fame and esteem. All the girls in their little Catholic school outfits you can handle. Hell, as if the possibilities of wild romps in the sack with a coed aren't enticing enough, I'll even pay you. I can offer you thirty dollars per story. It's all the paper can afford."

Slowly, Tyler lowered his chair back onto all fours. "Catholic schoolgirls, eh?"

"Sure, but maybe we should just focus on the thirty bucks at first. The girls will come later. Kind of like a bonus for working at the paper long enough."

"Yeah, I'm sure," Tyler said with a chuckle.

"So are you in?" Charlie asked, though he thought he knew the answer.

Tyler extended his hand across the table. Charlie's eyes lit up as he grasped it with his own in a firm handshake.

"I'm glad to have you on board," Charlie said.

He stood up and raised his glass of beer. In one swallow, he drained the drink and slammed the cup down on the table.

"I'm excited, Ty. I think this is going to be great! You remind me a lot of myself when I was an underclassman."

Tyler looked up at his new boss. "Is that an insult?"

"Ha! That's what I mean. You're a character, and soon you too will see that."

Tyler stood up. "Really though, I'm kind of excited. For so long now all I've been allowed to focus on is golf. It feels good to make a decision for myself."

"That's right," Charlie said, coming around the table and clapping him on the back. "It's going to be great. Just don't let your golf game slip too much. St. Alfanus needs that championship as much as the *Clarion* needs a press award."

Tyler chuckled. "You got it, boss."

"I'm not your boss yet," Charlie said. "You need to swing by the office and fill out the necessary paperwork. Then we can get you an assignment to cut your teeth on. From there, we'll be off to the races."

Tyler nodded. "Okay. How about right now? I mean, I have to go drop off my clubs, but I could head that way pretty quick."

"Sounds great, Ty!" Charlie said. "We'll see you in a bit. The *Clarion* is located in the basement of Cormac Hall. You can't miss it, unless you venture into the boiler room. Of course, the boilers should be a giveaway that you're not in the right room."

"Okay. See ya."

With a wave, Charlie stepped out of the clubhouse and bounded down the sidewalk. Cormac Hall was on the other side of the campus, but Tyler guessed Charlie would make record time. He was excited to have Tyler as part of the staff, and Tyler was excited too.

"I'll finally be able to be like Grandpa Al," he said to himself before slowly drinking the rest of his Coke.

When he was finished, he threw his and Charlie's cups away. Then he retrieved his golf bag and walked down the short outdoor ramp to the equipment room.

A staffer worked the desk every weekday from 7:00 a.m. until 8:00 p.m. All athletes were expected to keep any of their outdoor equipment in the room to prevent loss or theft. They could check out their own equipment anytime the desk was open, but they had to return it by closing that day so the clubs, tennis rackets, javelins, or whatever else could be safely locked away for the night.

Tyler thought the rule was a little strange, but he didn't mind. It saved him from having to keep his personal and his school-issued clubs all in his cramped dorm room. Besides, he liked talking with the girl who most often worked the desk. Her name was Brooke Nichols, and she was a petite, auburn-haired beauty. He often had to guard himself from getting lost in her dark green eyes.

Brooke was a senior at St. Alfanus studying to become an athletic trainer, and to make extra cash she worked at the equipment room. To Tyler's delight, she was working the desk that afternoon.

"Hey, Brooke," he said as he walked up to the counter.

"Hey, Tiger. How did you play?" Brooke asked as she pulled up the logging software used to monitor when and who checked out what.

Tyler shrugged. "Okay, I guess. It could have been better."

Brooke smiled at Tyler. He about melted. "Oh, I'm sure you did fine. You're the best one on the team."

"I don't know about that," Tyler said, blushing. "A lot of the guys are good too."

"You're so modest," she said. "It's sweet, but you need to knock it off. You need to get a little more intense and get that competitive edge. You need to win."

Tyler never knew how to react to such comments from Brooke. He wanted to flirt back, which is what he thought was happening when she called him things like "sweet," but then when she kind of lectured him with an intensity that belied her small stature, he didn't know what to think.

"I know, Brooke," he said, hanging his head.

"See, there you go," Brooke said. "Don't look down. Look me right in the eye and tell me to shove it!"

Tyler looked up with wide eyes of bewilderment. "What?"

Brooke smiled again. "You're too easy to mess with, Tyler."

Tyler mustered a weak smile. Brooke was domineering and due to her intensity, a little scary. But she was beautiful. What a mystifying combination. It truly boggled Tyler's mind.

Apparently he had been standing there speechless for too long. "Hello? Tyler?" Brooke said, waving a hand in front of his face.

Tyler snapped out of it. "Sorry. You must have really got to me that time. I don't know if I will ever recover," he joked, with more confidence than he truly felt.

Brooke laughed. "Oh, Tiger. Just when I think you're out for the count, you come swinging back. So you going to check those clubs in?"

"Yes, ma'am," Tyler said, lifting the golf bag up onto the counter.

With ease, Brooke grabbed the bag and placed it in its specified place. Then she officially checked the clubs back in via the computer system.

"You're all set," she said with a smile.

"Thanks, Brooke," Tyler said with a wave as he walked away. "I'll see you tomorrow."

As Tyler emerged back into the hot Texas sun, a large smile spread across his face. Was it because he just got done talking to a gorgeous woman? Not really, though it didn't hurt. More importantly, he was getting ready to do something he had secretly always wanted to do. He was going to be a journalist.

Tyler broke out into a slow jog as he made his way toward Cormac Hall. By the time he hit the front steps, he was sprinting.

Chapter Two

Tyler dove headfirst into his work as a reporter for the *Clarion*. He picked up as many stories as Charlie would throw his way, and he quickly began to gain the attention of the faculty for his clear and concise writing style and evident voice that each piece carried.

The first week he only wrote one story, but by the end of July, he was tackling as many as ten. With Charlie barely keeping pace, some stories didn't get printed right away.

"If we keep up this pace, we won't have to write a thing the last two weeks before the semester starts," Charlie often said. "We'll be that far ahead."

Tyler didn't care, though. He loved writing for the paper. He wanted to write about everything he could, and he got that chance. He covered everything from features about the janitorial staff to sports to religious issues relating to non-Catholic students attending St. Alfanus.

He received special attention for a story he wrote near the beginning of July about the school's budget. It was a dicey topic since it was a private school, but Tyler ran wild with the challenge.

"I can't believe they opened up to you like that," Charlie said, astonished by a rough draft of the story.

Tyler shrugged. "It's not like I uncovered anything earth-shattering. I just reported what they told me."

"Yeah, but I've tackled this story before," Charlie said, shaking the pieces of paper toward Tyler. "They've never been that candid."

"I guess I got the gift," Tyler said.

Charlie chuckled. "There it is. I knew that modesty bullshit was just an act. Your true colors are starting to show."

Tyler smiled.

"There is a problem with this story, though," Charlie said.

The smile disappeared from Tyler's face. "What?"

"It's too long!" Charlie shouted. "We might not have room for it all!"

He walked toward the end of the room and shouted around the corner. "If this fucking ad staff would sell a few more ads we could run this whole damn thing!"

Tyler smiled. Charlie's excessive swearing had taken getting used to, but now he almost enjoyed hearing it, especially when he was heckling the ad director, Joni Steen.

"Cram it up your ass, Charlie!" Joni yelled back. "You have the wonder kid now. I'm still saving our pennies through the summer by selling the entire paper on my own."

Joni came walking around the corner and poked Charlie in the chest. She was tall, nearly six-feet tall. She used to play volleyball for St. Alfanus, but she blew out her knee her sophomore year. She was entering her senior year with a major in business administration. She was probably headed for a desk job, but her body didn't show it.

Everything about Joni Steen was tight. She still sported six-pack abs, and her long legs and arms still rippled with toned muscle. She could have spiked Charlie's head through the wall, but she stuck with finger poking, which always looked like it probably hurt enough to get the point across.

Joni stepped back from Charlie as he rubbed his chest. She turned her head, causing her jet black hair to fly around her head, revealing the smooth, light brown skin of her complexion. Her brown eyes sparkled.

"Mr. Fox, do you agree with this bowel movement? Do you think I'm not doing my job well enough?"

Tyler shook his head. "No, ma'am."

"I didn't think so." She turned back to Charlie. "Would you like to rethink your position on this subject, Mr. Harrison?"

Charlie smiled. "Oh, calm down, Joni. I was just joking. Tell ya what, to make up for this I'll buy you some fried chicken. Or some watermelon."

Joni answered this with a hard slap to the back of Charlie's head. "Shut the hell up. You know I hate that racist bullshit."

"I was just joking," Charlie said, rubbing his head. "You know you're my girl."

"Not anymore, Charlie. That ship has sailed. And that little bitch giving you a blow job in the cafeteria helped fill the sail."

Charlie shrugged. "It was a mistake. You know I'm sorry."

Joni winked at Tyler. "How sorry? Sorry enough to take me to Hooks Pizza Place tonight?"

Charlie smiled. "But of course, my dear. Greasy pizza, loud music, and all the beer you can handle."

Joni and Charlie had dated, quite seriously at one time. And then Charlie did get caught in a tryst with a freshman in the cafeteria. Joni broke it off, but she never seemed mad. They continued to work together and be close friends. From the onset, Tyler suspected it was still more than a friendship and the joking about going on dates was actually quite true. He hadn't asked Charlie about it yet, though. The time would come. Probably after one of their unwinding sessions after sending the final page of the weekly issue to the press. They were becoming pretty close friends.

Since Tyler started, Charlie included him in on his weekly ritual. After the last page was sent, Charlie bought a six-pack of beer and went to the football stadium at the north end of campus. He used a key Tyler didn't care to know how he got and unlocked one of the entrances. Then he went to the top of the stands to drink and smoke cigars.

Tyler never drank in high school, so he rarely succumbed to Charlie's peer pressure to enjoy a can. However, Tyler liked the smell of the cigars, and he began to smoke one every week with Charlie.

"Well, I'm hungry. And thirsty. I will take you up on that offer now," Joni said.

Charlie smiled at Joni. "Your wish is my command. See you later, Tyler."

The two left, and Tyler sat down at a computer to edit some of the Charlie's stories as well as the columnists' weekly babbling before he went home to his dorm room on the west side of campus.

The most thrilling part of working for the *Clarion*, other than beginning to make a few real friends, was his golf game. It had improved, not weakened as he had feared taking on another responsibility might cause. He was hitting the ball better than he ever had before.

Life in Hooks was good for Tyler. He missed being home and spending time with his family, but he felt he was gaining a new family within St. Alfanus.

It wasn't until August 15, four days before the fall semester began, that things changed, and it was a change that would haunt Tyler's dreams for the rest of his life.

Tyler and Charlie had just finished the customary "Back To School" edition of the *Clarion*, and the two were driving back to campus from the Hooks gas station with a six-pack in tow.

Charlie pulled a cigar from his shirt pocket. "Get in the glove box and get my lighter," he said as he put the stick of tobacco into his mouth.

Tyler popped open the glove box and retrieved the lighter. Charlie took it and flicked a flame to life. He slowly lit the cigar, blue smoke rolling out of his mouth as he puffed to get the cigar good and lit.

Charlie offered a cigar to Tyler.

"Not tonight," Tyler said. "It is nice out. I think I will go for a run later."

Charlie rolled his eyes. "You're a health nut. John Daly is a golfer, and that fat sonofabitch always has a smoke dangling from his lips. You don't need to do all that running. Just swing the club."

"There's more to it than that," Tyler said, looking up at the night sky. "Besides, I like to run."

"It's that damned runner's high, isn't it? Well, I tell you right now, all those endorphins coursing through your body can't be any better than a few puffs on a good stogie."

They drove the rest of the way to the campus in silence. Charlie quickly navigated his old Chrysler Cirrus into the football stadium parking lot, killing the lights on the car as soon as the wheels crossed into the lot.

He pulled up in front of the entrance he preferred, and the two got out. Tyler carried the beer while Charlie unlocked the gate.

It didn't take long for them to get to the top of the stadium seating. They sat down and Charlie puffed on the cigar.

"So I think this week's issue is a good one," Charlie said looking down at the artificial turf of the football field. "Like better than any of the other welcome-back issues I've been a part of."

Tyler nodded. "It sure looked good. We pulled together a few good features about the coming year, and I think the calendar on page six is solid. It is really going to be valuable to the students."

Charlie agreed. "Yes, indeed. I can't wait to see students all over campus reading it. That's going to be awesome."

A long pause stretched out through the night. Then Tyler decided to ask the question burning in his mind. "What's the deal with you and Joni? Are you two a thing?"

Charlie laughed. "We were, as you know. Now, things are complicated. We still fuck. Often. But she won't date me. That stupid freshman that seduced me in the cafeteria messed everything up."

"She seduced you?"

"Well, maybe it wasn't exactly like that, but it still messed things up." Charlie took a drink of his beer. "What about you? Why don't you have a sex buddy?"

Tyler shrugged. "I don't know. I guess I just haven't had time. I had a girlfriend back home, but I broke it off with her when I moved down here."

Charlie pitched the empty can over the top of the railing. It clinked on the ground. "I see. At least you're not gay. I worried about that."

Tyler looked at Charlie. "Are you serious? You thought I was gay?"

Charlie laughed. "Lighten up, Ty. I was just yanking your chain. Really, though, what are your plans after this place? You going to be a journo?"

"I don't really know. I wouldn't mind being a journalist. My grandpa was a reporter at a small weekly back around home, but I guess I haven't decided what my future holds. I've got time. What about you?"

"I would love to work at a big paper, but I won't get to. My old man just wanted me to get a college degree. He didn't care what in. As soon as I graduate, though, I'm heading back home to Dallas to take over the family construction business."

Tyler smiled. "You? Manual labor? I don't think I understand."

Charlie cracked open a third beer. "You clearly don't. I'll be the guy who goes out and estimates and bids jobs. That's why it would be great if I could marry Joni. She could handle the business stuff, and I could make sure we keep getting work."

"You love her, don't you?"

"I guess," Charlie said, shrugging. "But enough of this kind of talk. I've got beer to drink."

Tyler slapped him on the knee. "And I've got running to do. I'll leave you to it."

"You want a ride back to the dorms?"

"No. The walk will be my warm-up."

"Okay. See you later, buddy."

Tyler waved and bounded down the metal bleachers. He got into his dorm room and quickly changed. Grabbing his MP3 player, he left the dorms for a jog he would never forget.

Chapter Three

Alison Alcott slowly walked down the cart path on the St. Alfanus golf course; the night sky filled with shining stars and the glowing moon lit her way. Her flip-flops made quiet clicks against the concrete, but even she couldn't hear it. The sound of locust buzzing in the trees was nearly deafening.

Her nighttime trip on the course was a special occasion. She was a freshman at St. Alfanus, and she had grown up in Fort Worth. She was no stranger to St. Alfanus, though. Her father was an alumnus and the current college president. She had spent a lot of time on the campus grounds for various campus functions, including homecomings, graduations, and donor banquets.

Alison had been on the course before for alumni golf tournaments with her father, but that night her father was not invited. He didn't even know she was there.

Last year, during one of her frequent visits to St. Alfanus from Fort Worth, she had met a local boy named Robert Ray Turner. He was a twenty-year-old ranch hand who lived in Hooks and worked south of town on a small ranch that generally lost money each year. He graduated from Hooks High School near the bottom of his class. He wasn't a bright boy, and he was known around town as a drinker and fighter, even though he wasn't old enough to drink in the local bar he frequented. Alison didn't care about any of this, though. She found Robert Ray rugged and handsome, and she thought he had a huge heart.

Alison's first year as a college girl was starting in the coming days, and she wanted to celebrate by having a romantic night under the stars with her boyfriend.

Boyfriend. Just the thought of the word sent chills down her spine. She had just turned eighteen a few weeks ago, and now she could date with her father's permission, not that such mandates from her father had stopped her before.

Several boys had been a part of her life back in Fort Worth, but they were just that—boys. Now she was dating a man.

Thoughts of her cowboy swam through her head as she deftly navigated the golf course. She was heading to the most secluded hole on the course: Hole No. 14.

When she got to the green, she shrugged the backpack she was carrying down off her shoulders. She unzipped it and pulled out the blanket she had brought. After spreading it out on the grass next to the cup, she stood and tucked her brown hair behind her ears.

"This is going to be great," she said to the locust in the trees as she tucked her thumbs into the belt loops of her jean skirt.

Thanks to the locust, she never heard anyone coming up behind her.

Suddenly a hand covered her mouth, and the crook of an elbow wrapped around her neck. She was pulled back against her assailant.

Alison attempted to scream, but the sound was muffled by the hand and lost in the buzzing of the locust. Panic began to rise in Alison's chest, but then she felt a rough hand on her thigh. It crept up her leg and beneath her skirt. As the hand neared the border of the thong she wore, she moaned slightly and ground back against her captor.

The hand left her, and she was released. She turned around to see Robert Ray standing before her beneath his cowboy hat, with his left hand dangling at his side and his right resting on his large belt buckle.

"Hey, Ali," he said.

Ali blushed and lightly hit Robert Ray in the stomach. "You scared the hell out of me."

"I know," he said, laughingly, lightly. "It didn't take you long to start enjoying it, though."

Alison stepped up to him and wrapped her arms around his waist. "I knew it was you, that's all."

"Whatever," he said, embracing her back.

Then he bent down and kissed her deeply.

When they separated, both were out of breath. "Did you bring us a nice spread?"

"Yes, sir," she said turning away from him and bending over to get a six-pack of beer out of her backpack.

Robert Ray enjoyed the sight of Alison bending over at the waist to dig in the backpack. "Whoa doggies. That's a daisy of an ass poking out right there."

Alison peeked back over her shoulder at Robert Ray. "You like that?" She shook her hips.

Robert Ray let out a grunt and stepped up behind her. "You better believe it."

Alison turned around into his arms and kissed him again before leading him to the blanket. They each popped open a beer and drank in between kissing and exploring each other's bodies with their hands. Soon Alison was wearing nothing but her skirt. Every other article of clothing had been removed.

Soon the cans of beer had been tossed to the side, and they were entangled in frenzied lovemaking. Alison's cries and Robert Ray's grunts of pleasure were answered only by the locust.

Unknown to the two young lovers, a person hid in the nearby trees watched the couple make love.

After watching for a while, the observer reached over to a tree trunk and lifted a Colt OHWS .45-caliber, semiautomatic pistol. A large silencer was attached to the end of the barrel. Hanging from the gun was a small leather bag positioned over the chamber slide to catch the spent rounds. The moonlight reflected from water of the pond made the gun glimmer in the observer's hand, and the weight of the firearm felt good to him.

The observer decided it was time. Leaving the protection of the trees, the would-be attacker crouched low and crept toward the green. Alison was on top of Robert Ray. Her hands were planted on the grass on either side of his head. His hands were grasping her hips, guiding her up and down. The assailant continued forward and tugged on the ski mask hiding his identity.

With his knees brushing the grass, the gunman quickly reached the edge of the sand trap that hugged the edge of the green. He looked up. Alison was lying by herself on the blanketed green. The observer's eyes darted back and forth, trying to locate Robert Ray.

He saw him. He was staggering toward the gunman. Both his hands were being used to keep his pants from sliding back down to his ankles.

The gunman didn't know what was happening, but he dropped to his belly in the grass. The overhanging tree branches cast a shadow over him, causing his black and green camouflaged shirt and pants to disappear into the blades of grass.

Robert Ray stumbled off the green and to the precipice of the sand trap. He began to urinate. The gunman looked up and saw Alison was lying on her back, staring up at the sky.

The gunman tucked the gun into the waistband of his pants and crawled forward. His hand landed on the handle of the sand trap rake.

Quietly the gunman got into a crouched position a few feet from Robert Ray. The gunman gripped the rake, and when Robert Ray seemed to be nearly done relieving himself, the gunman jumped up and ran forward, swinging the rake in a high arch over his head.

The rake smashed into Robert Ray's face. The gunman heard the crunch of cartilage breaking as blood gushed from the cowboy's nose.

Robert Ray barely made a sound. The grunt of pain was easily masked by the buzzing locust, and Robert Ray fell face first into the mixture of sand and urine at the bottom of the sand trap. He was unconscious.

The gunman tossed the rake on top of Robert Ray and looked back at Alison. She hadn't moved, so the gunman began to make his way toward the naked girl stretched out on the blanket.

As he neared Alison, the gunman removed the gun from behind his back and clicked off the safety. Alison must have heard the noise.

"Hey, cowboy," she cooed. "Are you ready for another ride?"

The gunman didn't answer.

"Cat got your tongue?" Alison asked, rolling over.

Her eyes went wide with terror when she saw the gun leveled at her. Tears instantly began to stream down her face, and the blanket beneath her became wet as she lost control of her bladder muscles.

"Oh god," she gasped. "No. Please no."

The gunman stepped forward. Alison clawed her way backward. One of her hands found a full can of beer. She hurled it at gunman. He easily sidestepped the toss and took another step forward.

"Leave me the fuck alone!" she yelled, but there wasn't a lot of volume behind the shout. She was nearly panting with fear.

The gunman took another step forward, putting Alison at his feet. He swung one booted foot and kicked Alison in the shoulder, spinning her around. She landed on her back.

Looking up at the gunman who loomed over her from above her head, she began to whimper.

"Robert Ray," she cried. "Help. Please help."

The gunman raised his weapon and aimed it at Alison's forehead. He held the aim for a moment, causing Alison's body to be wracked with convulsions of fear. She closed her eyes. Her mouth continued to form the words "no, please, help," but no sound escaped her throat.

The gunman squeezed the trigger. The gun made almost no sound. The bullet struck Alison in the center of the forehead. Her body twitched, and then it went still as blood began to cover the green around her.

For good measure, the gunman shot Alison three more times. One bullet pierced Alison's jugular vein. Another punched a hole in her right lung, and the final bullet tore her stomach and intestines apart.

The gunman put the gun back into his waistband and began to jog back across the green. When he got to the sand trap, he saw Robert Ray was crawling out of the sand. The gunman pulled his foot back and kicked him in the side of the head. Robert Ray slumped back over into the sand trap.

Resuming his jog, the gunman went back to the trees in which he had been hiding. He ducked through the branches and waded into the water. Soon he sank below the surface and disappeared as he swam away from the golf course.

As he swam, tree branches scraped and pulled at him, tugging at his shirt, jeans, and mask. Between his frantic splashing and the snapping branches, someone could have easily heard him, but the killer was too focused on getting away to worry about that.

Chapter Four

The warm night air gently blew across Tyler's chest. He was jogging a zigzag pattern across the campus. Early in his run, he had removed his shirt and tucked it into the back of his gym shorts. Music filled his head from the earbuds lodged in his ears that were connected to the MP3 player in his shorts pocket.

As he ran, he blotted sweat from his forehead with the sweatband he wore on his wrist. With the song he was listening to winding down, Tyler slowed to a walk before coming to a stop. He looked around at the part of campus he was on. Light poles lit the sidewalk he was standing on, but the moon illuminated the rest of campus. Normally dew would have been glistening in the grass, but it was still warm enough out that nothing had formed yet.

Tyler took a deep breath. He began reflecting upon where his life had brought him. He had a job he enjoyed. He was beginning to become close friends with Charlie. His golf game was as good as it had ever been.

I guess St. Alfanus was the right choice after all, he thought.

Tyler had several offers to attend various schools. He hadn't really wanted to go to a Catholic college. He was a Lutheran, and though the similarities with Catholics were many, he wasn't a Catholic and didn't think he would fit in.

Ultimately, the decision came down to money and Tyler's urge to venture away from his hometown, even though he loved where he had grown up. St. Alfanus fit the bill perfectly. The golf coach, Mark Grower, had worked tirelessly to get Tyler as many scholarships as possible to cover nearly every expense—including tuition, room, and board—he would incur to attend college. He worked it out so all Tyler had to pay for every semester were his books for classes.

Few people knew of the deal Tyler had, and he kept it quiet. He knew NAIA student-athletes didn't get full-ride deals. Schools couldn't give full-tuition athletic scholarships, and it was rare for St. Alfanus to dish out enough academic scholarships to cover the balance. He wasn't sure what Coach Grower had done to get him, a golfer, all that financial support, and Tyler didn't think he wanted to know. He figured some clandestine business dealings had been put into place to secure some of the obscure scholarships he had received, and he figured ignorance was bliss.

Thinking about his road to St. Alfanus and the *Clarion* was an interesting path, and Tyler found it interesting the path was the fairway of a golf course.

Golf had brought him to the small Texas college. It was while playing golf that Charlie had approached him about joining the *Clarion*'s staff. Golf was the center of Tyler's universe, and he was happy about that. He loved the sport.

Tyler decided to jog through the golf course.

He started at the No. 1 tee box. He jogged down the fairway and around the No. 1 green because he didn't want to hurt the putting surface. He did the same for the next eight holes, which brought him back up to the clubhouse.

Tyler stopped and leaned against a sidewalk railing. He looked up at the sky. The moon was still full. The air was still warm. He decided to finish his tour of the golf course before heading back to the dorms.

Before he knew it, Tyler was jogging over the tee box of the hole he hated the most—the extremely difficult No. 14.

As he glided down the center of the fairway, he saw someone standing on the green around the hole's dogleg. Tyler came to a stop. As he watched, the shadowy figure clumsily walked toward the flagstick that reflected the moonlight streaming through the tree branches. Then the person, who Tyler concluded was a man, fell to his knees. A scream shattered the night air, loud enough to be heard over Tyler's MP3 player.

Tyler yanked the earbuds out and let them dangle from their cord around his neck. He took off, sprinting toward the green.

As he neared the No. 14 green, Tyler saw before him what looked like a scene out of a crime drama, though much more graphic than fit for television.

The man, who looked like a stereotypical cowboy minus the shirt and hat but complete with the tight jeans and cowboy boots, was crying and bellowing up at the night sky. Clutched in his arms was a naked girl. She had a gaping bullet hole in her forehead with more in her neck, chest, and midsection. There was blood everywhere. Empty and full beer cans were strewn about, and there was a matted blanket lying on the grass next to an open backpack.

Tyler felt his stomach turn, and his legs became rubbery with fear.

The man saw Tyler come running up. "Did you do this, you motherfucker?" he screamed, still holding the girl. "I swear to god almighty I'll cut your goddamn balls off for this!"

Tyler stopped. He shook his head. "No. No. I didn't do this. I was just going for a run." Tyler tasted phlegm at the back of his throat as he looked at the dead girl, and he broke out in a cold sweat.

"Well then, help me!" he screamed.

Tyler fished his cell phone out of his shorts pocket. As he tried to ask the man if he had called 9-1-1, he lost control and vomited, dropping his phone in the process.

"Help me, asshole!" the cowboy shouted. "Somebody fucking killed my sweet Ali!"

Tyler nodded as he wiped his mouth on the back of his hand and frantically felt the grass for his phone. "Okay. Okay," Tyler said as he found his phone and began dialing the number. "What's your name? And what's hers?" Tyler's mind was racing.

Seeing that Tyler was trying to help, the man attempted to calm down. "My name is Robert Ray Turner. Her name was . . . is Alison Alcott."

Alcott. That name registered briefly, but he was too scattered to know why. "Okay. I'm going to call for help," Tyler said as he pressed send.

The 9-1-1 operator picked up quickly. "9-1-1. What's your emergency?"

"Someone's been shot," Tyler said hoarsely. "Her name is Alison Alcott. She is on the No. 14 green at the St. Alfanus golf course. One other person is here. His name is Robert Ray Turner. He says he is her boyfriend."

"Is anyone hurt?" the operator asked.

What a stupid question! Tyler thought. I just said someone was shot. Who isn't hurt after being shot. "She's dead. Has to be. It looks like she was shot in the head and chest. There's blood everywhere. Please help!"

"We'll have police officers and EMS crews there," the operator said.

Tyler hung up and began to dial another number out of instinct. Robert Ray wasn't paying much attention. He was crying and stroking Alison's hair.

The phone rang a few times before it was answered. "What do you want, Ty? I'm fixing to enjoy a midnight rendezvous with Joni."

"Charlie. Something horrible has happened. Some girl named Alcott has been killed on the golf course. On the No. 14 green," Tyler said in almost a whisper.

"What? Why? Just because you are crazy enough to play a round of golf in the dark is no reason I should come photograph your hole-in-one."

"No, Charlie, listen," Tyler hissed in a panic. "I don't know what to do."

Charlie heard the fear in Tyler's voice. "Oh shit," Charlie said, and hung up.

Tyler looked at his phone in confusion and slipped his phone back into his pocket. He wasn't sure why he had called

Charlie. He had done it almost without thinking. Then he was acting out of instinct again. He was walking toward Robert Ray. Tyler wanted to help him, but he didn't know how.

Who would do something like this? he thought. It was so horrible. Tears began to seep from the corners of his eyes, and he vomited again.

Tyler shook his head slightly as he approached Robert Ray, trying to clear his clouded thoughts.

"So what happened?" Tyler asked numbly.

Robert Ray looked up at him as he continued to stroke Alison's hair. His face streaked with tears, sand, and blood. "What the fuck does it look like, man? Someone killed her. Shot her dead. They busted me in the head good. I didn't even know what happened. Last thing I remember I was taking a leak in the sandbox back there." He gestured behind him a jerk of his head. "Next thing I know I'm crawling out of sand with a broken nose. I make my way up here and find Ali all shot up and bloody. Who the fuck would do this?"

"It's horrible," Tyler said. "I'm so sorry this happened."

"You're sorry? That sonofabitch who did this is gonna be sorry. I'm going to kill that motherfucker."

Tyler let a moment of silence spin out between them as his world went in and out of focus. "Well, I hope you find them. Whoever did this deserves what they get," Tyler said without realizing it.

"You're goddamned right."

"So what were you guys doing out here tonight?"

Robert Ray was slowly regaining some composure as he talked with Tyler. "Well, Alison was going to start school here in a few days. Freshman year, you know? We wanted to celebrate. Kind of have, like, a romantic evening under the stars. Ali said she thought this place would work because it was so hidden. Said she'd seen it when she was up visiting her old man different times. He's the college president here."

Tyler nodded. "Okay. But you didn't see anyone out here who could have done this?"

"Just you, but that was later. You didn't do this, did you?"

Robert Ray appeared to be getting agitated again. "No. I swear. I was just jogging," Tyler said.

Robert Ray eyed him with newfound suspicion. "So what's with all the questions?"

"I don't know. I just want to help you catch this psycho who did this. Sorry. I'm an idiot."

Robert Ray continued to look at Tyler. "Okay. I guess."

Sirens began to sound in the distance. "Looks like help is about here. I'm going to get out of their way."

Robert Ray looked confused. "Okay." He nodded, adding, "Yeah. Yeah. Thanks, man. What's your name?"

"Tyler Fox."

Suddenly he seemed to lose interest in all the talking. Robert Ray turned his shocked gaze back down at the bloody and naked body of Alison Alcott. He began to cry again.

Tyler slowly backed away. Suddenly his legs gave out, and he collapsed to the grass. When someone put a hand on his shoulder, Tyler almost screamed but stopped the shriek before it escaped his throat.

He turned around and saw Charlie standing there. He had his camera in hand and was looking at the green.

"Charlie? What are you doing here?" he asked.

Charlie patted him lightly. "You don't look good, Ty," he said with concern in his eyes.

Tyler struggled to find words. "She's dead."

"That's some fucked-up shit," Charlie said. "I've got a couple good photos. The moon is playing nice tonight. I need to get a couple more with a flash, though."

"What?" Tyler asked disgustedly.

"This has to be reported, Ty. I mean, the president's daughter getting murdered. We have to report this," he said.

"The president's daughter?" Tyler asked.

"Yeah. Alison Alcott. That's the college president's daughter."

Tyler nodded. He knew the name had sounded familiar.

"I've seen this kind of shit before. Clearly this is your first time. The shock will wear off. Just hang in there. I'm going to get some more shots."

"That's going to piss off Robert Ray."

"Who's Robert Ray?"

"The cowboy holding the dead girl. He said he was dating Alison," Tyler said detachedly.

Charlie shrugged. "He's probably too freaked out to kick my ass right now . . . I hope."

Charlie walked closer to Robert Ray and Alison. He fired off several pictures, the flash illuminating the entire green. Robert Ray didn't even seem to notice.

Walking back to Tyler, Charlie said, "There it is. I got some good ones. Just as good as the police photog is going to get."

"This kind of stuff doesn't happen often in Hooks, Ty," Charlie said. "So let's be away from the crime scene when the cops get here."

Charlie helped Tyler to his feet, and the two walked over to the cart path a safe distance from the green so it wouldn't look like they had been too close. They stood in silence for a moment, just staring at the green and listening to Robert Ray sob.

"Who the fuck would have done this?" Charlie asked quietly.

Tyler shook his head. "I don't know." He then turned and vomited into the grass again.

More silence. Then Charlie asked, "How are we going to cover this?"

Tyler turned and looked at his friend, the fearless editor of the *Clarion*. "That's kind of your call, isn't it?"

"I guess so," Charlie said, nodding slowly. "But as far as I'm concerned we're working this one together."

"Why? You have more experience. Besides, I can't deal with this.

"Who cares about experience? You found it, and the shock will fade. You can do this. You are as much a part of this as I am. More so, really."

"Yeah, but I've never covered anything like this before. I'm new at this newspapering stuff. This whole thing is making me sick."

"That doesn't matter. You've got the stuff. I know it. I'm not claiming to be a genius at reporting, but as far as I can tell and from what your teachers have said, you've got some serious talent."

"I don't know," Tyler said, scuffing his shoe on the concrete of the cart path. He pulled the T-shirt out of his waistband and wiped his face. He tucked it back in his shorts. He was too hot to wear it.

"Shut the fuck up. We, you and I, are doing this. We have to, really. It is our journalistic responsibility, and we might even be able to win a Texas Intercollegiate Press Association award."

"Is that the only reason you want to cover this story? To win an award?" Tyler found himself almost disgusted with his friend. He was already sick to his stomach from what he had seen and from what he knew the people closest to Alison would be going through, yet Charlie was getting all excited about some stupid award.

Sensing he had offended Tyler, Charlie clapped him on the back. "I'm just kidding. About the award, that is. We really do need to cover this. We are the news source of this campus, and this happened in our back yard."

"That's true," Tyler said, shrugging weakly. "I just want to find out who did it. The story won't be finished until that comes out."

Charlie nodded. "Yep. We need to work toward that. We need to start talking to people right away."

Tyler nodded. Sirens could be heard. They were getting close. "I just feel bad for Alison's family. And Robert Ray. This is horrible."

"Yes. Yes it is."

They stopped talking. Tyler was lost in his thoughts about a family dealing with the murder of a daughter, and Charlie was trying to figure out how to go about covering the story that was beginning to unfold at St. Alfanus.

Soon headlights and flashing emergency vehicle beacons appeared around the dogleg of hole No. 14. A St. Alfanus campus security jeep was leading an ambulance and a Bowie County Sheriff's Department cruiser down the center of the fairway.

"The cavalry has arrived," Charlie said.

The caravan rolled to a stop in front of the green, and paramedics piled out of the back of the ambulance with a stretcher. A sheriff's deputy jumped out of the car and ran toward Robert Ray, gun drawn.

"Get your hands off of her and get on the ground!" the deputy shouted.

Charlie and Tyler watched. "That's Deputy Randall Bonner. He's an asshole," Charlie said.

Deputy Bonner grabbed Robert Ray with one long, muscular arm and tossed him to the ground. A look of confusion and terror covered Robert Ray's face.

"He didn't do anything," Tyler hissed.

"That doesn't matter. Bonner always thinks he has to assert himself. I'm sure that urge is even greater for him since it is a murder. Small-town cop bullshit. Besides, Robert Ray is going to be their top suspect. He was the one here when the murder happened."

Deputy Bonner shoved Robert Ray's face into the grass and slapped handcuffs onto his wrists as Robert Ray protested. "I didn't do anything!" he shouted. "Some sick motherfucker killed my Ali! Arrest him! Not me!"

Deputy Bonner easily hoisted Robert Ray to his feet and took him to the police cruiser to put him in the back seat. Charlie lifted the camera and fired off shots, a few with and a few without the flash.

On the green, the paramedics were working on Alison's body, though Charlie and Tyler both knew they weren't going to succeed in bringing her back to life.

The campus security guard noticed the camera flashes and approached Charlie and Tyler.

"What the hell are you doing here?" the middle-aged man asked as he got close.

Charlie smiled. "Good evening to you too, Officer Jones."

"Shut up, Charlie. It's not a good evening, and you know it."

"Come on, Nick. Don't be like that. We're just doing our job, just like you."

"Don't call me by my first name. And you don't have any business being here."

Charlie shook his head. "That's bullshit, Nick. We have as much right to be here as anybody else. We're with the campus newspaper."

Officer Jones looked over his shoulder at the green. Deputy Bonner was stringing up yellow crime scene tape, and the paramedics were preparing to put Alison's body onto the stretcher. "Charlie, I know I've helped you out before, but that doesn't mean we are friends. You can't be here."

"We have to be, though. Unless you don't want to talk to the guy who made the 9-1-1 call."

Tyler looked at Charlie with wide eyes. Officer Jones saw this. "You?" he asked, pointing a stubby finger at Tyler. "You called this in?"

Tyler nodded uncertainly. "Yeah. I was jogging and came upon Robert Ray holding Alison in his arms. He was hysterical."

Officer Jones considered this a moment. "So how do I know you didn't shoot her?"

"Come on, Jonesy. He's a *Clarion* reporter. He wouldn't have done this. Besides, he was with me. At the football field. Just like I am after every successful production of the paper."

Though Tyler didn't know it, Charlie had gotten his key to the football field from Officer Jones after he agreed to not write a story about the security guard getting a drunk-in-public citation in New Boston a few summers back.

"Okay. Maybe," Jones said, once again looking over his shoulder. "What's your name, boy?"

"Tyler Fox."

"The golf stud?"

"Yes he is," Charlie said.

Officer Jones exhaled loudly. "Do you promise, swear on your momma's grave, that you didn't kill Alison?"

"Of course," Tyler said, insulted to even be considered a suspect.

Officer Jones nodded. "Shit. Okay. I can't stop Deputy Bonner from questioning you. But I can make sure you don't get hauled in with Robert Ray. Randall and I went to Hooks High School together. We're old friends."

"Why are you friends with assholes, Nick?" Charlie asked.

"Shut up, Charlie," Tyler said.

"Yeah. You need to keep your damn mouth shut, Charlie. I'm trying to help you guys out. And Randall isn't an asshole. He's just a little rough around the edges."

Charlie shrugged. "If you say so, Nick. And thanks for the help. Can we expect more of the same later? For the story?"

Officer Jones looked at Charlie. "Story? You've got to be kidding."

"We have to cover this. Someone has to be held accountable for the shit they pulled tonight."

Officer Jones said nothing for a moment. Then he nodded. "You're right, Charlie. Someone needs to burn for this."

"So you'll help us?"

"I don't know. I guess. Some. Not a lot, though. And if I see my name in the paper at all, I'll stop telling the maintenance crews that all those fucking beer cans you leave at the football field aren't a big deal, that they're nothing more than some stupid high school punks having a little fun. You get busted for those empties, and your ass will be kicked out of school."

Charlie smiled thinly. "Thanks, Officer Jones."

Officer Jones ran his hands through his graying black hair. "Fuck me."

From the green, Deputy Bonner shouted. "Nick! What have you got over there?"

Giving one last glance at Charlie, Officer Jones turned and shouted back, "Just reporters for the campus paper. One of them actually called the police when they found this."

"Okay," Deputy Bonner shouted. "Bring that one here and tell the one with that camera to stay away from the victim!"

Charlie nodded. "You got it, Officer Jones. I'll just get a shot of the green with the tape up and maybe a picture of Robert Ray in the car, if Bonner tells me he is a suspect, of course."

"Yep. Sure. You boys come with me," Officer Jones said, walking toward the green. Charlie and Tyler followed.

As the three neared the green, Deputy Bonner walked up to them. "Oh no. Hell no. What is Harrison doing here?"

Charlie flashed a grin. "Deputy, I'm just doing my job. Same as you and Officer Jones here."

"Fuck you, Harrison."

"Now, Randy, should you really be talking to me this way?"

Tyler looked at Charlie. *Why does this guy hate Charlie, too?* he thought. What have I gotten myself into?

"Cut the crap, Harrison. Why are you here?" Deputy Bonner's face was becoming red, matching his bushy hair and overgrown mustache.

"Covering an important story. What kind of newspaper would the *Clarion* be if we didn't tackle the murder of the college president's daughter?"

Deputy Bonner shook his head. "It's not much of a paper anyway, so I don't see what the problem would be."

"That's insulting. We're students, sure, but we are the only news source for Hooks. Lord knows *The Bowie County News* rarely leaves the New Boston city limits to cover what's going on here. This is a big fucking deal. This needs to be covered, and the asshole who did it needs to be brought down."

"How do I know you didn't do it?"

Officer Jones interrupted. "He didn't do it, Randall. I can account for his whereabouts."

"What about this kid?" Deputy Bonner asked, pointing at Tyler.

"That's Tyler Fox," Officer Jones said. "He was with Charlie most of the night. Until he went for a jog. He's the one who made the call to the police."

Deputy Bonner eyed Tyler. "Is that right, son?"

Tyler nodded.

"So how do I know you didn't do it?"

Tyler began to speak, but Officer Jones once again jumped in. "He's solid too, Randall. Take my word for it."

Deputy Bonner looked at Officer Jones. "This is a homicide investigation. No one should be above suspicion."

"I know, Randall, but we go way back. You know I don't just stand up for anybody."

This seemed to be enough to satisfy Deputy Bonner. "Okay. But I still need to get a statement from you, Mr. Fox."

Tyler nodded, and Charlie stepped forward. "Can I ask a few questions quick?"

Deputy Bonner looked annoyed.

"Please, Deputy," Charlie said. "You know me well enough that I wouldn't be asking if it wasn't important. Alison was part of the St. Alfanus family. Justice needs to be done. I want to report on this in hopes that anything we publish will shake loose more information."

Though the deputy clearly disliked Charlie, Tyler could see that he realized Charlie was right. Putting the story out publicly would be better than keeping it quiet and letting the Hooks rumor mill run rampant. "Okay. But make it quick."

Charlie talked with the officer for nearly ten minutes. Deputy Bonner answered all of Charlie's questions with long, drawn-out answers that hedged around giving direct responses to the questions. Deputy Bonner repeatedly said that he couldn't talk about too many details because the investigation was ongoing and just getting underway, but he did say that he believed most of the questions concerning the crime would be revealed sooner, rather than later.

Through all of it, though, Deputy Bonner did give Charlie the information Tyler figured he was seeking. He said the investigation was being treated as a homicide and that Robert Ray Turner was a suspect at that point. Other than that, Charlie and Tyler knew as much as the police did, which wasn't a lot.

"Okay," Deputy Bonner said. "That's enough. I need to talk with Mr. Fox here."

Charlie nodded. "All right. Thanks, Deputy. Will be you be available later for more questions?"

"I guess so," Deputy Bonner said with a shrug. "Sheriff Giles will be in from New Boston first thing in the morning. Should I tell him you will be contacting him in the next few days?"

"That would be perfect," Charlie said.

Deputy Bonner sighed. "Okay. Mr. Fox, if you'll come with me . . ."

Tyler followed the large sheriff's deputy away from Charlie and Officer Jones. As Deputy Bonner began to ask Tyler questions about where he was prior to the incident and what he saw when he came upon the murder scene, Charlie began snapping pictures. He even took one of Robert Ray as he sat still crying in the back of the police cruiser. The ambulance left with lights flashing but no sirens.

When Deputy Bonner was finished, he started to walk away, but Tyler stopped him. "Deputy, was I any help?"

At first, Deputy Bonner seemed confused. "Why?" His eyes narrowed. "You feeling guilty about something?"

Tyler shook his head. "No. I just think what happened is horrible. I've never seen anything like this. I want you to catch the person who did this."

"Oh," Deputy Bonner said. He softened some. "What you provided is as much as I could have hoped for. The only way it could have been better was if you did it and broke down and coughed up a confession right here on the spot."

"I bet," Tyler chuckled nervously.

"Listen, kid, we'll get this guy. I promise."

"Have you ever dealt with this kind of stuff?"

Deputy Bonner hesitated. "No. But that doesn't mean we won't get the killer. Cops go through a lot of training that they hope they never have to use. We know what to do."

"Okay."

"You going to help Harrison write this story?"

"I don't know. Yeah. I think so," Tyler said meekly, looking at the ground.

"Why? Why are you going to write this story?"

"Because I found it . . . at least that's why Charlie said I needed to be a part of it."

"No. Why do you want to write it?"

"I want to do whatever I can to help catch the guy. No one should ever be killed, especially like Alison was. In such a . . . vulnerable state."

Deputy Bonner nodded. "Good. I was hoping that was what you were going to say. Just promise me you'll share information you come across with me. We need to work together."

"Okay. So you'll do the same?"

His eyes narrowed. "You've been around Harrison too long . . . But yeah. I'll tell you everything I can."

Tyler smiled weakly. "Thanks. So why are you so friendly with reporters? I imagine most cops would not be this willing to talk."

Deputy Bonner shrugged. "I'm usually not, especially with Harrison. But . . . I have to admit he runs a pretty good paper, even for a student, and this is a big deal. I'm man enough to admit that it is one of the biggest cases I have worked on. I've dealt with deaths, but usually they are kids who drink and drive. Knowing Harrison, you two will probably be able to find stuff out about Alison's life that I couldn't hope to, as much as I hate to say that. If we end up working against each other, it won't be good."

"I understand."

Deputy Bonner put a thick hand on Tyler's shoulder. "You seem like a good kid, Mr. Fox. I'm glad you are here, and

I'm glad you are working for the paper. Hopefully you can keep Harrison grounded."

The officer walked off, and Tyler started back up the fairway, away from the green. Charlie came jogging up beside him.

"What were you and supercop talking about?" he asked.

Tyler shrugged. "I was just talking to him about what he asked me. He was pretty easy. Never accusatory. I asked him 'why?'"

"What?" Charlie asked, lightly hitting Tyler in the shoulder. "Why the fuck would you ask him that? Now he's going to think you had something to do with this whole mess."

"No. No, he won't. During the interview he said he wasn't suspicious of me, and our little conversation confirmed that. He knows where I, we, stand. He knows we just want to figure out who did this."

"You're sure?"

"Yes."

"Okay," Charlie said, exasperated. "What else did he have to say?"

"Well, he just wanted to work together. He said he would give us what information he could if we didn't keep anything important from him."

Charlie grabbed Tyler's arm and stopped him. They were near the tee box, out of sight of the green. "Please, Ty, please tell me you didn't agree to that."

Tyler looked Charlie in the eyes. "I did."

"Fuck! Why would you do that? You never tell a source you'll check things out with them first. We don't need his okay to publish stuff. For shit's sake, we go to a private school. The administration could pull that card and force prior review, but even they know that. He's got you pegged for a newbie, and you played into his hands. You're just a chump to him."

This angered Tyler. He shoved Charlie's hand away. "Listen, I knew what I was doing. He isn't going to screw us over."

"That's what you think. He hates me. He'd love nothing more than to embarrass me and make me look disreputable, which will hurt the *Clarion*."

"You don't know that."

"Yeah. I do. He hates me."

"Why? What did you do to make him hate you?"

Charlie smiled slightly. "Well, I fucked his daughter. He caught me with her in her room. He lives here in Hooks. She told me he was gone for the night to a meeting in New Boston. She was wrong."

Tyler shook his head and looked down. "Great."

A look of embarrassment crossed Charlie's face. "Sorry, man. I should have told you before he talked to you."

"Yeah. You should have."

"Sorry."

"Well now what? I've already messed up by agreeing to talk to him. I guess you should just handle this on your own. If I'm not reporting, he can't expect me to share information. I won't know anything."

"Nonsense. You're still working this with me. It's going to take two people. Besides, he knows the *Clarion* isn't a big operation. He'll assume you know something even if you don't, and he'll be pissed that you aren't sharing."

"Well, that's perfect."

"Don't worry about it. We'll both still cover it, and we'll go ahead and play by the rules you have set up . . . as long as we need to."

Tyler cocked his head to the side. "What do you mean?"

"Well, we have the First Amendment we can hide behind if we have to. We won't have to tell him things if we don't want to. We'll give him little morsels of information in order to keep him talking to us, but we'll hold back the things we need. With luck, we'll get this uncovered and rescue little Randy by laying it all out for him. In the paper, of course."

"I don't know, Charlie. That sounds pretty unethical, and you're always preaching ethics, such as getting all sides of the story and whatnot."

Charlie nodded. "Ethics isn't a black and white world. It's pretty gray. He crossed a line too when he put pressure on you to keep him in the loop. He's trying to do his job just as we are. It's almost a game. We have to play it all the way."

Tyler was silent.

"If you have to, you can just say I won't let you talk about it. That's how it works in the real world. Reporters have to answer to their editors."

"Couldn't I get into trouble if I went back on our little agreement?"

"Maybe, but it's nothing to worry about. He might try to get you with a contempt order, but we can call in some free legal help. There are people student newspapers can contact for that sort of thing. Don't worry."

"Contempt?" The air gushed out of Tyler's lungs. "Couldn't that mean jail time?"

Charlie nodded slowly. "It could, but we won't let it get that far. Randy won't know we are holding stuff back if we don't tell him everything we know. I mean, do you really expect him to be totally open with you?"

"I guess not."

"Hell no, he won't tell you everything. It's a game. Like I said."

"It just feels wrong to play a game over someone's death."

Charlie draped an arm around Tyler's shoulders. "That's just the way it is, Ty. This is the real deal. It's not the stupid campus bullshit we've been covering all summer."

"How do you know all this? You've never worked anywhere but the *Clarion*."

"I've had some good mentors. I've reached out to professionals I admired, and a few of them have been kind of enough to take me under their wings. I'll be contacting them tomorrow morning about this. They'll help guide us in the right direction."

"You sure?"

"Yeah."

"I'm trusting you right now."

"As you should."

"So who are these mentors? Are they any big names?"

Charlie hesitated. "Relatively. They've covered some big stories in Texas and Louisiana. Just like you don't have to reveal everything to Randy, I'm not going to give away all my sources either. I will let you meet with the ones who agree to advise us on this deal, though."

Tyler nodded. "Okay. Fair enough."

They began to walk again. Neither said anything again until they arrived back at the clubhouse. Charlie broke the silence.

"You okay? We good?"

"Yeah," Tyler said. "I'm okay."

"Are we though? Are you mad at me for anything?"

"No," Tyler said, shaking his head. "I'm not mad at you. You were doing what you are supposed to do. You were trying to teach me stuff. I do wish you had told me all the back story of your history with Deputy Bonner, but that's not a big deal. You've convinced me it will all work out."

"Good, Ty. I wouldn't want my ace reporter pissed off at me."

"I'm your ace?"

Charlie smiled. "Well, technically you're my only reporter, but you're also my friend. I don't want to fight over this thing. I want us to work together to blow the lid off this motherfucker."

Chuckling, Tyler said, "I want that too."

Charlie nodded and smiled. "Right on." He started to walk away. "Get some rest. We've got some serious work to do in the morning. People to talk to. Plans to make. It's going to be crazy for a while. Probably until the killer is caught."

"It actually sounds kind of fun."

"Yes it does, and in its own way, it will be."

Tyler waved good-bye. "See you in the morning. Tell Joni hello."

"I will. After I make up for the time I missed out on with her already tonight," he said with a wink as he walked off.

Tyler smiled slightly and walked back to the dorms. He went into his room and took a shower. When he stepped out, he wiped the steam from the mirror and looked at his reflection. His face, drained of color, was lined with stress, and dark circles were forming under his eyes.

"This is serious," he said to himself. "I never expected to get into anything like this, but I guess I'm in too far to turn back now, huh?" he asked the reflection.

The face staring back at him didn't answer, but Tyler knew what it would have said: Yes. He was in deep enough that he had to see it through to the end. He felt drawn to joining the *Clarion*'s staff, and maybe it was supposed to be like this. Maybe he was supposed to be a journalist, and maybe he was supposed to cover such a big story.

It was a lot of pressure, but Tyler had to admit he was in some sort of sick way excited about the opportunity to cover this story. He wasn't excited that Alison Alcott had been murdered, but he thought the process of the reporting would be enjoyable in its own way. He was excited to be a real journalist covering more than student government.

Tyler left the bathroom and crawled into bed. Sleep came quickly, but it was fraught with dreams that haunted him.

Chapter Five

Tyler was golfing. It was the middle of the night, but he was golfing. The moon shone brightly above him, illuminating the course. He teed off from the No. 12 tee box and was able to easily track his ball as it sailed through the air and landed a good two hundred yards down the center of the fairway.

As he lugged his bag toward his ball, he glanced at his scorecard. He was only two strokes above par. He was playing a magnificent game. "I wish all the tournaments were played at night. I'm playing great," he thought to himself.

He finished that hole with a birdie, and he parred No. 13.

He teed his ball up as he prepared to tackle the treacherous No. 14. He surveyed the fairway. He lined up to play it safe and lay up at the bend of the dogleg, but then he changed his mind. He turned slightly and aimed for the trees marking the fairway's change of course toward the green. He didn't usually go for the green, but he was playing so well he figured it was worth a shot.

Tyler pulled the clubface back from the ball and swung forward. He connected well, and the club striking the ball made a satisfying ping as he found the driver's sweet-spot.

The ball sailed through the air climbing higher and higher. It didn't reach the peak of its path until it was nearly to the trees. Then it began to descend and dropped out of sight behind the treetops.

Tyler picked up his golf bag and slung it across his back. He walked down the fairway and quickly reached the dogleg. From there, he could see his ball sitting a few feet from the hole on the green. The ball was illuminated by a beam of moonlight that was penetrating the trees. The rest of the green was shrouded in darkness.

Smiling broadly at such a great shot, Tyler began to jog toward the green, his clubs jingling in his bag.

As he approached the green, his eyes began to adjust to the dark, and he saw he wasn't alone on the course. Two people were on the green. Getting closer, Tyler began to make out what the two were doing.

It was a man and a woman. They were having sex. Both were completely naked. The man was on top of the woman, who was moaning and gasping in pleasure as the man grunted with exertion and enjoyment.

Less than 50 feet from the green, Tyler let the golf bag slip from his shoulders and fall to the ground and walked closer. Now he could see the two people. The man was Charlie, and he was having sex with Alison Alcott, except it wasn't exactly her. She had red hair.

Alison's nails dug into Charlie's shoulders as her breathing began to quicken. Charlie groaned loudly, seemingly enjoying the pain of the nails cutting into his flesh.

A scream escaped Alison, and suddenly the two weren't alone on the green. Deputy Bonner was standing near them, his service pistol drawn and pointed at Charlie.

Tyler tried to say something, but he was frozen. He couldn't talk or move his arms, yet his feet carried him ever closer to the three.

Then Deputy Bonner spoke. "You motherfucker."

Charlie looked up. "Oh shit."

Alison craned her neck and looked up at Deputy Bonner. "Daddy!"

Charlie rolled off of the girl who Tyler thought was Alison and scrambled to his feet, covering his crotch with his hands. He began to back away from his lover. The girl sat up and turned to face Deputy Bonner. She covered her chest by crossing her arms over her breasts.

"I told you to stay away from my daughter, shit bag. Now I catch you out here fucking her on the grass like you two are a couple of damn animals. It ends tonight," Deputy Bonner said. He cocked the gun.

"Daddy, no!" the girl said jumping up and running toward Charlie, who hadn't stopped backing away from the business end of the gun.

Deputy Bonner fired three shots just as Alison got in front of Charlie. The bullets tore into her, and she dropped to the green in a pool of blood. Charlie screamed and dropped down next to her.

"No! Dammit! No!" Deputy Bonner howled as tears streamed down his face, and he sank to his knees.

Suddenly Tyler was unfrozen. He screamed, and suddenly he sat up in his bed. He was drenched in sweat.

He kicked his sheet and comforter away and stood up. His legs were shaky, but he walked to the bathroom and flipped on the light. He looked at his face in the mirror. His eyes were wide with terror.

"Holy crap," he said breathlessly.

He filled a cup with water and drank it quickly. He splashed water on his face and toweled off. Then he went back into his bedroom. The digital clock on his nightstand read 2:37 a.m. in bright, blue numbers. He had been asleep for less than two hours.

Tyler crawled back into bed and quickly fell back asleep. He didn't dream the rest of the night.

Chapter Six

Charlie rolled over again and looked at the clock on his nightstand. It was just after 4:00 a.m., and the bedroom of the small house he rented just outside of Hooks was suffocating, even with all the windows open. The air conditioner didn't work, and the landlord was an elderly man who didn't move too fast in getting things fixed. The rent was cheap, though, so Charlie couldn't complain too loudly.

He swung his feet off the edge of the bed and stood up. He looked at Joni lying on the other side. the sheets were shoved down to her feet. She was lying on her stomach wearing nothing but a pink thong. She was beautiful, and Charlie wanted to crawl back into bed, wake her and express his love for her, which he knew she reciprocated even though she put up a front of anger toward his previous transgressions.

He couldn't do it, though. He was too bothered by what he had seen on the golf course. That was why they were at his house instead of in Joni's dorm room. When he had arrived back to her room from the course and told her what had happened, she said she didn't feel safe being on campus, so they gave up the coolness of the dorms for the heat and security of his rental.

Charlie walked to his closet and grabbed a T-shirt off of a hanger and took it with him out into his living room. He dropped it on the back of his recliner and grabbed a lighter and cigar out of a kitchen cabinet. He went out the front door and sat down on the front porch swing. Even though he was only wearing a pair of gym shorts, it was warm outside. It was going to be a hot day.

He lit the cigar and began to puff on it as he thought about the previous night's events. He felt bad for his first impulse of wanting to cover the murder just for fame and glory. Seeing how scared Joni was, he now sided with Tyler. He wanted to cover the crime to bring the killer to justice.

But why Alison Alcott? Sure, she was the college president's daughter, but if someone wanted to get back at him for something, why not just attack him directly instead of going through his daughter?

There had to be a reason. Maybe it wasn't an attack directed at President Alcott. Maybe it was directed at Alison herself, but she was just beginning her time at St. Alfanus. How would she have made any enemies already, especially ones who would kill?

Something began to dawn on Charlie. He had reported on Alison Alcott before, but he couldn't remember when or why.

"I need to go to the office and look at the archives," Charlie said to the early morning air.

He snuffed out his cigar in a coffee tin filled with sand and went back inside. He went to the bedroom and gently crawled onto the bed. He kissed Joni on the cheek. She woke up and looked at him sleepily.

"I'm going to campus to deliver the paper and work on some stuff," he said in a whisper. "Call me when you want me to come pick you up."

She smiled. "Okay. Be careful."

"I will. Love you."

"Love you too, babe." She went back to sleep.

Charlie left the bedroom and put on a pair of sneakers. He pulled his T-shirt on as he left the house and climbed into his car.

Arriving at St. Alfanus, Charlie saw the campus was quiet. He was sure Officer Jones was still at the crime scene. He probably wouldn't leave that post until investigators had finished combing the area for clues.

He parked in front of Cormac Hall and walked into the building. He unlocked the door of the office and went to his desk. The message light was flashing on his phone, so he picked up the receiver and called his voicemail. The message was from Hayley "Ginger" Godin. She was entering her junior year, and she worked for the *Clarion* as the photo editor and reporter. She was good and in her message said she was going to be arriving back on campus that morning after spending the summer touring Europe with her family. They had money, and since beginning work at the *Clarion* her freshman year, she had always gone on lavish trips over the summers.

Charlie dialed her cell phone number. Her voicemail picked up. He left a message for her to come to the office as early as possible because there had been a murder on campus, and they needed her right away.

Charlie guessed the message might spook her, but it would not scare her away. She wanted to work for a large newspaper after she graduated, so she would be anxious to get to work. Charlie often wondered why she didn't attend a school with a traditional journalism program, but he knew the answer despite his ponderings. She was a Catholic through and through. She had even attended an all-girls Catholic high school in Indiana where she grew up, and since St. Alfanus was known to be an exceptional Catholic college, her parents, both alumni, urged her to attend the Texas school.

With Hayley dealt with, he turned on his computer and began to search the archives for Alison Alcott.

First, Charlie just found pictures of Alison attending various college functions with her father and mother. Then her name began to appear in stories. The first one was a quote from her when her father was presented with an award of service to St. Alfanus. Then there was a story of her intent to attend St. Alfanus. Finally, her name appeared often in stories about the St. Alfanus Presidential Scholarship.

St. Alfanus was a close-knit community, so as soon as she threw her name into the hat for the scholarship, she was considered a favorite to receive one of the three scholarships offered. It was common knowledge that students with family members working for the college usually got preferred treatment in such matters. It wasn't exactly fair, but few people complained. It was just how business was done at St. Alfanus.

Charlie found a list of the top ten finalists for the scholarship: Andrew Hackney, Kara Bauer, Alison Alcott, John Anderson, Mallory Lux, Bethany Laureth, Paul Stramel, Carl McRae, Sheena Hespe, and Eric Fields. From that list of ten, it was pared down to the three scholarship recipients through essay writing and interviews. At the end, Alison Alcott, Mallory Lux and Eric Fields were chosen.

Charlie printed the stories and pictures in which Alison was involved. He put them in a manila folder and sat them on the corner of his desk. He leaned back in his chair, propping his feet up on the desk.

He was trying to figure out what to do with the information. It really gave him little more to work with. Alison, though the president's daughter, was just a freshman. She had little history with the college, and now she had no chance to make a history. Her life had been snuffed out prematurely, and it pissed Charlie off.

"Fuck," he said aloud.

Charlie stared at the wall for nearly fifteen minutes before he came up with an idea to chase. It wasn't necessarily going to pan out, but at least it was an avenue to pursue. He would try to talk to the other two scholarship winners and see if they knew anything about Alison.

This idea caused a few more to pop into his mind. He would also talk to her roommate. Freshmen were required to live in the dorms, and though school hadn't started, Charlie figured it was likely Alison and her roommate had already spoken in order to arrange moving in and who was going to bring what to the room.

Also, he would talk to some of the people who didn't get the scholarship. Maybe they knew Alison too. Maybe they became acquainted with her through the application process.

It would be difficult to talk to the students who didn't decide to pony up the tuition and attend St. Alfanus anyway, but those who had enrolled should be easy enough to contact.

Charlie dropped his feet back off the desk and began to type on his computer. St. Alfanus, though a private institution, was relatively open. The college founding fathers believed that they should promote, not conceal, the good work they were doing. This included enrollment statistics. They published numbers as well as names of those enrolling.

On the St. Alfanus web site, Charlie found the list of incoming freshman. He copied the names into a word processing document and did a search for the seven names of the people who didn't receive the scholarship. Four names showed up: Carl McRae, Bethany Laureth, Paul Stramel and Kara Bauer.

"I'll turn Ginger loose on these when she gets in," Charlie said to his computer. "She's good at finding people on campus and getting them to talk."

Charlie then navigated his internet browser to the *Bowie County News* site. There was nothing posted about the murder, so Charlie checked out the *Texarkana Gazette*. They had a brief story, no photos, but they did have a statement from Deputy Bonner.

"Shit," Charlie said, pushing away from his desk. "This would happen after we sent the paper to press. We need to get a damn web site. Now it's going to look like we were scooped."

Suddenly there was a knocking on the office door. Charlie got up and answered. It was a man dressed in a blue work shirt and jeans. Stitched on his breast pocket was the name "Drew."

"Hey, Drew."

"Hey, Charlie. I just saw there were lights on, so I thought I would tell you that the paper is here," the man said. "That's some crazy shit that happened here last night."

Drew was a pressman for the *Bowie County News*, which printed the *Clarion*.

"Yeah it was. The News have anything on it yet?"

Drew smiled. "Now, Charlie, you know I can't tell you anything about that. Same as I can't tell the reporters or editors what you have in your paper. That's the agreement."

"I know, Drew. We're on the story, but I was just wondering how bad we were going to get our asses kicked, since we're just a weekly."

Drew nodded in condolence. "I understand. I'll just tell you I heard there is going to be a press conference at the crime scene at 10 a.m. That's all I can tell you."

"At the crime scene?" Charlie asked, his face crumpled in confusion. "That's kind of strange, don't you think?"

Drew shrugged. "That's Sheriff Giles for you. It's an election year, so the dumbass probably wants to make a big show of this to make all the voters see how serious he is about his work. If he doesn't get reelected, what else would he do? He isn't qualified for shit."

Charlie chuckled. "I suppose you're right."

"Well, here's the paper," Drew said, tapping his foot on one of the many stacks of newspapers tied together with plastic bindings.

"Thanks, Drew."

Drew nodded and went back up the stairs that led out of the basement. Charlie went to a storage closet and got a wheeled metal cart. He loaded the papers onto it. He shut off the office lights and left. He didn't bother locking the door.

He pulled the cart loaded with fresh newsprint to the other end of the hallway and used the service ramp to take the papers outside. He began to distribute the papers. As he did so, he pondered the next course of action. He had to get Hayley talking to the students, and now he had to cover the press conference.

The sun was burning through the morning clouds, making it hotter out. Charlie took off his shirt and draped it over the handle of the cart. He delivered the paper as his thoughts swam about how to cover Alison's murder.

The last stop of Charlie's paper route was the golf course's clubhouse. The doors were locked, which wasn't normal but not surprising, considering what had happened. Charlie left the stack in front of the door. He wheeled the cart, which still held one stack of papers for the *Clarion*'s office use, over to a few benches that surrounded a series of picnic tables overlooking the No. 9 green and the practice green, on their respective sides.

Charlie pulled a paper from the final stack and sat down on a bench. He thumbed through the thick edition and was quite pleased. Everything looked good, and it was full of high-quality articles, photos, and infographics that would leave every reader brimming with knowledge about St. Alfanus.

Except the murder of the college president's daughter.

"Damn," Charlie said. "I wish we weren't a weekly."

He stood up and shoved the paper back into the stack and began pulling the wheeled cart back to Cormac Hall. He put the stack of papers in the office on the reception desk and was just finishing putting the cart back into the storage closet when his cell phone rang in his pocket.

He fished it out and looked at the screen. It was Joni. He punched a button and put the phone to his ear.

"Hey, babe," he said.

"Hey," came Joni's voice through the receiver. "Everything okay there?"

"Yeah. I just got done delivering the paper. It looks great. You did a great job on getting ads for this one. Our budget is going to be looking good after this."

"That's good, but how is campus?"

"Quiet. Not too many people milling about. The golf course was locked up, which really doesn't surprise me. I didn't see Jonesy around. I figure he's out guarding the crime scene. Other than that, if I didn't know any better, I'd say it was a normal day."

"Okay. Well, you want to come home?"

Charlie could hear in her voice that it wasn't a request for a ride to campus. "You think I should?" he asked with a sly grin.

"Yes."

"But why?"

"Don't fuck around, Charlie. We were both too shook up last night, but I feel safer here at your house. You need to get your ass home."

"Okay. See you in a bit."

Charlie hung up and ran out of the basement to his car. He quickly drove home and parked in front of his house. Joni was sitting on the porch swing. When she saw him pull up, she stood. She was wearing her thong and a tight, white tank top that left little to the imagination.

Joni leaned over the railing and stared at Charlie with a seductive smile as he got out of his car and walked up the front walkway. "It's about time," she said. "I thought I was going to have to start without you."

Charlie climbed the steps and took her in his arms. Their lips locked. One of his hands cupped her bare behind, and her fingers locked into his hair.

Without letting go of each other, they went back into the house and to the bedroom to burn off the tension they both felt from the previous day's events.

Chapter Seven

Tyler woke up and looked at his nightstand clock. It was nearly 9:00 a.m. He never slept that late. He couldn't believe it. Of course, the events on the golf course and the nightmare had surely exhausted him, so having his body reclaim a few lost hours of sleep made sense. Still. Getting up at nearly midmorning meant he was late.

He jumped out of bed and quickly showered and got dressed in some workout clothes. He grabbed a breakfast bar from the top of his dorm room's minifridge, shoved his MP3 player and cell phone into his pocket and bolted out the door.

He ate his meager breakfast as he left the dormitory, and then he plugged his MP3 player's earbuds into his ears and took off at a jog. He subconsciously decided to alter his normal route and avoid the golf course. He took off on the outskirts of campus.

After nearly an hour of running, the sun was beating down on him, and the air was becoming oppressively thick with humidity. He peeled of his T-shirt and tucked it into his waistband as he came to a stop. He wiped his brow on the back of his hand and looked around. He hadn't really been focusing on where he was jogging. He had just been aware that he was still on campus.

Tyler found himself on the golf course, the No. 17 hole to be exact. He shut off his MP3 player and could hear the squawk of radios and people talking. Tyler knew what he was hearing—the police were at No. 14 investigating Alison's murder.

Without thinking or hesitating, Tyler began to cut across the fairways toward the source of the sound. He entered one of the tree rows flanking the No. 14 fairway and peeked out the other side. He was just at the bend of the dogleg, and from his vantage point, he could see several investigators milling around looking for evidence. As he watched, one investigator picked up Alison's clothes, blanket, and backpack and put each item in separate, labeled bags. Another investigator was collecting the beer cans.

Off to the side of the green, standing in the shade of a tree, was Deputy Bonner, Officer Jones, and a tall man with a round stomach sticking out over his large belt buckle. He was wearing clothes similar to Deputy Bonner. He had a gun strapped to his hip and wore a sheriff's star on his chest and the center of his large, tan cowboy hat.

The three men were talking, but Tyler was too far away to hear. He had to get closer. He rapidly made his way through the trees until he was near the green and just a few feet away from the three men. Mosquitoes buzzed his ears as they ventured away from the nearby pond, but Tyler silently swatted them away and listened intently to the conversation in case something important was being discussed.

Deputy Bonner shook his head. "You're right, Nick. I feel bad for the family too. How would you cope with this?"

"I don't know," Officer Jones said. "It's a horrible deal. Whoever did it needs to have his dick cut off. Shooting a poor girl like that. The bastard probably got his jollies shooting her while she was bare-assed on the green."

Sheriff Giles spat a long stream of tobacco juice onto the sidewalk the three stood on. "That's for sure. Course, I couldn't blame the cocksucker for enjoying the view. That little Alcott had a body."

Officer Jones and Deputy Bonner chuckled uncomfortably at the sheriff's off-color comment about the murder victim. "Speaking of which, Bill, you and the crew think this was a sex crime? You think that boyfriend of hers did it?" Officer Jones asked.

Sheriff Giles scratched his stomach and spit again. "I don't reckon so."

"Well, how can you be so sure, Sheriff?" Officer Jones asked.

"I can't. Yet. But as soon as we get all the reports back from the labs and whatnot, I'm sure that's what it'll say. Any sex that happened here was consensual, and that boyfriend of hers, Robert Ray Turner, he's too dumb to think about beating himself up to make it look like they were attacked."

"So are we going to clear him today and let him go?" Deputy Bonner asked.

"Hell no," Sheriff Giles said with a hearty laugh. "That little pissant can sit in the tank for a while. He's been in enough trouble getting in fights at bars he isn't old enough to be that drunk in that I think it is just fine if we hold him for a bit."

"But we can't hold him too long," Deputy Bonner said. "We could get in deep for that. Some hippie lawyer would love to swoop in and make a mockery of the Bowie County Sheriff's Department."

"I know. I know. We'll just keep him long enough to show him that he shouldn't fuck around with us anymore. Then we'll turn him loose."

Deputy Bonner nodded and swatted a mosquito on his neck.

"Those mosquitoes are thick down here because of that pond. I damn near get eaten alive every time I come down this way," Officer Jones said.

"I imagine so," Deputy Bonner replied.

After a few moments of silence, Officer Jones spoke again. "So, if Robert Ray didn't do it—who did?"

Sheriff Giles and Deputy Bonner looked at the campus police officer. "That's what we're hoping to find out," Sheriff Giles said.

"Well, yeah. Of course, but how are you going to do it? Is all the evidence there to capture the killer?" Officer Jones asked.

Sheriff Giles turned and faced Officer Jones. He tilted his hat up, revealing cheeks beaded with sweat and dark eyes squinting more in frustration than from the sun. "Officer Jones, are you questioning the ability of this office to solve this case?"

Officer Jones shook his head. "No. No sir. I was just wondering, that's all. I mean, I was here last night. It just didn't look to me that there was a whole lot of evidence. I didn't even see any shell casings."

"Listen here, security guard," Sheriff Giles said, jabbing a long, thick finger into Officer Jones's chest. "Let me handle the police work. You just keep making sure no one shits in the front drive's fountain."

Officer Jones took a step and looked at the ground. "Yes sir."

Sheriff Giles sneered. "That's what I thought. Now, Deputy Bonner, what else can you tell me about this that I already haven't covered with Officer Jones here?"

Deputy Bonner gave Officer Jones a look that said he was sorry, and then he began. "Well, there's not a lot else. Like Nick pointed out, there were no shells around, though the victim was clearly shot four times. In the head, neck, chest, and stomach. I figure we'll be able to at least get the size of the gun from the bullets inside her, but that's probably about it. You know as well as I do that we don't have the resources to do some of that TV bullshit and get fingerprints off the bullets buried in the poor girl."

"True," Sheriff Giles said, nodding slowly. "Anything else?"

"I suppose so. The boyfriend, one Robert Ray Turner, said he got smashed in the face while peeing in the sand trap over there," Deputy Bonner said, pointing a few feet from where they were standing. "There was blood on the sand. Any urine probably soaked away already."

Sheriff Giles nodded and then shouted at one of the investigators. "Hey! Make sure you get some of the sand that doesn't have blood on it! We need to look for piss too!"

An investigator on the green waved a hand at the sheriff and walked toward the sand trap with a bag and small shovel in hand.

"Anything else?"

"Honestly?" Deputy Bonner said, shrugging his shoulders. "We ain't got shit. From everything I've seen, there's no evidence a killer was even here, except for a dead girl."

Pulling a handkerchief from his back pocket, Sheriff Giles removed his hat and wiped his forehead. Once he was dried off, he replaced his hat but kept the handkerchief in his hand. "I hate to say this, but I think you're right. Without a miracle like the killer coming forward and turning himself in or a surprise witness surfacing, we're fucked, and I'm going to be without a job. It is an election year, you know."

Deputy Bonner patted his boss on the back. "Don't worry, Bill. We'll figure it out."

"I hope so," Sheriff Giles said. Suddenly he hacked and spat a large wad of chewing tobacco into the grass beside the cart path. "I hope so indeed, but we can't let the vultures know we don't have anything. We've got to go to this press conference and paint a picture of us handling things. We'll be sparse on the information. Just enough to give them something to report. Nothing more. Sound good?"

Officer Jones and Deputy Bonner nodded in agreement.

"All right," Sheriff Giles said. "Let's head to the clubhouse for this press conference. I can't imagine too many reporters will be there, but you never know. This is a big deal in this part of Texas."

The three walked over to Officer Jones's golf cart and climbed aboard, with Deputy Bonner standing on the back where golf clubs would be placed. The cart's frame groaned with all the extra weight and leaned slightly to the passenger side where Sheriff Giles sat.

As the golf cart drove away, Tyler took another look at the investigators. They were being thorough and weren't paying attention to anything but their work, so Tyler left his hiding place in the trees and began walking quickly up the cart path toward the clubhouse. As he walked, he fished out his cell phone and called Charlie, who answered on the third ring.

"Ty. Where are you?" he asked.

"I'm heading to a press conference at the clubhouse," Tyler said.

"The clubhouse? Shit. I was told it was at the crime scene."

"No. I just heard the cops talking about it. It is at the clubhouse."

"Okay. Cool. Then I'm not running as late as I thought . . . Wait. How did you hear the cops talking about it?"

"I was jogging, and I took a jog through the course. I came across the investigators looking the green over, and I saw Officer Jones, Deputy Bonner, and some tall, fat guy who looked like a sheriff all talking."

"Yep. That's Sheriff William Giles. What an assbag."

"Anyway, I snuck up behind them and listened to what they had to say. I heard about the press conference."

"And?"

"And what?"

"You had to have heard more. Giles runs his mouth."

"I'll fill you in later. I'm just about to the clubhouse."

"Okay. I'm almost there too."

Tyler hung up and put the phone in his pocket. He broke out into a run and quickly arrived at the clubhouse, where the outdoor patio was bustling with activity.

A lectern was set up. A couple of microphones were set up, and a handful of digital audio recorders were there too. As Tyler arrived, he saw Charlie, with camera around his neck, placing his recorder with the rest of them.

Tyler met Charlie toward the side of the patio. He was leaning against the railing. "Nice of you to join me, Ty," Charlie said with a grin.

"This place is kind of a zoo," Tyler said, looking around and ignoring Charlie's welcome.

Charlie shrugged. "It's not too bad. We've got a radio station, TV station, and newspaper here, each from both Dallas and Tyler. From what I've heard from talking with a couple of the reporters, they are all helping each other out due to the long distance from home these folks had to travel. The radio stations are going to give audio to the others in their towns. TV crews are going to provide video. Newspapers are doing print stories. You get the idea, right? Otherwise, it is just the *Bowie County News* and the *Texarkana Gazette* for local media outlets. Oh, and us, of course."

"Of course. So this is a pretty big deal, eh?"

"For this area, you're damned right. For Tyler and Dallas? Not really. They have bad stuff like this happen all the time. However, this gives them an excuse to provide their annual coverage of this part of the state so they can continue to claim to cover all of Texas."

"Nice."

"Oh, for sure. These other media outlets are nothing but a bunch of bloodthirsty vultures. They only come to town when they have something negative to report on. They could give two shits about Hooks. They just want to get something juicy to cover."

Tyler nodded. "That's not good. They're going to benefit from Alison's death?"

"Sadly, yes. That's how this game is played. It's not always pretty, but it's a business too."

"You've talked a lot about this 'game' lately."

"That's because you need to understand it. You've got skills, but you have to understand this stuff. Even though we're at a college paper, we're in the bigs now with this murder."

"Okay."

"Great, now, before Sheriff Giles and his band of merry gentleman come out, how about you cover up your nipples? You don't look the least bit professional without a shirt on."

Tyler's eyes went wide. "Oh crap! I forgot I didn't have my shirt on! It's just hot and . . ."

"Right," Charlie said, waving his hand at Tyler. "Whatever you say. Just put your shirt on."

Tyler pulled his T-shirt on just as Sheriff Giles and Deputy Bonner stepped up to the lectern. Officer Jones stood off to one side behind them, alongside Paula Garcia, the St. Alfanus director of marketing and public information.

Sheriff Giles stepped up to the microphones and tapped them obnoxiously loud. "These things on? Everyone ready?"

An annoyed looking TV cameraman from the Tyler NBC affiliate was standing closest to the lectern. "Yes. It is working. Please don't hit those. It's expensive equipment."

"Oh. Sorry," Sheriff Giles said, flashing a politician's smile. "Then I guess we'll get started."

He cleared his throat. "Okay, folks. I'll tell you from the get-go that we are still early in the investigation. Information is quite sparse at this time as myself and my investigators only arrived here this morning. Even so, there are a few things we know and I can share with you. Luckily, the family of the victim has agreed to allow us to release her name. So, here it goes. At approximately 11:30 p.m. Thursday, one Alison Alcott was shot and killed on the fourteenth green of the St. Alfanus golf course. She was the daughter of St. Alfanus College President Gerald Alcott. Four bullets struck Alison. All of them were fatal wounds. We have one person being held for questioning, and we are looking for suspects in the matter. There was one person with Alison at the time of her death. He appears to have been assaulted at the time of Alison's death. Suspects are also being sought in this case, though we anticipate the same person will be behind both acts. The Bowie County Sheriff Department is handling the case and anticipates locating the person behind this as soon as all the evidence has been processed. At this time, I would field a few questions?"

"What was she doing on the golf course that late?" one reporter shouted out.

"At this time, we do not know, but we plan to interview those close to her and see if we can determine her reasons that way," Sheriff Giles answered.

Another reporter shouted, "Who was she with? Was it her boyfriend? Does he have a name?"

"She was with a man that appears to have been her boyfriend. We can't release his name at this time."

"Then does that mean he is being held for questioning? Is he considered a suspect at this time?" the same reporter fired back.

Sheriff Giles nodded. "Yes. The boyfriend is the one being held, and he hasn't been ruled out as a suspect."

"What kind of gun was it?" a radio reporter asked.

"We won't know that until all the evidence has been gathered."

"Did you find the gun that killed Alison?" a television reporter asked.

"We can't discuss that until all the evidence has been gathered and processed."

"Was there any sign of a struggle?" the reporter from the *Bowie County News* asked.

"No. It doesn't appear so from our initial investigation, but further work will have to be done to determine that for sure."

"How is President Alcott dealing with this?" the *Bowie County News* reporter followed.

"I can't answer that. Missus Garcia, the college's public information director, will discuss such matters after I have answered questions you have for me."

"Have you ever dealt with anything like this?" the Texarkana Gazette reporter asked.

Sheriff Giles eyed the reporter. "If you are asking if we'll be able to solve this, I assure you we will. A poor young girl was killed here in Bowie County, and we won't stop until we have the murderer behind bars."

The members of the press began to shout out questions about Sheriff Giles's experience and if the crime scene was being handled properly. The sheriff shook his head throughout all the shouting before finally clearing his throat loudly.

"No more questions, please," he said.

"Are you refusing to discuss your ability to properly handle this case?" a Dallas newspaper reporter asked.

"I assure you we will handle this just fine," Sheriff Giles said with a touch of anger. "Now, Missus Garcia will speak to you."

Sheriff Giles stepped back away from the lectern, and Paula Garcia stepped up to the microphones.

"Hello," she said with a Spanish accent. "My name is Paula Garcia. I am the St. Alfanus director of marketing and public information. I have come here today to give a brief statement concerning the tragic incident that has occurred on this campus. I will not be answering questions afterward.

"Alison Alcott was to be a freshman here when school starts on Monday. Alison was a scholar during her high school days and devoted follower of Christ, and she was expected to do well here at St. Alfanus. She is, as Sheriff Giles said, the daughter of St. Alfanus President Gerald Alcott. President Alcott is quite devastated by what has transpired, and he and Missus Alcott are grieving. In honor of Alison's life, a candlelight vigil will be held Sunday night. The president and first lady will be in attendance. At this time, that is all I can say. More information will be made available as necessary."

Mrs. Garcia stepped back as a barrage of questions where shouted at her. Sheriff Giles stepped back up to the microphones, waving his hands to quiet the crowd.

"Okay, okay," he said as the reporters quieted down. "That concludes this press conference. When we have more to tell you, we will let you know."

Sheriff Giles and Paula Garcia then left the patio and went back into the clubhouse. As the reporters began to disperse, Charlie retrieved his recorder and joined Tyler on the sidewalk outside of the patio.

"Giles doesn't have shit, and he knows it," Charlie said.

Tyler nodded. "He wasn't very forthcoming, was he?"

"Nope," Charlie said, shaking his head. "He got really rattled when the other reporters started pointing that fact out. There's more than just a murder case riding on this. His re-election is on the line too."

The two began to walk away from the golf course toward Cormac Hall.

"Why didn't you ask any questions?" Tyler asked.

Charlie shrugged. "Giles probably would have ignored me. Besides, the other reporters got as much out of him as possible. I wouldn't have had any better luck, and besides, we already know more than he told them. We were there. We saw the crime scene."

"True, but what do we really know?"

"Not a lot. We know where and how many shots hit her. And we have your interview with Robert Ray. Speaking of which, we have his name. He told it to us himself. We don't have to wait for Giles to tell us."

Tyler nodded, and they continued walking. Eventually Tyler asked, "Do you think they'll catch the killer?"

"I don't know, but I think we might have as good as a shot at solving this as the cops. This is our campus. We have more access to people than the cops will. People around here will trust us easier."

"So how are we going to cover this?"

Charlie smiled. "That's what we're going to figure out as soon as we get back to the office."

They walked the rest of the way to Cormac Hall in silence. Both Charlie and Tyler thought about how worthless the press conference was. Charlie knew it was just a bit of grandstanding on the part of Sheriff Giles since he was up for re-election, and Tyler wondered if all press conferences were as devoid of information as that one—all Sheriff Giles did was dodge questions. Charlie thought of uncovering the murderer to win awards and bring prestige to the *Clarion*, and Tyler strained to recall every detail he had seen and heard in hopes he could come up with a way to solve the crime and put Alison's killer in jail for the sake of the college and her family and friends.

Without realizing it, the two entered Cormac Hall and went down to the office. They went inside, and Tyler was jolted from his thoughts by the sight of a beautiful, red-headed girl sitting at one of the desks.

She looked to be about Tyler's height, and her long, toned legs were sticking out of short, plaid shorts that matched the flip-flops on her feet. Her skin was slightly tanned, but she looked darker thanks to the white tank top stretched across her supple breasts.

As the two entered, she turned, her blue eyes looking at them closely. Then she broke into a vibrant smile.

"Ginger!" Charlie said. "Good to see you!"

He quickly walked toward the girl, and she met him halfway. They embraced. When they let go of each other, he turned to Tyler. "Tyler, this is Hayley Godin. Also known as Ginger for obvious reasons. She's our photo editor and a pretty good reporter too."

Tyler extended his hand. "Nice to meet you."

She shook his hand firmly as she looked him in the eye. The handshake lasted longer than seemed necessary, and her eyes never left his. "Nice to me you too . . ."

"Tyler. Tyler Fox."

She let go of his hand but didn't stop looking at him. Her eyes sparkled. "Tyler Fox. Seems appropriate."

Confusion crossed Tyler's brow, but before he could ask what she meant by the comment, Charlie spoke.

"You're here just in time," he said. "The shit's hitting the fan."

Hayley nodded. "I heard there was a murder. Poor girl. What happened?"

"She got shot while fucking her boyfriend on the golf course."

She gasped. "Oh man! Did the boyfriend do it?"

"No," Tyler said, surprised he found his voice.

"Yeah, he got beat up by the killer," Charlie said. "That hick isn't smart enough to set this up. It was done too well to be the work of him."

Hayley thought about this a moment by staring down at the ground. Then she looked up, her eyes carefully looking over Tyler before looking at Charlie. "So give me the details. What's the plan? We need to find the bastard that did this."

Charlie and Tyler filled her in on everything they knew, and soon the three were planning out the next issue of the *Clarion*. After a few hours of discussion, coverage of the murder was all sketched out.

"So let's recap," Charlie said. "I'm going to talk to the administration, instructors, and campus security to get a feel for how this affects the college and campus life. Tyler, since you already got an interview out of Robert Ray, you are going to cover that angle. You're going to build a profile of who he is by talking to family and friends, maybe even him. Ginger, you're going to talk to Alison's roommate and students on campus. Between Ginger and me, we'll compose a profile and obituary about Alison. Between Tyler and me, we'll come up with a story about the murder. How am I doing so far?"

"So far, so good," Hayley said.

Charlie smiled. "Great. I was also thinking that, Tyler, maybe you should write an editorial about this. I know you were pretty fired up about the killer being caught and how awful this is, so maybe you should take a stance on this for the paper. What do you say?"

Tyler shrugged. "Sure. I could do that."

"Well, okay," Charlie said. "That does it. I think we have a plan."

"Sure does," Tyler said, "but won't we need other news in the paper besides this?"

Charlie nodded with a smile. "Yes, but we can hash that out tomorrow. We need to focus on the big story first. I mean, we'll need stories about the first week of school, changes to scheduling, activities news and whatnot, including previews of the sports teams, but we can assign those tomorrow. Those will be relatively easy to handle compared to this murder stuff."

"What about the design of the murder package?" Hayley asked.

"The twins will be here tomorrow. I got an e-mail this morning."

"Who are the twins?" Tyler asked.

Hayley turned to him. "They are Misty and Alex Mitchell. They're a brother and sister duo. Their dad operates one of the most successful graphic design firms in Missouri. The whole family is devotedly Catholic, so they came here and helped bring the *Clarion* a sharper look."

"Yeah. They're great. They'll come up with something sharp, I'm sure. I'm just going to tell them all the stuff I want to include and let them run wild," Charlie said.

"Cool," Tyler said.

Charlie looked at his watch. "Holy shit. It's almost six. I guess we should call it a day."

All three of them stood up. "Oh, and Ginger, I've got photos for you to edit. I'll let you have the memory card Monday or something."

"Sounds good," Hayley said.

"You going to be available for the vigil tomorrow? We'll need all hands on deck."

Hayley flashed a vibrant smile. "Of course. I wouldn't miss it."

"Well, see you all Sunday?" Charlie asked.

Hayley walked to the door. "See you, Tyler."

Tyler smiled. "See ya."

She left, and Charlie looked at Tyler. "No good-bye for me?"

"I guess not," Tyler said, still looking at the door.

"I'm over here, Ty."

Tyler looked at him and smiled sheepishly.

"I know. I know. She's fucking hot."

"Yeah."

"And she seems to have taken a liking to you right off."

"I don't know."

"I do. She was eyeing you like a piece of meat."

Tyler chuckled nervously.

"It's funny. When I hired you, I promised girls. Catholic schoolgirls. That's what Ginger is, you know."

Tyler shook his head.

"I'm just saying don't dismiss it. I've known Ginger for a while now. I've never seen her date anyone, but I have seen her get what she wants in everything else. She's relentless. If she wants you, she'll have you."

"Is that bad?"

"Hell no!" Charlie laughed. "You need to hit that!"

"Hit that?"

"Don't play dumb. You know what I mean."

"Do you have to say it like that?"

"Yes. Yes, I do, but enough talk about your new piece of ass. You said you heard Sheriff Giles talking with Deputy Bonner and Nick. What did they have to say?"

Tyler sat back down. "Well, first Sheriff Giles talked about how good looking Alison was, especially naked."

"That sick bastard."

"Then they said they knew Robert Ray didn't do it because he wasn't smart enough to think of beating himself up to make it look like he wasn't involved. They said he got beat up while peeing in the sand trap. The sheriff also said he was sure it wasn't a sex crime. He said Robert Ray and Alison probably had sex, but it was consensual."

"Yeah, it looked like they were having a romantic evening, judging by the blanket and beer."

"Of course, Sheriff Giles said he wasn't going to release Robert Ray until he had to. Said he wanted to keep him from causing more fights at the bars. He also said they didn't find any bullet casings or anything. He said they didn't have anything to solve the case. He said they needed a miracle."

Charlie smiled. "The *Clarion* could be that miracle."

"You think so? You think we'll be able to do what they can't?"

"We've got more access around here. Those dumbasses won't be able to talk to the people we will."

Tyler nodded.

"So what else did they say?"

"That was about it. Officer Jones seemed like he really wanted the killer brought to justice, but Deputy Bonner stayed pretty quiet. Just toed the line in front of his boss. Of-ficer Jones spoke up, but Sheriff Giles made him shut up."

"Prick."

"And he was saying how worried he was he wouldn't get reelected this year."

"That stupid sonofabitch!" Charlie exclaimed. "That's all he's worried about. He doesn't care if the killer is caught. He just wants to keep his job."

Tyler nodded again.

"Good work, Ty," Charlie said, clapping him on the back. "Why don't you head home and get some rest. You look tired."

"I kind of am. Couldn't sleep well."

"Me neither," Charlie said as the two walked to the door and left. "I don't think I slept at all really."

"I know how you feel," Tyler said as the two emerged from Cormac Hall. The evening was warm, but a nice breeze was blowing.

"I'll talk to you tomorrow, Ty. I'm going to spend some time with Joni tonight."

"Have fun," Tyler said as the two parted ways.

When Tyler got back to his dorm room, he turned on the television and flopped down on the bed. He didn't even see what was on. He fell asleep instantly.

Chapter Eight

Tyler woke up drenched in sweat. He had the nightmare again.

"Man," he said to his empty room.

He looked at his nightstand clock and saw it was just after 8:00 a.m.

"At least I slept all night this time," he said as he crawled out of bed.

The television was still on from the night before. A morning news program was being broadcast, so he turned up the volume. The anchor on the screen was talking about the murder at St. Alfanus. He listened for a moment but grew tired of the speculation being discussed. He flipped the channel to a sitcom and went into the bathroom.

For a moment he considered going for a jog, but for one of the first times since he had begun high school, he didn't feel like exercising. Instead, he got ready for the day and went back out to his bed and sat down. He fired up his laptop and grabbed his MP3 player from the nightstand. He decided to write up what he could remember from when he talked to Robert Ray so he and Charlie could get to work on the story and he could develop questions for Robert Ray's family and friends, if he could get them to talk.

Soon Tyler was lost in the work. He didn't stop, working through lunch and late into the afternoon. He even started work on the editorial Charlie had assigned him. He didn't stop working until his cell phone rang shortly before 6:00 p.m.

Tyler scooped up his phone and looked at the screen. It was Charlie. Accepting the call, he answered, "What's up?"

"Not much," Charlie said. "What are you up to?"

"Working."

"Working? On what?"

"I've been writing up notes from when I talked to Robert Ray and coming up with questions to ask his family and friends. I've also been outlining that editorial you asked me to do. Say, is it going to have my name on it?"

"No. It is going to be an unsigned editorial representing the opinion of the entire paper. Basically, without the author's name, it will have all our names. You feel me?"

"Yeah."

"Great. Now stop working. We're going out."

"What?"

"Yep. Put on your party dress. We're going to Irene's."

"What's that?"

"It's the bar in Hooks. Owned by Irene Worthington. She's a tough old bag. Don't ever mess with her. Anyway, we're going dancing. I hope you know how to two-step."

"Well, I don't. And I can't go to a bar. I'm not old enough."

"Don't be such a baby. This is Hooks. If you can see over the counter, you can buy a drink. Besides, this was Hayley's idea. She said she wanted to go blow off a little steam before classes start Monday, and she told me specifically to make sure your ass was there."

"Is Joni going?"

"Of course Joni's going."

Tyler was silent.

"So are you coming or what?" Charlie asked impatiently.

"Sure," Tyler said in defeat.

"Good. Because Joni and I are at your door."

Loud knocking then began. Tyler hung up and answered the door. Joni was standing there wearing a cowboy hat, yellow cowboy boots, blue jeans, and a yellow T-shirt. Charlie was wearing jeans, work boots, and a baby-blue pocket T-shirt.

"Wow," Tyler said as he let them inside.

"We look good, don't we?" Joni asked as she ruffled Tyler's hair.

"Very country," Tyler agreed.

"Country? Hell, we look like we just came off the range, if you ask me," Charlie said. He looked at what Tyler was wearing. "Okay. That outfit might fly in Goessel, but this is Texas, Ty. You've got to look the part a little more."

"I don't have any redneck clothes."

Charlie shook his head. "Why do you have to be so difficult? Listen, put on a pair of jeans and a T-shirt. If you've got boots of some sort, that's great, but if you walk in there wearing those khaki shorts, that red polo, and flip-flops, you'll probably get your ass kicked because the locals will think you're gay."

Rolling his eyes, Tyler opened his closet and looked around. He found a pair of tattered jeans and a white T-shirt. "How are these?"

"Great," Joni said. "What about shoes?"

Tyler sighed and leaned farther into the closet. After rummaging around at the bottom for a moment, he stood up with a pair of brown boots.

"Holy shit," Charlie said. "Those are almost cowboy boots. Where did you get them?"

"Honestly, a friend of mine gave them to me as a graduation present because he thought it was hilarious that I was moving to Texas."

"Well, the joke's on him, honey," Joni said, smiling. "Get dressed. Your lady is waiting."

"My lady?" Tyler asked as he pulled off his polo and slipped the T-shirt on.

"Yeah, Miss Hayley," Joni said. "Sounds like you made quite the impression."

"Charlie talks a lot," Tyler said, stepping into the bathroom to change into the jeans.

"True, but I could hear her talking to him on the phone. She was very insistent that you come out tonight," Joni said, cocking a hip and resting an elbow on it.

Tyler came back out of the bathroom and began slipping the boots on. "Whatever," he said.

The three left the room and went up to the next floor on the other end of the building. Charlie loudly rapped on the door. It swung open, and Hayley stepped out.

Tyler thought for a moment his heart stopped. He couldn't believe how good she looked. She was wearing skin-tight jeans with purple cowboy boots. She had on a long-sleeved pearl-snap shirt. The sleeves were rolled up to her elbows, and the buttons were undone at the neck all the way down to her chest. Her red hair flowed around her face.

"Hi guys!" she said happily as she shut the door behind her. "Looking good, Tyler."

Charlie and Joni exchanged a look.

"You look good too, Hayley," Tyler said, smiling, his cheeks burning with embarrassment.

"Thanks," she said, winking at him. "So shall we get going? I want to start early so we can finish late," she said to the trio with a sly grin.

"Hell yes!" Charlie said. "Let's get it on!"

The four loaded into Charlie's car and made the short drive to Irene's. As they stepped out of the car, they could hear country music blaring inside the building.

"I haven't got to dance all summer," Hayley said as they approached the entrance. "Charlie, you going to dance with me?"

Charlie shook his head and grinned. "Sorry, Ginger. Can't. I've got a woman," he said as he hooked an arm around Joni's waist and kissed her on the cheek.

Hayley pouted her lips and looked at the ground. "Well, shoot. Who will dance with me then?" She leveled her gaze at Tyler.

Tyler stammered. "I will. I mean. I'll try. I've never two-stepped before."

Flashing a broad smile, Hayley said, "Don't worry. I'll teach you."

Inside, the group found a table in the middle of the bar near the dance floor. Charlie went off and came back with four red beers.

"What's this?" Tyler shouted, turning the glass mug in his hands.

"It's beer! Come on, Ty!" Charlie said.

"Oh. Well, why's it red?"

"There's tomato juice in it," Hayley said into Tyler's ear. "It's good."

Tyler shrugged and took a sip. "Wow. That is good."

"Yep. After tonight you won't be turning down my offers for beer . . . at least I hope," Charlie said, taking a long drink from his own mug.

As he set his glass down, Joni grabbed his hand. "Let's dance!"

The two went onto the dance floor and began dancing to the upbeat country music, leaving Hayley and Tyler at the table.

"I'm really glad you came out tonight," Hayley said. "Charlie told me you weren't much of a partier."

Tyler blushed. "Well, no. Not really. But I figured since you just got back into town it was worth it."

She smiled. "You're sweet."

Tyler smiled back at her.

"So you want to learn to dance?"

"Sure."

Hayley took Tyler by the hand, and his heart jumped. She pulled him onto the dance floor and began to teach him how to two-step. After three or four songs, he began to get the hang of it.

When the music slowed and the lights dimmed for a slow dance, Tyler began to leave the dance floor, but Hayley pulled him back and wrapped her arms around him, nestling her head into the crook of his neck. He put his arms around her and pulled her close. She sighed.

Nearby Charlie saw the two dancing. He nudged Joni and told her to look. Tyler saw them staring at him with smiles. He smiled back, and Charlie winked at him.

When the dance ended, all four *Clarion* staffers gathered back at their table. Charlie said he was going to go get them another round of drinks, and he took Tyler with him. As they stood at the bar waiting for Irene to take their orders, they talked.

"She likes you, Ty," Charlie said with a grin. "I told you."

Tyler smiled. "I guess so."

"So? What do you think of her?"

"She's hot and seems pretty cool, but we just met. I don't want to read too much into it."

Nodding, Charlie said, "That makes sense, but I think you two will be an item before long."

Tyler began to protest, but then they both heard a couple of men start arguing.

"You better shut the fuck up, man," one guy was saying. "There's no way Robert Ray did that. He loved that girl. He was ring shopping for her."

"Whatever," the second guy said. "There's no way that rich bitch's daddy was going to let that happen. He's got a temper. He probably knew he was going to get shot down, so he shot the little cunt down right after he slipped it to her."

"Fuck you!" the first guy said.

As Charlie and Tyler watched, the first guy grabbed a beer bottle and smashed it over the head of the second guy. With blood gushing from his forehead, the guy staggered backward, then lunged at Robert Ray's supporter. The two crashed into a table and fell to the floor, fists flying.

Friends of both men joined in on the fight. Irene yelled at the group and came around the bar with a baseball bat in hand.

"Y'all knock this shit off!" she shouted.

They paid no attention, and the fight quickly began to grow into an all-out brawl.

"Oh shit," Charlie said. "The girls!"

The two turned and saw Hayley and Joni getting pushed around as people pushed their way toward the fight.

Charlie reached the girls first. He grabbed Joni and began to pull her toward the door, but he couldn't get a hand on Hayley to take her with them. Just as Tyler got to her side, a large cowboy took a punch to the side of the head and stumbled into Hayley. Tyler shoved him to the side. The guy caught his bearings and turned on Tyler.

As he threw a punch, Hayley screamed. Tyler ducked the drunken man's attack and threw a right jab that connected with the man's jaw. He followed with a left uppercut that sent the man reeling and landing on his back on the dance floor.

Hayley clutched Tyler.

"Let's get out of here," he told her.

She nodded, wide-eyed.

As they left the bar, the lights inside came on, and sirens could be heard in the distance. At Charlie's car, Tyler looked Hayley over. "Are you okay?"

Hayley nodded. "I think so," she said, fighting back tears.

"Good," he said, hustling her into the back seat. Charlie had the engine running.

"Holy shit!" Charlie said. "Everyone all right?"

Everyone said they were, and Charlie quickly backed his car out of its parking spot and left the bar. They drove in silence for a while. Hayley cuddled up against Tyler in the back, and Joni clenched Charlie's hand as he drove.

Eventually, Charlie spoke. "That sucks for you, Ty."

"How so?" he asked.

"Those boys fighting are the people you need to talk to," Charlie said, glancing in the rearview mirror at Tyler. "They must be Robert Ray's friends."

"Great."

"Did you get a good look at them?"

Tyler shook his head. "Not really."

"That's okay. If you come and talk to Irene about it Monday, she'll be able to tell you their names. Hell, they'll probably be there Monday night."

Tyler couldn't believe what he was hearing. "You want me to do a story about this?"

"Yes," Charlie said. "It is part of the story. People are edgy about what happened, and the people in that fight seemed to know Robert Ray."

Tyler sighed and settled deeper into the seat. Hayley held onto him tighter.

When they pulled into the dormitory parking lot, Charlie turned and looked at Tyler and Hayley. "Joni and I are going to go stay at my place. You two okay here?"

Tyler nodded. "I think so."

"Okay. I'll call you tomorrow. We can meet up before the vigil."

"Okay," Hayley said, getting out of the car.

"See ya," Tyler said and stepped out.

With a wave, Charlie and Joni drove off.

"Wow," Tyler said to Hayley as they watched Charlie's taillights disappear. "That was nuts."

"Yes it was," Hayley said.

"He's a hard-core journalist though, isn't he?" Tyler asked. "He instantly started looking at angles to cover this."

Hayley smiled weakly. "Yep. He's good. It seems strange sometimes, but that kind of drive is what is needed, I guess."

"I guess so."

"I'm tired," Hayley said. "Will you walk me to my door?"

"Of course."

The two went into the dormitory and went to Hayley's room.

"My roommate is probably sound asleep," she said as they stood in front of her door.

"You have a roomie?"

"Yeah," she said. "You don't?"

Tyler shook his head. "Nope. My coach arranged it so I wouldn't have one because I would be coming and going so often he didn't want my practice schedule to bother someone else."

"Lucky you."

"I guess."

They stood staring at each other for a moment. Then she spoke. "Thanks for saving me tonight."

Tyler blushed. "It was nothing."

"No. It was something. It was great. You dropped that guy like he was nothing."

Tyler began to speak, but Hayley stopped him with a finger pressed to his lips. Then she leaned in and kissed him.

At first Tyler let her kiss him, but soon he was kissing her back. One of his hands settled on her butt, and his other slid up to her neck, his fingers locking into her silken hair. Her hands clutched his neck and shoulders.

After a while, they broke their embrace, both breathing heavier than normal.

"Goodnight, Tyler," she said as she unlocked her door.

"Night, Hayley," Tyler said as she opened her room.

"See you tomorrow," she said, stepping inside.

"See ya," he said as she pulled the door shut.

Tyler went back to his room, his mind reeling—first a fight and then a kiss. It had definitely been an interesting night.

Chapter Nine

With his hand wrapped in a bandage, Tyler met with Joni, Charlie, and Hayley at the *Clarion* office thirty minutes prior to the start of the vigil for Alison Alcott. Everyone was dressed respectably for the occasion but practical to work. They had a lot to do during the ceremony honoring the killed St. Alfanus student.

Charlie began to lay out the marching orders. "Hayley, you and I will be running cameras. Don't be afraid to get close and get emotional shots. We need those. Tyler, you need to take notes like you've never taken notes before. All three of us will try to get quotes and reactions from students in attendance. If you see anyone you are supposed to talk to as we discussed Friday, catch them now. With classes starting tomorrow, we might not be able to get in touch with them in time otherwise. Lucky for us they are holding off on the Rosary and whatnot until after the remembering portion of the evening. That will give us extra time to talk to people who chose not to stay for the entire ceremony."

Everyone nodded. "What about me, Charlie?" Joni asked.

Charlie smiled. "Just look good and be noticed. The three of us will be working and probably end up bothering someone for intruding on this. That's a load of crap, but we have to play the PR game. You're the friendly face of the *Clarion*. Be noticed. Show support. Paint the rest of us in a positive light so we won't be scorned for doing our jobs."

Joni nodded.

"Okay," Charlie said, slinging a camera over his shoulder. "Let's do it."

The four went outside and began walking toward the main drive as dusk descended upon St. Alfanus. Candles were being lit among the large number of people in attendance. A stage was set up in front of the crowd. President and Mrs. Alcott were seated there alongside Paula Garcia, Officer Jones, Sheriff Giles, and Deputy Bonner, as well as various professors and administrators.

Hayley struck off from the group and began snapping photos and jotting down names of people in the images. Charlie did the same.

"I'm going to stick with you, Ty," Joni said.

"Okay," Tyler said as he made his way to the front of the crowd directly in front of the stage.

Soon, Father Mike Holmes stepped to the lectern and flipped on the microphone. The public address system buzzed momentarily as electricity coursed through the system.

"Hello everyone," Father Mike began. "On this, the eve of the new school year, we gather for a somber reason. A tragedy has struck our beloved St. Alfanus, and as a campus and community, we must come together and support one another as we grieve and attempt to understand God's reason for taking one of our own at such a young age."

Behind him in the crowd, Tyler heard people begin to sob.

Father Mike then launched into a long discussion of who Alison was. Her parents sobbed heartily as he spoke.

As Father Mike wrapped up his obituary for Alison, he gently slapped the lectern at which he stood. "Alison's death shall not be in vain for she perfectly represented all that St. Alfanus represents. This institution is based on the values of our Lord and Savior Jesus Christ, community, conversion of life, love of learning, listening, excellence through virtue, hospitality, stability, stewardship, prayer, and work. Alison was a faithful servant of the Lord. She served her community well, and she cherished learning, which is why she chose this esteemed place of learning. She was a hospitable soul, a person who was always available to listen and lend a shoulder to cry on. She was a leader with her peers, always guided by prayer. Our St. Alfanus himself would be proud to have said she attended a college of his same name. St. Alfanus was a Benedictine archbishop. He was a monk at Monte Cassino until appointed the archbishop of Salerno, Italy. Alfanus assisted Pope St. Gregory VII on his deathbed. So it begs the question, why was Alison taken from us so early? That is only for the Lord to know and reveal in due time. What we can take from her death is this: St. Alfanus took care of his own, and in Alison's death we shall all learn to take care of each other. St. Alfanus is built on such values, so her death can only mean it was time for us to once again be reminded of caring for each other and putting faith in the plans the Lord has for us."

Father Mike crossed himself and stepped away from the microphone. More people in the crowd cried. Paula Garcia stood and strode to the lectern.

"President and Mrs. Alcott wish to thank everyone for attending and showing support in this time of personal tragedy for them. They asked me to tell you all that they are confident the perpetrator behind Alison's death will be brought to justice because, as Father Mike just said, St. Alfanus takes care of its own. That has long been the motto of this institution, and they are comforted by the fact that one day the evildoer who has wrought such pain to this campus and community will face judgment both here on Earth and in the afterlife. Now, the student body president, Dean Carr, will speak. Followed by a close friend of Alison's. Then Father Mike will lead us through a Rosary."

Paula Garcia sat back down and a thick young man wearing a suit stepped forward.

"Hello," he said into the microphone. "My name is Dean Carr. I am your student body president. I will keep my comments brief. I just wanted to let President and Mrs. Alcott know that Alison will be missed. She was a scholar whose attendance at this great college was much anticipated. And to you, my fellow students, fear not. This will not diminish the great experience St. Alfanus has in store for us this year. It will only intensify the joys we will feel as we will experience them knowing that one of our own is no longer here to feel them with us. St. Alfanus has a grand history, and we will not let down the legacy left by Alison."

Charlie came up beside Tyler as Dean Carr spoke. "It's hard to believe, isn't it?" he whispered.

"That she's gone?" Tyler asked in a hushed tone.

"No. That he's gay. Hard to think a gay dude would get elected student body president at a religious college, isn't it?"

"How do you know that?" Tyler asked, aghast.

"Trust me," Charlie said quietly. "Besides, you should be able to tell. I mean, listen to him go on and on about Alison as if she'd been here for four years. She hadn't even taken a class on campus, yet this douche is ready to put her up on pedestal next to Alfanus."

Tyler shook his head as Dean Carr thanked the crowd for its time and stepped away from the microphone.

Then Brooke Nichols stepped up to the microphone.

"Brooke?" Tyler asked out loud.

"You know her?" Charlie asked, starring at Tyler.

"Yeah," Tyler said. "She works at the golf course."

"Hello," Brooke said into the microphones as she blotted her eyes with a tissue. "My name is Brooke Nichols. I was-am-a close friend of Alison's. We went to high school together, and we were going to be roommates this year. I've waited a long time for her to move here for good. It was always a joy when she came to visit her parents, and I was excited to spend my final year at St. Alfanus with her as she experienced her first official year as a student here.

"Alison was a great person. I just can't understand why someone would have done this to her. She never would have hurt a fly. I loved her like a sister."

Brooke then broke down. Paula Garcia came forward and helped her back to her seat as Father Mike stepped forward and solemnly began the Rosary. Some of the crowd dispersed, but a majority stayed, their tear-soaked faces lit by the glow of the candles.

Charlie, Joni, and Tyler slowly worked their ways to the edge of the crowd and waited for Hayley, who they could see periodically popping up and shooting pictures of people crying, praying or doing both.

Eventually she joined them, her eyes rimmed red from crying, and they silently went back to Cormac Hall, but they didn't go into the *Clarion* office.

Enjoying the night air, Charlie said, "So did we get anything?"

"I did," Hayley said. "I got some great pictures, and now I know who Alison's roommate was going to be. That's a very helpful lead."

"Yes indeed," Charlie said. "Speaking of which, Ty, didn't you say you knew her roommate?"

Tyler nodded. "Yeah. She works the equipment shed at the golf course. I have to check in my clubs with her after I practice."

"What do you know about her?"

"Not much. She's never talked about Alison to me. Of course, why would she? Until now, there's been no reason for her to come up in conversation."

"True," Charlie said, looking up at the sky. "Well, at least we have a lead. Shall we get together in the morning to figure out the rest of this week's paper?"

"I think so," Hayley said. "I'm going to look through the photos tonight and organize the quotes I got."

"I'll probably do the same thing," Tyler said. "I feel like we need to get the murder stories written so we can get the first-week-of-school stories tackled."

Charlie agreed. "Sounds like a plan."

Charlie and Joni then walked off together, and Hayley and Tyler headed toward the dormitory.

"This was tough," she said as they walked.

"Yes it was," Tyler said. "It took all I had not to start crying."

"I wasn't able to hold it in," Hayley said with a light chuckle as she dabbed at her eyes. "I didn't know the girl, but I just feel awful for her family and friends."

"Me too."

Silence spun out between them. Then Hayley spoke again. "So you know Brooke? Alison's roommate?"

"Kind of," Tyler said with a shrug. "I only talked to her when I was checking in my clubs after practice. She was always nice."

"You think she'll talk to me?"

"I'm sure."

"I hope so," Hayley said as they walked up the front steps of the dormitory. "This is going to be hard enough. I don't want to have to fight with someone to talk about their dead friend."

Tyler nodded.

"Well, I guess I'll see you tomorrow?"

"Yep."

"Good," Hayley said. She lightly kissed Tyler on the cheek and went to her room.

Tyler watched her go. Once he was sure she was safely in her room, he went to his room. He felt disgusted with himself. He should be focused on the murder of Alison Alcott, but instead he found himself wondering what the future was between Hayley and him. She seemed to like him. Twice now she had kissed him, but Tyler felt inclined to attribute that to her just feeling vulnerable due to the murder.

"What could she possibly see in me?" he asked as he sat down with his laptop in hand and began typing notes.

The next day the *Clarion* staff met early at the newspaper's office and got to work. Everyone took assignments for how to cover the first week of school, and they all went about their tasks as time allowed between their classes. Charlie only had one class, English Literature, on Mondays, so he went to it and sat at the back of the lecture hall in Cormac Hall. The teacher, Dr. Arthur Laureth, was also Charlie's academic adviser and the *Clarion*'s official faculty adviser, though he did little with the paper. The *Clarion*'s adviser was the adviser purely in title because the paper needed a college staff member to be involved before St. Alfanus would allow the campus newspaper to exist. Dr. Laureth wasn't the first adviser of the *Clarion*, but he was the most recent, agreeing to take the job so Charlie could continue to keep the paper running. Dr. Laureth knew little about journalism, but he was happy to help keep the paper alive by signing his name on the dotted line and agreeing to fill the position. As long as the editor did the job well, the faculty adviser had little to do with the paper, which helped preserve its freedom to report without interference from the college. The position was more of a safety net for St. Alfanus. It kept them out of any legal problems brought on by having a rogue paper on campus, but the way the *Clarion* advisers had operated also kept the college from censoring or demanding prior review of the paper. It was a good relationship.

After class, Charlie went to the front of the room and stopped Dr. Laureth.

"Hey," he said.

"Hello, Charlie," Dr. Laureth said, peering at Charlie over his half-style reading glasses that completed his scholarly look of a sweater vest, dress slacks, polished shoes, and balding head. "What can I do for you?"

"I just wanted to talk to you about this murder business," Charlie said.

Dr. Laureth's eyes narrowed. "What about it?"

"Well, I just wanted to let you know what we had going for this week's paper."

"Okay," Dr. Laureth said slowly.

"We don't have a lot. The cops don't have a clue as to who did it, and we don't have a lot more than they do."

Dr. Laureth's eyes softened. "I see. Well, just do your best. It's sad to say, but sometimes murderers get away with it. That's a sad truth of life."

"I guess, but St. Alfanus is known for taking care of its own. Won't that help bring the killer to justice?"

Dr. Laureth laughed. "Charlie, I don't mean to sound crude, but the notion that this place takes care of its own generally refers to money. And I fear there is no amount of money that will miraculously uncover the killer."

Charlie nodded. "I guess not."

"You know I don't know a lot about journalism, but you've got a lot of talent, Charlie. Don't let this bog you down. You're two semesters away from graduation. Cover this story as best as you can, but also begin to prepare for your life after St. Alfanus. You've got a bright future. I'd hate for you to come up short of your potential because of this."

"Okay," Charlie said, a bit confused.

"Okay. Now, I hate to cut this short, but I've got to get ready for my freshman English class. It is going to be a zoo, especially because one of the students won't be there."

"All right," Charlie said, turning to leave. "Thanks for your time."

Outside of Cormac Hall, Charlie lit a cigarette and thought about what Dr. Laureth had said. It was puzzling to him, but it also made some sort of sense. St. Alfanus was a private college. Money had to play into many decisions.

Charlie finished his cigarette and went down to his office. He called President Alcott's number. Paula Garcia answered and told him the president wouldn't be making any statements for a while.

"Shit," Charlie said as he hung up and stared at the wall.

Across campus, Hayley walked up to the dorm room that she had been told was the one Alison Alcott had been assigned to. She knocked rapidly on the door.

Brooke opened the door and looked at Hayley. "Can I help you?" she asked.

Hayley quickly looked at the floor. Brooke was wearing no clothing except a sheer robe that left nothing to the imagination.

"Oh, uh. Hello," Hayley said to the floor. "Is this a bad time?"

Brooke shrugged. "Not really. What do you need?"

"I'm, I'm, I'm a reporter for the campus paper, the *Clarion*. I was hoping to talk to you about Alison."

"Oh. I guess that would be okay, and don't be so shy. We have the same body parts, you know," Brooke said, gently pulling Hayley's chin up so their eyes met. "Please come in."

"O-Okay," Hayley stammered. "Do you need to finish dressing?"

Brooke smiled coyly and winked at her. "So what would you like to know?" she asked as they sat down next to each other on the dorm bed, ignoring Hayley's question.

"Well," Hayley said, looking around the room and trying to avoid the sight of the nearly nude girl on the bed next to her. "I guess first, how are you holding up?"

Brooke shrugged. "All right. It's just hard, you know. We were really close. We went to high school and elementary school together. We spent almost every summer together. I was so excited to have her coming to St. Alfanus with me."

"How did you two get so close?"

"Summer camp. That's when we first met. Sure, we'd seen each other at school before, but it was at summer camp when we became so close."

"What kind of camp was it?"

"It was a softball camp. Neither of us was very good. We just enjoyed playing. We learned a lot at those camps."

"Like what?"

Brooke chuckled. "I don't know if I should really get into it."

"It'll be fine. What did you learn?"

Brooke thought for a moment. Then she blurted out, "Sex."

Hayley's jaw dropped. "Excuse me?"

"Sex," Brooke repeated. "But it wasn't the kind of sex people usually associate with softball. It was all about boys. See, there was a baseball camp on the other side of the campus the camp was held on. No one ever stayed in their own rooms at those things. Boys were on the girls' side and vice versa."

"And that's how you and Alison became so close?" Hayley asked, stunned.

"Yes," Brooke said nodding. "Alison was new to the camp, and I had been there a year. Since I recognized her from school, I took her under my wing. By the end of the second year, we had our pick. We learned how to get what we wanted from whichever cleated god we chose to inspect the jockstrap of."

Hayley couldn't believe what she was hearing. "President Alcott's daughter?"

Brooke smiled. "Yes, but please don't print that. There's no sense in bringing that up. It's over now."

"Right. The murder. Maybe we should focus on that?"

"I think that would be best," Brooke said, getting up and retrieving a bottle of water from the minifridge next to her door. "Want anything to drink?"

"No thanks," Hayley said. "So, since it seems Alison might have . . . enjoyed the company of men, did she have a lot of boyfriends?"

"Alison? Heavens no!" Brooke exclaimed, sitting back down. "She was never serious about any of them. They were just our toys. Until she met Robert Ray Turner last spring. She was really into him."

"He's the one who was with her when she died, right?"

"Yep. Alison told me she and him had planned a romantic evening on the golf course. She didn't tell me, but I knew what she had planned."

"So do you think he did it?"

"Not a chance. Robert Ray worshiped the ground she walked on, and he damned well should have. There was no way he was going to get anything hotter than Alison, especially living around here."

"So what do you think happened?"

"I don't know," Brooke said, her mood turning from flirty to angry. "But if I ever find out who that sonofabitch is, I'll personally rip his nuts off."

"Who do you think could have done it? Did Alison have any enemies?"

"No. Alison was a sweet girl," Brooke said, her eyes filling with tears. "She never hurt anyone. Sure, she might have left a few broken hearts along the way, but that's to be expected. She was beautiful and smart and knew what she wanted."

Hayley sat for a moment. "This is a tragedy, isn't it?"

Brooke nodded, reaching for a box of tissues. "Yes. I realize I must not have seemed too upset over it when you arrived, but I've been doing everything I can to put it out of my mind. She was like my sister. I don't know what I'm going to do without her."

"I understand. Everyone copes differently. Once, when my grandmother died, I cracked jokes. People thought I was incredibly insensitive, but that's just how I dealt with it."

"I know what you mean."

"Well, thanks for your time, Brooke. If you think of anyone who might have had it out for Alison, let me know, okay?"

Brooke walked Hayley to the door. "I will."

As Hayley stepped outside, she stopped and turned to face Brooke. "One last question. Were you and Alison, uh, ever romantically involved?"

Brooke smiled. "Just like any girls we had experimented, and this year might have brought a bunch of new experiences. Why? See something you like?" Brooke asked as she stretched herself seductively into the doorway.

Hayley blushed. "No. No. Not me. I-I was just trying to be thorough."

"Okay. If you change your mind, you know where to find me," Brooke called as Hayley quickly walked down the hallway.

Holy shit! Hayley thought to herself. She's a freak!

Even as she thought it, though, Hayley was surprised by her own desire that had been stirred up, and she began to wonder what Tyler was doing.

She pulled her phone out of her pocket and dialed his number. The call went straight to his voicemail.

"Shoot," she said to herself as she went outside and sat at a picnic table beside the dormitory.

Hayley couldn't believe herself. She was crushing on Tyler Fox, and she had just met him. What was more troubling to her was how listening to Brooke's crass descriptions and flippant attitude toward sex had got her a bit worked up. Hayley didn't consider herself a prude. She had been with boyfriends before, and those relationships had gone far beyond what most would consider proper for a devout Catholic. Catholics were humans too, after all. No, sex didn't bother her. She enjoyed it. What bothered her was how exciting it was to hear another female talk so openly about it. That never would have happened where she grew up. Sex was obviously a vital part of life, but it wasn't discussed. Just briefly talking about Alison's and Brooke's sex lives caused Hayley to feel hot and flushed, leaving her longing for the warmth of Tyler's embrace as she'd felt it on the dance floor and at her doorway Saturday night.

Hayley looked at her cell phone. She'd been sitting outside for almost thirty minutes thinking about Tyler.

"Jesus," she said, standing up.

Then from behind her came Tyler's voice. "Hayley?"

She spun around, and her face lit up at the sight of Tyler. "Ty! How's it going?"

He smiled. "Good. Just got out of class. I don't know why I signed up for physics. I hate math. And science. Physics is like the worst of both those worlds. What are you doing?"

Her eyes darted away from his for a moment. "I was just sitting outside. Enjoying the afternoon."

"Not really much of an afternoon left."

"No. I guess not."

"So what are you doing tonight?"

"I don't have any plans yet," she said, her heart skipping. This is ridiculous! she thought. I'm older than he is, yet I'm acting like a schoolgirl. A naughty, Catholic school g-Stop it!

Tyler nodded as he came up next to Hayley. "Well, I was going to go do a quick piece on the football team preparing for the first game of the season next week. If you wanted to go with, we could go grab a bite to eat afterward."

Yes! she screamed in her head. "That would be fun," she told him.

"Cool," he said, smiling. "Let me just go drop off my books, and we can head that way."

"Okay," Hayley said through a broad smile. "But, do you have a car? How can we go eat?"

"Oh," Tyler said with sudden understanding crossing his face. "Crap. I don't have a car."

Hayley stepped closer to him. "Well, we could walk, couldn't we?"

"I suppose. If we go into Hooks to eat, though, that could mean like a couple miles of walking."

Despite herself, she slipped her hand into his. "That sounds like a wonderful time. Just the two of us. Walking under the stars."

Tyler slowly grasped her hand in his. "You're right. That does sound like a good time."

Together they walked up to his room and dropped off his schoolbooks. Then they went and watched the football team practice before heading off toward Hooks. Rarely did their hands separate the rest of the night.

Chapter Ten

After a full day of classes Tuesday, Tyler met up with the rest of the *Clarion* staff in the newspaper's office. If anyone had asked what classes he had attended that day, he wouldn't have been able to give a decent answer. He had thought about Hayley all day. After a great night with her, he was giving up on the notion that she was just feeling vulnerable, and he was trying to mentally prepare himself for what he saw as inevitable—they were going to become a couple. It frightened him some because he had never had a serious girlfriend, but he enjoyed spending time with Hayley so much he knew it wouldn't take a lot for him to get over his hurdle of fear.

Upon entering the *Clarion*, though, he no longer had time to think about the new woman in his life.

"Ty," Charlie said, emerging from his office. "Between me and you, we have all the normal stories covered, I think. Hayley is going to wrap one up today. Otherwise, we just have Alison Alcott stories to worry about. When are you going to go talk to Irene and the fellas that got into the fight?"

"I don't know," Tyler said, dropping his backpack to the floor.

"Wrong answer," Charlie said, slapping him on the back. "The correct answer is tonight."

"Okay. Tonight."

"You're a good man, Ty. I'll even drive you to Irene's since you are such a good guy."

"Thanks," Tyler said, sitting down at a computer. "When are we going?"

"Soon. I want to get there early enough to give you time to talk to Irene before Robert Ray's friends hopefully show up."

"Okay."

"Did you and Hayley have a nice walk last night?" Charlie asked with a grin.

"How did you know about that?"

Still smiling, Charlie said, "Jonesy. He's stepped up his patrols since the murder. He told me this morning during our daily news briefing that he saw you and that lovely redhead leave and then come back a couple hours later. Said it looked like you two had been to Hooks on foot."

Tyler stared silently at his blank computer screen for a moment. Then he said, "Yeah. It was a nice walk."

Charlie laughed. "I bet it was. You two fucking yet?"

Tyler turned to Charlie, his cheeks burning with embarrassment. "What? No."

"Not yet, eh? I'm sure you will soon. So how are the Alcott stories coming?"

"Okay, I guess," Tyler said, booting up the computer. "I'm ready to sit down with you and write our story. After tonight I guess I'll have the Robert Ray piece, and I've about got the editorial done."

"Good. Get them done by tomorrow night. I'm having the twins come in early to get a start at laying this sucker out. I want to get it to the press as soon as possible Thursday so we can get it onto campus first thing Friday."

"Okay."

"Great. Let me go talk to Joni for a second, and then we can head out."

Tyler surfed the internet for a while and then left with Charlie. They arrived at Irene's, and Charlie ordered food and a beer at a table. He sent Tyler to a barstool. The sounds of a juke box and men playing pool filled the air, mingled in with the scent of smoke and stale beer.

Irene was a short, gray-haired woman who always seemed to have a cigarette dangling from her lips. Years of hard work and sweat under the sun and in the smoky bar left her skin looking like worn leather, but her eyes were vibrant green and revealed an energy Tyler doubted he would ever have.

"Hi," he said. "My name is Tyler. Can I talk to you for a bit?"

Irene looked at him. "Why?"

"Well, I'm from the *St. Alfanus Clarion*, and I'm working on a story about the murder of Alison Alcott."

The bar suddenly became quiet to Tyler. He could even hear the hum of the neon signs hanging on the wall behind the bar. "You are?" Irene asked, her eyes cutting through him like high beams to fog.

"Yes."

"And what makes you think I have anything to say."

"Well, I've spoken with Robert Ray, and I know he didn't do this. But the police are still holding him. I'm wanting to talk to people who knew him and can vouch for him. I was told he frequented this place. I was here Saturday night, and it seemed like that fight that broke out was because other people believe he is innocent too."

Irene looked at him a moment. Then she grabbed a shot glass and a bottle of whiskey. She poured a healthy shot and swallowed it as if it were water. "Okay. I'm listening."

"Great. First, thank you for this, and I just wanted to tell you that I really like this place. I'm from Kansas, and this is by far the best bar I've ever been to."

"Stop flirting. I'm too old, and you're too young to get into my pants."

Tyler was taken aback. "I wasn't trying to flirt."

She waved a hand at him and poured herself another shot. "Just ask what you have to ask."

"Okay," Tyler said, swallowing hard. "Let's just cut to the chase. Do you think Robert Ray did this?"

"No."

"Why?"

Irene then started talking about Robert Ray. She didn't stop for nearly an hour, during which time she went through four cigarettes. By the time she was finished, Tyler felt like he knew Robert Ray like a brother.

During Irene's narrative, Tyler learned that Robert Ray Turner had grown up outside of Hooks on a farm. His mother had left him and his father when he was three, and his father adopted the habit of bringing Robert Ray into Irene's to eat because he couldn't cook. Irene took Robert Ray in as one of her own. She helped raise the young man, who she admitted wasn't the brightest but had a big heart. As he entered high school, Irene said she put him to work in the bar, sweeping floors, scrubbing toilets and carrying kegs. He was a hard worker, Irene said. He would work on the farm all day and then come work in the bar during the summers. His father was proud of him, and though Irene admitted she probably shouldn't let him drink in her bar since he wasn't yet old enough, she couldn't help it. She loved the young man, and she wanted to take care of him. She confided at first she was worried when Robert Ray began talking about a new girl-friend he had. He had dated a couple of tramps before, and Irene didn't want to see him with another one of those. How-ever, when she finally got to meet Alison Alcott, she was relieved. She knew Alison's father might not take the news of his daughter dating a local cowboy well, but the young couple was working on a way to break the news.

"So now I guess they don't have to worry about it," Irene said at the end of her story. "It's a shame. He really loved her, and that's why there is no way he did this. Sure, he liked to fight in the bar and outside the bar, but the next day if he ran into the person he'd fought with, he'd smile, slap them on the back and laugh with them about how good of a fight it was."

Tyler nodded. "Wow. You know, when I first met him, I saw how tore up he was over Alison's death. I knew there was no way someone could be pretending to feel that kind of pain."

"Exactly," Irene said, lighting another cigarette. She took a long drag and then said, "So you were wanting to talk to some of his friends?"

"Yeah. If I could," Tyler said.

Irene nodded. "Johnny! Peter! Get over here!" she shouted.

Two gruff-looking men put down their pool cues and sauntered over to where Tyler sat at the bar.

"Tyler Fox," Irene said. "This is Johnny Hooper and Peter Colby. They are two of Robert Ray's best friends, and as you can tell by the black eye Peter's sporting, he was here for Saturday's fight."

Peter extended a thick hand and shook Tyler's. Johnny, wearing dirty bib overalls, wiped his hand on his pant leg and shook hands with Tyler as well.

"Boys, Tyler here works for the paper, and he is a supporter of Robert Ray. He wanted to talk to some of Robert Rays friends for a story. Play nice," Irene said just before she walked off to tend to the cash register.

"Hi," Tyler said.

Both men nodded hellos.

"How long have you two known Robert Ray?"

"All our lives," Peter said with Johnny nodding in agreement.

This is going to be an enthralling interview, Tyler thought. Then he said, "Okay. What do you think of this murder and people saying Robert Ray did it?"

"He didn't do it," Johnny said with sudden anger, "and anyone who thinks otherwise can come in here and say so. We'll beat his ass."

This time Peter nodded in agreement.

"Okay. Why is this something Robert Ray wouldn't do?"

"He doesn't even like to hunt. The only time he'll kill something is if a coon or coyote is messing with his garden or cows," Peter said.

Something clicked in Tyler's mind. "Does he have a gun?"

Johnny nodded his head. "Yeah. He's from Texas. He's got a shotgun and a rifle."

"No pistols?"

"What the hell would he need one of those for? You can't shoot a coon off the roof of the barn from across the yard with a fucking pistol. You need a rifle," Peter said.

Tyler nodded. "Okay. Is there anything else you'd like to say about the situation?" Both men shook their heads.

"Okay. Thanks."

The two walked away and went back to their game of pool. Irene came back up to the bar where Tyler sat. "Not a bunch of talkers, are they?"

Tyler chuckled. "No. Not at all."

Irene nodded with a smile. "They're kind of lost without Robert Ray. He was the charismatic one. Those two are workers. Strong as all get out. The three of them together was a nearly unstoppable force. They could get things done. Robert Ray could do the talking and the work, and those two could outwork anyone in Bowie County, easily."

"It sure looks like it. Their handshakes hurt a little."

This pulled a laugh from Irene. "Oh, Tyler. You're an interesting kid. You come back in here any time."

Tyler smiled. "I will. Thanks a bunch, Irene."

She waved and went to clean a few beer mugs. Tyler walked over to where Charlie was sitting.

"So you won over Irene on your first try?" Charlie asked with a big smile. "That might be a bigger story than the murder."

Tyler shrugged. "I can't help it that I don't have such a nauseating personality as you."

Charlie laughed. "Ty, I like you more and more every day. Let's get out of here."

On the way home they discussed what Tyler had learned, and by the time Charlie dropped him off at the dormitory, Tyler was ready to write.

By the next morning he had written all his articles, including the editorial. All that remained was the story he and Charlie were writing together.

Chapter Eleven

At the *Clarion* office, Charlie and Tyler were hunkered over a computer finishing up the murder story when Hayley came in.

"Ginger!" Charlie yelled. "Did you talk to those scholarship winners I gave you the names of?"

Hayley smiled. "Yes sir. None of them had anything bad to say about Alison. All had glowing responses to my questions about her, and they all just wanted to express how bad they felt about her death."

"Damn," Charlie said, standing up. "I was hoping we'd get some sort of lead about who did this."

"You really think someone would have killed her over a scholarship?" Tyler asked from his chair.

Charlie shrugged. "I don't know. I went and talked to Dr. Laureth, the newspaper's adviser, and he said St. Alfanus was all about how deep your pockets were. Scholarships equal money. I guess I was just grasping at straws."

"Guess so," Hayley said, taking a seat next to Tyler. "Here I thought St. Alfanus was a place of God."

"There was a murder, Ginger," Charlie said.

"True," she said with a nod. "So now what?"

"Now you need to get the rest of your stories written. Ty and I are done," Charlie said as he stretched his arms toward the ceiling.

Hayley gave a mock salute. "I'm on it, boss." She fished a flash drive out of her jeans pocket and tossed it to Charlie. "All the photos are ready."

"Sweet," Charlie said, taking the flash drive into his office and plugging it into the back of his computer to look at them.

"How are you doing, Ty?" Hayley asked, placing a hand on his knee as soon as Charlie was engulfed in looking at the photos.

"I'm good," Tyler said, covering her hand with his own. "And you?"

"Better now," she said with a sly smile.

Tyler grinned. "Yeah?"

"Yeah."

"So you think you've got a few good stories for this issue?"

"Of course," she said, placing both hands on the keyboard. "I might be a photog, but I'm no slouch reporter."

Tyler stood and put his hands on her shoulder. Giving her a gentle squeeze, he said, "I figured so. I'll leave you alone so you can get to it."

Tyler wandered into Charlie's office and looked at the photos over Charlie's shoulder.

"These are great," Tyler said.

Charlie turned and faced Tyler. "I know! I'm excited to see them in the paper!"

The next day, Charlie got his wish.

The twins showed up at 3 p.m. and got to work. With the entire content of the edition ready, they started with the inside pages and left the front page for last. They spent nearly three hours on the cover, but at the end, Charlie was very excited with the result.

As Joni, Tyler, Hayley, Charlie, and the twins sat in the football bleachers enjoying a celebratory beer, Charlie congratulated his staff.

"Everyone, this was a tough issue, but we kicked ass!" he said, cracking open another beer.

"That editorial Tyler wrote was awesome," Alex Mitchell said.

"Yeah," agreed Misty Mitchell. "It gave me chills."

"Hopefully it will hit home tomorrow when the campus reads it," Charlie said.

"With the great front page and the stellar stories, there's no way it won't," Hayley said, hugging Tyler as she sat next to him.

"Here's to the *Clarion*!" Joni said, raising her can of beer.

"Yeah!" the group said as they raised their beers to the sky.

Chapter Twelve

Friday morning, Charlie and Tyler met at the *Clarion* by 7:00 a.m. They arrived at the office doors happy to see the week's issue of the *Clarion* had been delivered.

Tyler reached for a copy, but Charlie stopped him.

"Not yet," he said. "Let's deliver them first."

At a record pace, the two split up and got the paper delivered to all the campus distribution points. Charlie had one bundle of papers in his arms.

Without saying a word, they rushed into the office and cut the plastic straps binding the papers together into the bundle.

Each grabbed a copy, and instinctively each turned to the back page. They both wanted to see the cover last.

The sports and general news pages looked great. The opinion page, anchored by Tyler's editorial, hummed together beautifully.

Looking at each other, they turned to the cover.

Charlie yelled in joy, and Tyler smiled so wide he feared his face was going to get stuck. They gave each other high fives and congratulated the other on the great work.

In the center of the page was a great shot of the crime scene stretched across the entire page. Below it was the murder story. A biography of Alison started next to the murder story with a picture of her taken from her photo on file for her student identification card. An obituary, only the fourth student obituary to ever run in the *Clarion* and the first that didn't deal with a car accident or terminal illness, ran next to Alison's biography.

A piece about campus security and student reaction came next, followed by the story about the lone suspect—Robert Ray. Next to the Robert Ray story was a photo of him sitting in the back of a police cruiser. He was crying and dripping with blood.

Another short story about the police press conference and who President Alcott was came next.

Anchoring the bottom of the page was a story about the vigil, complete with emotional pictures and pullout quotes from Father Mike.

Each story had its own headline, but stripped across the top, above the crime scene photo and below the *Clarion*'s flag, was a huge, bold headline.

It read: Murder at St. Alfanus

PART TWO

Chapter Thirteen

Alison Alcott's murderer sat in his car. He looked at his watch. It was nearly 7:00 p.m., and it had been almost three months since he had shot Alison while she sat in her own juices and the ecstasy of recently finished sex.

"Slut," the killer spat to the empty car. "She got what she deserved. She was spoiled and never earned anything she got. She deserved to die."

He opened the car door and stood next to his vehicle, looking up at the neon sign proclaiming the establishment to be Irene's.

Fall Break was upon St. Alfanus, just as it came around every October, and the killer figured things had calmed down enough that he could go out and enjoy a drink.

The killer walked inside, and no one appeared to notice, even though a large number of the patrons filling the bar were college students celebrating Fall Break. The fact that the break didn't officially start until the next day, October 12, didn't bother them. And why should it? It was customary for the St. Alfanus professors to call off classes on the day Fall Break begins, even though a special, half-day schedule had been implemented to accommodate the break.

The killer found a barstool and sat down. The bar's owner, Irene, came up to him from the other side.

"What can I get you?" she asked roughly.

The killer smiled. "I'll have a scotch and water, please."

She nodded and went off to fix his cocktail. As she did so, the killer looked at his surroundings. A curled newspaper caught his attention. He plucked it off the bar top and unfolded it. It was a copy of the latest *Clarion*, the campus paper of St. Alfanus.

On the front page of the paper was a note saying the *Clarion* wouldn't be publishing the week of Fall Break, so the paper was nearly a week old.

The killer skimmed the front page. He saw a short story of continuing coverage of Alison's murder. No new leads had come out, though Robert Ray Turner had been released. The *Clarion* teased an eventual interview with Alison's boyfriend, though no specific date for that interview to be published was mentioned.

The killer tossed the paper aside. Stupid kids, he thought. You can keep writing about it until your fingers bleed, but they aren't going to find me out.

Irene brought his drink to him. He thanked her and took a long sip.

As he enjoyed his beverage, he took in the sights and sounds of the bar. The country music was blaring, and college-aged men and women were dancing, rubbing on each other, laughing and drinking. They were having a great time.

The killer so enjoyed watching the scene he didn't notice the large fellow sit down next to him until the man slapped him on the back.

"Hey, buddy!" he said. "How the hell have you been? You haven't been by here in a while."

The killer nodded. "I've just been busy."

"I hear ya there. Been having trouble with keeping cattle in the pastures. Had a hell of a time figuring out where they were getting out, but I got it licked."

"That's good," the killer said, feigning interest.

"Yep. So that's some crazy-ass shit going on at the college, eh?"

"Yes it is."

"Do you know who did it?"

"No," the killer said, laughing to himself on the inside.

"Me neither, but boy I wish they'd find him. The kids have to be scared to death being on that campus."

The killer turned and looked at the dance floor writhing with college students. "From the looks of it, they're doing just fine."

The man turned and looked at the dance floor as well. "I don't know. Maybe they're just blowing off steam."

"Maybe," the killer said, turning back to his drink.

"Well, I hope they don't feel worried to be on campus."

"Me too," the killer said.

"Say, you know what seems awfully weird? They haven't found the gun that did it yet. I mean, the news said the bullets in Alison were .45-caliber bullets, but no one has said anything about a gun. Strange, ain't it?"

The killer nodded, though thoughts began to run through his mind.

From across the bar someone called the man's name. "Holy shit! That's my cousin! I haven't seen him in forever! I'll talk to you later, buddy!"

With that, the killer was once again alone to enjoy his drink, but he wasn't able to enjoy it much.

The gun.

The killer had committed the perfect crime, but he had lost the gun. He wasn't sure where it had ended up. He feared he had dropped it at the murder scene, but he hadn't been arrested yet, and there'd been no mention of guns or spent rounds in any reports. The lack of any spent rounds made sense because he had taken precautions against the fired shells flying all over the place, but no gun still worried him. He didn't want to be caught, so in a way no news was good news. However, it still bothered him because he didn't know where the gun was either. He needed to find it, just to be sure the police wouldn't.

Suddenly the scotch and water lost its appeal.

He paid his tab and left the bar. As he drove home, he wracked his brain trying to figure out where the gun could be and where he hadn't already looked.

Chapter Fourteen

Charlie sat on the edge of the St. Alfanus fountain slowly smoking a cigar. He had sunglasses on to shield his eyes from glaring sun. His head pounded. Taking a deep, ragged breath, he exhaled until his lungs were empty. The amount of alcohol he had drunk at the party last night was fuzzy. He didn't even remember getting home, and Joni was mad at him for something he assumed happened during his drunken stupor. She wouldn't even talk to him when he woke up that morning.

"At least it is Fall Break," he said to the still air.

He and Joni had had plans to spend the break together, but judging by the literature book she hurled at his head when he asked about those plans, he guessed he was on his own for the time being.

She'll get over it, he thought to himself. She always does.

Fights like this were rare between them, but when they happened they were always knock-down, drag-outs.

From across campus he heard the sound of whistles and yelling. Football practice didn't stop for break. Not that it mattered. The only way that team could be helped was with steroids and a coach who didn't use "Coaching for Morons" to learn how to coach a collegiate team.

Charlie flicked his cigar into the fountain and began walking toward his car. He had somewhere to go since Joni wouldn't be talking to him.

He pulled his cell phone out of his pocket and looked at the time. It was almost noon, so he called Tyler.

"Hello?" came Tyler's voice after three rings.

"Hey," Charlie said as he continued to walk. "What're you up to?"

"Packing."

"Packing? Where you headed?"

"Hayley invited me to go spend the break with her out at her parents' cabin at the Lake of the Ozarks."

Hayley and Tyler had become quite serious since the first day of school, so Charlie shouldn't have been surprised. Yet he felt deflated. "Oh."

"Why, man? What's up?"

"Nothing. I'm just going for a road trip and was going to see if you want to tag along."

"Oh. Sorry. Joni isn't going?"

"Nah. She's having a bitch fit about something. God knows what I did this time. Don't worry about it. Have a good break."

"Okay. Thanks, man. Be safe."

Charlie smiled. Since it had been months since Alison Alcott's murder and the killer hadn't been caught, the two had taken to wishing each other safe travels. Just in case. "Will do, man, but you know there ain't nobody that can fuck with me."

Tyler chuckled. "Okay. Later."

"Later."

Charlie hung up and began scrolling through his contacts. Alison's killer was exactly the reason he needed to make a road trip.

He found the number he was looking for and pressed the call button. On the other end, the phone rang and rang, but Charlie didn't give up. He knew he was there.

After nearly a minute of ringing, a gruff voice picked up. "Hello?"

"John."

"Who is this?"

"John Graham. I'm hurt you don't recognize my voice."

Silence.

"Hello?"

"I'm here. Is this that little asswipe Charlie Harrison?"

"The one and only."

"What the fuck do you want?"

"Is that any way to talk to an old friend?"

"A friend? You've got to be kidding me! Because of you I'm out of a job!"

Charlie smiled grimly. John Graham had been an ace reporter in New Orleans when Charlie spent the summer there interning for *The Times-Picayune*. He had been assigned to shadow Graham, and as luck would have it, that was when Graham was covering a high-profile murder case of a rich tourist. Charlie had gone with him to the crime scene. Freaked out beyond belief, Charlie lost control and began screaming. They didn't know it then, but the murderer had been hiding nearby. He heard the screams and came out. A cop got shot, and Graham lost all his pull with the police department, which resulted in his firing because he could no longer produce as a police beat reporter.

"Listen, John. You know I'm sorry," Charlie said quietly.

"Sorry don't pay the bills, motherfucker!"

Charlie sensed Graham was about to hang up. "I know. I know. I'm so sorry, but I need your help. I'm working a murder case."

Graham didn't say anything at first. Then, "So? You want me to come and fuck it up for you like you did for me?"

Charlie shook his head. "No. I do need your help."

"I don't give a shit," he said.

Sighing, Charlie said, "Look, if I could take it back, you know I would. I was young and stupid. I was just a freshman."

More silence. "Do you need another check? I could have my dad send you one."

"Your daddy's hush money ain't what I'm after. I should have just sued you like I had planned instead of agreeing to settle."

Charlie didn't know how to respond. "Okay."

Graham didn't say anything.

"Well, never mind then. I'm just in over my head and thought maybe you could help guide me. I always looked up to you when I was in high school reading your work. You inspired me, but I fucked everything up. So I'll stop bothering you."

Charlie held his breath. He hoped Graham's ego would like hearing he was someone's idol, and his heart would soften enough to feel sorry for a college student. Most of all, though, Charlie hoped the journalist in him wouldn't let him turn down a juicy story.

Graham exhaled loudly into the phone. "Fine. Fine. Stop crying. What do you want?"

Charlie smiled and finally started breathing again. "Help. The college president's daughter was shot shortly before school started this semester. I keep running little briefs about how the investigation is going, but those stories are shit because the investigation isn't going anywhere. The cops around here suck, and I'd like to break the case open, but no matter how I try to look at the story, I can't come up with any new way to approach it."

"I see."

"So? Will you help?"

After a long pause, Graham said, "I guess."

"Yes!" Charlie shouted into the phone.

"Jesus, kid. Don't blow my eardrums out."

Kid. That's what Graham had called him when he was an intern. It was a sign of endearment. Charlie knew he was back in his good graces as much as he could be. "So can we meet?"

"Meet? Why?"

"So I can show you everything."

"Okay."

"Okay. You still living outside of Dallas?"

"Yep."

"I'll get in the car right away."

"Great," Graham said with thick sarcasm.

"You're really excited, aren't you?"

"Bite me. The only reason I'm agreeing to this is because I couldn't stand to stay away from a story like this."

"Always a journalist. That's why I like you."

"Being a journalist all the time isn't always good. Just ask my three ex-wives."

Charlie laughed. "I'm on my way. Dust off the couch for me."

"You can sleep in your goddamned car," Graham said and hung up.

Charlie smiled broadly and put his phone back in his pocket. He quickly drove home and packed. Joni wasn't there, so he left a note on the marker board stuck to the front of the refrigerator telling her where he went.

By 12:30 p.m., Charlie was heading toward Dallas.

Chapter Fifteen

The sun was just beginning to dip over the horizon when Tyler and Hayley arrived at her parents' cabin. Tyler started to get out of Hayley's car, but she stopped him.

"Wait," she said, placing a hand on his knee.

Tyler stopped and looked at her with a smile. "Yes?"

Hayley bit her lower lip as she searched for the right words. "Ty, I'm really glad we found each other."

"Me too."

She smiled and leaned close. She kissed him deeply, her hand squeezing his knee.

When they separated, they both were smiling as they looked deeply into each other's eyes.

Hayley broke the silence. "Let's go."

They unpacked the vehicle and got themselves settled into the house. At Hayley's suggestion, they changed into bathing suits and went out on the dock.

Tyler dove into the water headfirst. The cold water cascading over his body made his lean, muscular body shimmer, so Hayley dove in after him.

When she came up for air, she looked around but didn't see Tyler. Then she felt a pinch on her butt. She let out a squeal as Tyler emerged from the water and wrapped his arms around her. He kissed her on the neck.

She pushed away from him and turned around to embrace him. They kissed deeply as his hands gripped her hips and hers held tight to his shoulders.

They continued to swim around lazily, each never being out of reach of the other.

As the sun disappeared from the sky and stars began to twinkle, Tyler pulled Hayley close. "This is wonderful. Thank you so much for inviting me."

Hayley kissed him on the chin. "I wouldn't have wanted anyone else to come with me."

"This place is beautiful, but nothing compared to you."

"Oh, Ty," Hayley said, blushing. "Stop."

"I'm serious. Don't you love it here?"

"I do," she said, hugging him tighter. "Especially the water. Look how clear it is."

Tyler looked around. "I don't know. It doesn't seem too clear to me."

"That's because it's dark now," she said. "Tomorrow you'll see. When I was a kid and came up here with my parents, I used to dive to the bottom and see what I could find."

"Ever find anything good?"

"The coolest thing I ever found was an old toilet seat and a license plate."

"Wow."

Hayley giggled. "Shut up. It was cool. Say, maybe tomorrow we can dive to the bottom and see if anything new is there."

"Okay. Why not tonight?"

"It's dark. And besides. I have something special planned for tonight."

She wiggled out of his embrace and swam to the ladder on the dock. Tyler watched as she slowly climbed up the ladder. He was in awe of how her small bathing suit clung to every curve of her body, stirring a deep yearning to be closer to her.

Once on the dock, Hayley carefully wrung the water out of her fiery hair. She looked down at him still in the water. "Come inside," she said with a devilish grin. "Get us a couple drinks and wait for me in the living room."

Then with grace, she lightly ran down the deck toward the cabin. Tyler swam to the ladder and climbed out of the water.

Inside he grabbed a couple of beers from the refrigerator and sat down on the couch. Cracking open one of the beers, he took a long drink. Even then he was surprised at how much he had come to enjoy the taste since less than six months ago he had never touched a drop of alcohol.

From the bedroom, Hayley said, "It's funny. When I wore this at the all-girls school I attended, it wasn't so tight."

As she finished her sentence, she entered the living room, and Tyler's eyes went wide, and his jaw dropped. She was wearing a sheer white shirt that wasn't buttoned but loosely knotted just below her breasts, which he could clearly see through the fabric. Barely covering her lower half was a short, pleated, black-and-white plaid miniskirt. She also had on white stockings.

"Do you still think it looks okay on me?" she asked coyly.

"I . . . I . . . I think it looks amazing," he stammered.

She smiled. "I hoped you would say that."

Hayley walked over to where Tyler was sitting and took the beer from his hand. She straddled his legs and sat down on his lap. "Ty. We've been together a while now. I love you, and I want to show you."

Tyler stared into her eyes as he brought his hands up to her silken thighs. Running his hands up toward the butt, he realized the miniskirt was all she had on.

"I love you too, Hayley."

She bent down and kissed him, running her hands over his damp chest. "Then let's go to the bedroom."

Tyler nodded.

She stood up, and as he did, she grabbed the front of his bathing suit and pulled him close. Kissing him again, she untied the front of his suit and slid her hands inside. He gasped.

Locking eyes with him, she smiled. "Looks like you're ready."

Tyler smiled sheepishly as she led him to the bedroom.

Chapter Sixteen

Midnight. That's when Charlie pulled into the driveway of John Graham's small home on the outskirts of Dallas. Charlie felt like he hadn't slept in days. The hangover combined with the long hours behind the wheel had taken their toll.

Climbing out of his car, Charlie grabbed his bag and went up to the door. He was just about to ring the bell when Graham stepped out of the porch's shadows.

"It's about time," he said.

Charlie turned to face him and dropped his bag on the wooden floor. Graham looked just as he always had. His salt-and-pepper hair was turning white at the temples, and his skin looked like worn leather from so much time in southern climates. A slight beer gut pushed against the sleeveless shirt he wore, causing the waist of his cut-off jean shorts to curl over slightly. A wad of chewing tobacco was tucked into his cheek, and his black, horn-rimmed glasses reflected the light from the streets. He was short but had long arms, one of which he extended and offered a thick hand with short, stubby fingers.

Charlie shook his hand. "Thanks for having me."

Graham rolled his eyes. "You're an idiot. I would never invite you voluntarily."

"Okay. Thanks for inviting my story and allowing me to come with it."

Graham snorted and spat off the front of the porch into an overgrown flower bed.

"So shall we go in and look things over?"

Shaking his head, Graham said, "No."

"What?"

"Not tonight. You look like shit, and I can smell the booze coming out of your skin. We'll sleep, and in the morning we'll go over stuff. Just leave the story shit on the kitchen table in case I get up before you. I don't need you breathing over my shoulder as I get caught up."

Graham pushed past Charlie and went inside. Charlie followed and threw his bag onto the couch. From the kitchen, Charlie heard the faucet running and Graham loudly drinking a glass of water.

He came back into the living room and pointed at the couch. "There's your bed. We'll see you in the morning."

Graham started to leave but stopped and turned back to Charlie. "One thing. I'm not going to do this for free."

A frown creased Charlie's brow. "But you said you didn't want any of my money."

"I don't want your money, dumbass. I want something more. I want to write a book about this, and you have to agree to cooperate fully with it. If this story is as good as I think it might be, I could finally do what I always told myself I would do when I was done working the newspaper business—write a best-seller."

Charlie shrugged. "Okay. Sounds cool, but what if the story doesn't turn out to be as good as you think?"

Graham smiled grimly. "Just pray it does. You're a good Catholic now. Ask one of your saints for a little help in that department."

He disappeared down the hallway and slammed his bedroom door shut.

"Pray it's a good story, Charlie," he said, mocking Graham. "What an ass. I hope to be just like him someday."

He laughed at his own joke and scratched the back of his head as he sat down. He looked over at the throw pillow on the end of the couch. It was the only pillow around, and the afghan on the back of the couch looked older than he was.

He stretched out on the couch and pulled the afghan over himself. Reaching up over his head, he clicked off the nearby lamp and quickly drifted off to sleep.

The next morning he was lured out of sleep by the intoxicating smell of coffee. Through bleary eyes, Charlie saw Graham sitting at the kitchen table poring over the case file Charlie had accumulated.

Staggering into the kitchen and fighting to keep his eyes open against the harsh glow of the bare light bulb, Charlie put a hand on Graham's shoulder.

"How's it going, buddy?"

"Don't touch me."

Charlie removed his hand.

"My bad. So, what do you think?"

"I think you're a shit magnet. Looks like everywhere you go something bad happens to someone good."

Charlie shrugged as he poured himself a cup of coffee. "I learned everything I know from you, boss."

"Don't blame me for that shit. I take no responsibility."

Sitting down across from Graham, Charlie said, "You know I'm just like you, and you love it."

Graham shook his head. "No. I don't love it. I think the world would have been a better place if you'd ran down your momma's thigh instead of being born."

"Are you flirting with me?"

A stern look from Graham shut Charlie up. "Sorry. I took it too far. But really, what do you think of the story?"

Graham took a long drink of coffee. "It's interesting, but you don't have shit now, do you?"

"No. That's what I told you. That's why I'm here."

"You're screwed."

"What! That's all you've got? Why the fuck did I drive here?"

Graham smiled. "Don't get your panties in a bunch. Just face it, you are screwed. I've a few ideas you could chase, but if they don't pan out, you're fucked."

Charlie stared at his former mentor and took a drink of his own coffee. "Okay," he said with a sigh. "I get it, but anything would be awesome right now."

Graham reached into his robe pocket and pulled out his chewing tobacco. He put a large wad into his cheek and picked up the crime scene photos Charlie had shot. "First and foremost, what happened to this poor girl is bullshit. The motherfucker that did this needs to be killed."

"You sound like my friend Tyler," Charlie sneered.

"Well maybe you should listen to your friend Tyler. He's not a cold-hearted asshole like you."

Charlie scoffed.

"Now, as I was saying. You need to get this figured out because from the looks of it, those cops are as worthless as tits on a boar."

"That's an understatement."

"So, you need to get a suspect list. There's nothing in any of your articles that lists any possible killers. That poor bastard boyfriend probably didn't do it, but you also need to get an exclusive with him."

"Okay. I figure I can swing the Robert Ray interview, but where do I start coming up with a suspect list?"

"Well, why would anyone want to kill that girl?"

"I don't know."

"Think. Does she have any enemies?"

"Not according to our reporting."

"So do you think she was a random target?"

"No way. Not the way she was shot."

"Exactly. So that means there's something there that you're missing. Maybe she did have an enemy. You need to look at it closer. No one should be above suspicion."

"Where do I start though? I mean, something has to stick out."

Graham drummed his fingers on the tabletop as he thought. "Well, if it were me, I'd start with the girl, Alison, first."

"You think she killed herself?"

"No, you idiot. What did she do that might have pissed someone off? Who was she?"

"I don't know for sure, I guess. One of my reporters talked to her roommate. It didn't make the story, but she told me Alison and her roommate were kind of sex freaks."

"Okay. So maybe it was a crime of passion?"

"Then that points things back at Robert Ray."

"That's why you need to talk to him. What else?"

"Well, the roommate also said Alison didn't have any enemies, and surely someone who claimed to be as close to her as she did would say if she thought someone might have done it."

"Maybe it was the roommate."

"What?"

"If they were sex freaks, maybe Alison took one of her roomie's boys away from her. That might piss her off enough to pull the trigger."

Charlie nodded slowly. "Maybe."

"What else do you know about Alison?"

"Not a lot. Just that she's the college president's daughter, so she's bound to be a spoiled rich kid."

"Money as a motive then?"

Charlie shrugged.

"Maybe she had a drug habit. Rich people can get those and keep it under wraps because they've got the money. Maybe a dealer didn't get paid and sought revenge."

"That's a stretch."

"Why? Because daddy's angel wouldn't be on drugs?"

"No. Because drugs aren't a big deal in those parts."

"Maybe it was a habit she brought with her."

"I don't know. I'm just not buying it. She didn't look like she was on drugs."

"And what exactly does a drug addict look like?"

"I don't know."

"Exactly," Graham said, slapping the table lightly. "I'm not saying I'm right. I'm just saying don't count anything out."

"Okay."

"Now, I worked with you enough to know you have a decent sense about these things. What came to mind right away?"

"Scholarship money. Maybe someone who didn't get the scholarship she got offed her."

Graham smiled. "You're not as dumb as you look, kid. That's good. Did you chase it?"

"Some. My reporter didn't turn up much of anything."

"Your reporter? Do you do any reporting for this fucking paper?"

"I was working the murder itself," Charlie said defensively.

"Congratulations. How did that turn out? You get anything good from it?"

"No."

"That's what I thought."

Charlie looked at the clock hanging on the wall. He wasn't sure what time he had woke up, but it was almost noon. "Okay. This is all fine, and you've given me a lot to think about. But where do I start now?"

Graham stood up and spat the wad of tobacco into the trashcan. He grabbed a pad and pen from a cabinet before sitting back down. "Let's make a list of the top angles to pursue. First, the scholarship angle. Look at all those people closer. Then the boyfriend and roommate. Also maybe other students. Maybe someone was just jealous of her being a rich daughter of a college president. How's that sound?"

Charlie took the pad from Graham and looked it over. "Okay. You think that's it?"

His mentor shrugged. "Maybe. Maybe not. That's just how the crime beat works. It could be something totally different, but if I were covering this, this is how I would go about it."

Charlie stood up. "Cool. I'm going to grab a shower."

Graham nodded, and Charlie took a long, hot soak. When he got out, he dressed and walked back into the kitchen. Graham was still sitting at the table.

"One more thing. What about the murder weapon?" he asked.

Charlie ran a hand through his still wet hair. "I don't know. One hasn't turned up."

Graham stood up and smiled a toothy grin. "You find that gun, and you've solved the crime," he said, poking Charlie's chest.

Chapter Seventeen

Hayley woke up wrapped in the sheets, the cool cotton cloth feeling good against her bare skin. She rolled over and felt for Tyler, but he wasn't on the other side of the bed.

She squirmed her way out of the bedding and stepped on the hardwood floor. Grabbing a silk robe of her mother's hanging next to the bed and putting it on, she walked out into the living room.

Through the window she saw Tyler sitting on the deck with a mug of coffee in his hand. She poured a cup for herself and joined Tyler outside.

"How's it going?" she asked as she sat down in a chair next to him.

Tyler shrugged.

Clutching his hand with hers, Hayley asked, "Are you okay? You tossed and turned all night."

Tyler looked at her; his eyes were bloodshot as if he'd been crying. "I don't know."

Hayley set her coffee cup down and scooted her chair closer so she could hold both of his hands. "What's wrong?"

He looked down at the wooden deck. "It's nothing. Just a dream."

"About what?" she asked, her voice tense with concern.

Tyler looked at her and looked back down. "I've been having it since the murder. In the dream, I witness the murder. Every time it is different people doing the killing and being killed, but the end result is always the same. Last night, you got shot."

"Oh. You poor thing." She took his cup from his hands and crawled into his lap. Holding his face in her hands, she said, "It's over now. I'm fine. The dream is finished."

Tyler wrapped his arms around her. "I know, but it will be back. It's just so awful, and the longer it goes without the killer being caught, I think the dreams will continue."

Hayley kissed his forehead. "Well, let's do something to get your mind off of it for now. How about going diving like I talked about last night?"

Tyler nodded. "Okay."

Hayley smiled and stood up. She grabbed their cups and began to carry them back in, but she stopped and came back to Tyler's side. She kissed him on the cheek and whispered in his ear, "If it makes you feel any better, you were amazing last night."

Tyler smiled weakly and stood up to follow her into the cabin.

They changed into their bathing suits and went back out onto the deck. Diving into the water, they took turns going to the bottom, which Tyler found he could almost see.

For most of the morning, the two found nothing, and they were about to give up when Tyler decided to go down one more time beneath the dock.

On the lake floor he found a glass bottle. He pried it out of the mud and came to the surface.

"What did you find?" Hayley asked from the dock.

Tyler held the bottle up to her. "It's some kind of bottle with something in it."

Hayley plucked it from his hand as he ascended the ladder.

"There's a model ship in it," Hayley said, scrubbing away the grim. "And the corked end is still sealed. This is pretty neat."

Tyler shook water off of his body. "It's better than a toilet seat," he said with a grin.

Hayley laughed and shoved Tyler off the deck and into the water. She ran inside with the bottle as Tyler scurried up the ladder to catch her.

The rest of the little vacation was uneventful for the two. Tyler didn't have any dreams.

PART THREE

Chapter Eighteen

Charlie sat on his porch swing back in Hooks. Clutched in his hand was the sheet of paper Graham had scrawled on, making a list of avenues to pursue to uncover the Alcott murderer.

It was Sunday night, and classes resumed in the morning. Charlie reasoned he could get started right away, but contrary to Graham's advice, he was going to involve Tyler and Ginger. He needed help because there was a lot of ground to cover. Without assistance, the trails would grow colder, and the killer would surely get away. Not that Charlie really cared, but if the *Clarion* revealed the killer, an award was almost assured.

Even as the award crossed his mind, he felt a small twinge of guilt because Tyler would be pissed if he knew that was the reason Charlie was still chasing the story, but he didn't really care. Alison was nobody to him. An award would validate his entire college career and maybe help him convince his father he shouldn't take over the family business and stick with journalism.

Charlie wasn't overly hopeful that even winning something as prestigious as the Pulitzer would convince his father, but it was worth a shot.

Which left some key decisions to make. Where should he start on the list he held in his hand?

The answer seemed obvious. All of them.

Looking deeper into Alison would be the most difficult, but it could be done at the same time as fleshing out the roommate. Ginger could do both at the same time. Of course, just talking to the little nymph Alison called a friend wouldn't be enough. Charlie would talk to President Alcott himself. No one had been able to speak to him yet, but Charlie would make it happen. And to round out the investigation of Alison, Robert Ray would need to be contacted. Tyler could handle that since he had already begun covering that part of the story, and this would give him the opportunity to finish investigating Robert Ray himself.

But what else? Graham suggested other students. Fine, but that would be like finding a needle in a haystack. And if he was going to look at the entire student body, why not look into the faculty? A motive could come from anywhere, right?

Charlie stood up and went inside. He still hadn't heard from Joni, but first thing in the morning he would order some flowers delivered to her dorm room. That would begin thawing her out, and then maybe he could talk to her and smooth things over.

He crawled into bed and tried to go to sleep, but he couldn't. His mind was racing about how to catch the killer, become famous for it and rub it in the faces of Giles and his gang of merry men, especially Deputy Bonner.

After fighting for sleep until 5:30 a.m., Charlie got out of bed and got ready for the day. By 6:45 a.m., he was at his desk in the *Clarion* offices, going through e-mail and writing up story assignments for the next issue and the long-term murder coverage.

Charlie was just about to send out a mass text message to all his reporters when his phone rang. The caller ID said it was a campus phone number, so Charlie scooped up the receiver and cradled it against his ear with his shoulder. He continued to type his text message.

"*Clarion.* This is Charlie."

"Hello, Mr. Harrison," came a nasally voice.

"How ya doin'?"

"Just fine, thanks. My name is Dylan Parker. I'm the president of the local chapter of the National Catholic Student Coalition, and I must say I'm rather upset with your publication."

Charlie looked at the clock on the wall. "Dylan, can I call you Dylan? Listen, it's not even eight o'clock yet. Isn't it a little early to be mad at the paper?"

"Not at all, Mr. Harrison. I would have spoken with you sooner, but the fall break prevented this call from taking place."

Charlie set his cell phone on his desk and rubbed his face with both hands. "Okay, partner. What have you got?"

"Well, October 9 was the St. Alfanus Feast Day, which I'm sure you know is the day we as Catholics commemorate the work St. Alfanus did assisting Pope St. Gregory VII on his deathbed. Yet at such a devout college of the Catholic faith, the student newspaper did nothing to shine a special light on this. I sent you a note saying how the NCSC was planning a special ceremony, but you didn't run it. Instead, you ran that other filth about the death of a sinner."

Charlie sat up in his chair. "What? What did you say?"

"You heard me. Every week you run another story about Alison Alcott's murder, but the stories are all the same. You seem to just be keeping the story alive and the wound on this campus fresh for your own perverse reasons. If it isn't bad enough you can't just let people move on, you are holding her up as a martyr, even though she was killed while having sex outside of the confines of marriage."

Charlie couldn't believe what he was hearing. "You think it is good she was killed?"

"I would never wish death upon someone, but as Romans 6:23 points out, 'The wages of sin is death.'"

"Maybe this was her first time to sin in such a way. We're all human. Maybe she just slipped up."

"Please. She was well known for her promiscuity, even as a high school student here visiting her father. The sinful males on this campus often fawned after her, and she obliged because she seemed to have loose morals, which floors me considering who her father was . . . is."

"How in the hell would you know any of this?" Charlie asked.

"Please don't swear at me, Mr. Harrison."

"Sorry, but how do you know all of this?"

"I'm not at liberty to say. It is confidential."

"You're a student. You don't have to worry about confidentiality. Besides, are you telling me they confessed to you? If so, that's not good for you. Not a priest. You aren't qualified to take confession. You could get into some deep shit. On the bright side, though, your little organization would get some press. Probably not the kind you had in mind, but there's no such thing as bad publicity, right?"

Dylan was silent for a moment. "Mr. Harrison, I find it hard to believe you would do that to me."

"You don't know me very well then, Dylan. Of course, I can ignore the fact that what you are doing would probably get you kicked out of college, maybe even the church, if you just tell me what you know about Alison."

More silence, and then Dylan sighed. "Fine. Fine. Several of the boys that had had relations with her were attacked by a guilty conscience. As members of the NCSC, they confided in me. After three different people told me about having sex with her, it became clear to me she was a woman of ill repute. A sinner. I lost all respect for her then."

Charlie smiled to himself. "Okay. Did you ever get with her?"

"What!" Dylan shrieked. "Of course not! Intercourse is sacred and should be saved for marriage! I would never do that and go against God's will!"

"So you tried, and she turned you down?"

"I cannot believe what you are suggesting! I'm insulted!"

"Did you kill her, Dylan?" Charlie asked calmly.

"For heaven's sake no!" he screamed. "I've had enough of this! Good day, sir! And try to do your job better by actually covering the other things happening at this campus, especially the ones with religious significance!"

The phone line went dead, and Charlie placed the handset back into the cradle.

"Holy shit," he said to himself as he wrote Dylan's name down on the piece of paper Graham had given him. "I guess when I start to look into students, Mr. Parker will be the first one."

Charlie then picked up his cell phone and finished the text message. He sent it, which told Tyler and Hayley to meet him at the office by 8:30 a.m. for a special meeting. That left Charlie with twenty minutes to kill, so he left the office and went up to a vending machine to get a Coke and a bag of Funyuns-the breakfast of champions.

When his two reporters arrived, he handed out sheets of paper with the assignments typed on them. Tyler and Hayley sat closely together. To Charlie it seemed like something was different between them. He could guess what the break had meant for them, but he couldn't worry about it now.

"Okay," Charlie started. "Here's the scoop. I talked to one of my mentors over the break, and he and I came up with a plan of attack to try and wrap up this case. Of course, we also have other stories to do as well. Those are on the budgets I gave you too. But the priority needs to be the murder stuff. Knock the other crap off early and quickly. Time and care needs to be spent on the Alcott case."

Tyler looked up from his assignment sheet. "You've got all of us talking to the same people again. How's that going to help?"

Charlie smiled. "Listen. We have to start somewhere. I figured the killer was or based the shooting off of the stuff Alison was herself involved in or because of whom she was involved with. My mentor agreed with me. So, talking to these people again and in depth will help paint a better picture of who Alison was, which will hopefully point us in the right direction to bringing her killer to justice."

"Shouldn't we just ask the cops? Maybe they've already done this sort of thing," Hayley suggested.

"You've got to be kidding me right now, Ginger," Charlie said. "Those cops don't know the elbows from their assholes.

They can't figure this out, but we can. We're smarter than they are, and we're going to prove it."

Hayley pouted. "Okay. Fine. The cops are idiots. I get it, but do you think these people will talk to us again? And how do you expect to get President Alcott to even let you close to him?"

"Don't worry about Alcott. I'm on it, and as for the rest of them, use what you already know to get them to open up." Charlie eyed Hayley with a mischievous grin.

"Are you suggesting . . . ?" she asked, trailing off.

Charlie just smiled. "Okay. Meeting's over. We need to have made serious progress on this stuff by the end of the week, and don't forget your other stories and photos."

Charlie quickly left the office, and Tyler and Hayley looked at each other.

"This is going to be interesting, isn't it?" Tyler asked.

"I think so," she said. "I think so."

Chapter Nineteen

Later the next day, Tyler and Hayley walked hand in hand across campus toward the golf course.

"I really don't want to do this, Ty," she said, squeezing his hand.

"I know. It's weird, but Charlie said you needed to get the story. As much as I hate for you to do this, judging from the last time you spoke with her, it will probably work," Tyler said.

"I've just never done anything like this before. It seems wrong."

"Try not to worry about it. As soon as you get what you need, you're done."

"I guess," she said as they walked up to the clubhouse.

Going toward the equipment room, Hayley began to breathe heavily. "I don't think I can do it."

Tyler gently pulled her along. "You can do it," he said, stopping, shoving her forward and toward the desk where Brooke Nichols was staring at a computer screen.

Hayley began to slowly walk forward, and Tyler disappeared from sight. She looked back over her shoulder and saw he was gone.

"Dammit," she whispered under her breath.

As Hayley approached the desk, Brooke looked up. When she realized who Hayley was, she smiled.

"Hey. Hayley, right?" she asked, standing up from the stool she sat on and giving Hayley a once-over.

"Yep. It's me. How are you, Brooke?" Hayley asked, stepping up the counter and resting her hands on the smooth countertop.

"I'm good," Brooke said with a slight smile, her eyes burning into Hayley's. "What are you up to? Did you join a sports team or something?"

"No. I just came to say hi."

Brooke smiled a little more. "Really? Well that's nice of you."

"Yeah, well, I, uh, enjoyed talking to you the other day. Thought maybe we could do it again. Like tonight. I'm just kind of bothered still by what happened to Alison. Thought maybe talking to her best friend would help."

Brooke leaned both elbows on the counter and slid her hands over Hayley's. With a smile, she said, "I think I can do that. Want to come to my room after a bit? I get off in a couple hours. We could chat, maybe have a drink and a bite to eat. Whatever works. How's that sound?"

Hayley fought the urge to yank her hands from beneath Brooke's. "Sounds great," she said with a fake grin that probably sent the wrong message.

Brooke stood back up. "See you then."

Hayley gave a slight wiggle of her fingers as a wave good-bye before turning on her heels and walking away. Tyler was waiting for her on the patio outside the clubhouse.

"How'd it go?" he asked, standing to greet her.

Hayley looked at him and rolled her eyes. "I feel disgusting. I never should have told Charlie about how she hit on me."

Tyler nodded and attempted to hide a smile. "Probably not."

"I just can't believe I'm doing this."

"So it worked?" Tyler asked as they walked toward the dormitory.

"Yes. We're meeting at her room in a couple hours."

"You excited?"

Hayley punched him in the arm. "No."

Tyler started to tease her a little more but thought twice. "So what are you going to do until then?"

"Watch TV with you in your room while trying to think how I'm going to bring up questions I need answered," she said as they entered the dormitory.

At the appropriate time, Hayley left Tyler's room and slowly made her way to Brooke's room. She rapped lightly on the door, which was immediately pulled open.

No longer was Brooke's hair in a ponytail. It flowed around her face, and she was still wearing the same clothes, except she had removed her shoes.

At least she's not in a robe this time, Hayley thought as she flashed a fake smile and stepped inside.

"I'm glad we're doing this," Brooke said as Hayley took a seat on the edge of her bed.

"Me too," Hayley lied as Brooke settled in next to her on the bed a little too close for comfort as far as Hayley was concerned.

"Are you thirsty or hungry?" Brooke asked.

"Sure," Hayley said. "I could use something to drink."

Brooke stood up and went to her minifridge. She bent over at the waist in order to fish out two wine coolers. "Do you like these? It's all I have left."

Hayley took the cold bottle and twisted off the lid. "These are great."

"Good," Brooke said, smiling as she sat back down and took a drink from her own bottle. "So what would you like to do?"

"How about talk a bit?" Hayley asked.

"Okay. You start," Brooke said, taking another swig of the raspberry beverage.

Hayley sat for a moment staring at the bottle in her hands. She looked up at Brooke. "I want to know more about Alison."

"You're really torn up about her, aren't you?" Brooke asked with concern in her eyes.

"Yeah. I guess I am. I didn't realize it until after we spoke before. It's really . . . been on my mind a lot, I guess."

Brooke inched closer. "Well, how can I help?"

"Well, I'm afraid you might not be open to it."

"I'm open to a lot of things, Hayley. What is it?"

"For starters," Hayley said, locking eyes with Brooke, "I want to talk to you about Alison. For the paper. I really want to paint a picture of who Alison was. Better than the first article I wrote. I want people to feel the way I do. Not because I want everyone to be miserable. But because I want them to cherish life more. I have a whole new perspective now."

Brooke's eyes started to well up with tears. She put an arm around Hayley's shoulders and squeezed her in a hug.

It's working, Hayley thought. I can't believe it. This poor, naïve girl. I feel awful.

"If it will help you, I'd be glad to, and then afterward maybe we can grab a bite to eat together or catch a movie or something. You know, do something Alison would have enjoyed doing."

"Okay," Hayley said.

"So what are some of your questions?"

Hayley took a long drink from the wine cooler and quickly thought through all the questions Charlie had suggested to her in the text message she'd received just before going to Brooke's room. "First, can I record this so I don't have to mess with writing notes?"

"Sure," Brooke shrugged.

Hayley pulled a digital recorder out of her back pocket and turned it on. "Okay. Last time you told me Alison had no enemies, and you two were kind of . . ."

"Interested in sex?" Brooke offered.

"Yeah. Could she have made enemies because of her sexual appetite?"

Brooke shook her head. "No. We had a rule to never go after someone else's boyfriend, no matter how much we wanted to."

"So she never stole a boyfriend from you or anyone?"

"No. Especially not me. There was no need to steal. We shared a lot of times anyway."

"Oooh. Okay. So did you two ever get into arguments?"

"Sure. I guess so," Brooke said with a shrug. "What friends don't fight from time to time?"

"True," Hayley responded. "So did any of those fights ever go too far?"

Suddenly Brooke cooled toward Hayley. "Are you trying to ask if I shot my best friend in the whole wide world?"

Hayley was losing her, so she did what she didn't want to. She placed a hand on Brooke's knee. "No, sweetie. I was just trying to see if you ever saw Alison get really mad. So mad she might have done something to provoke a terrible response. Like a shooting. If she ever got that mad at you, then maybe she would get even angrier at someone else."

Brooke softened slightly and looked down at Hayley's hand, which she covered with her own. "Oh. Okay. Sorry. I don't mean to get defensive. This is still a sore subject for me too. But no. She didn't have a temper. Even when her parents aggravated her, she would just pout. She never said or did anything extreme out of anger."

"Did she have a good relationship with her parents?"

"Yes. She was the light of her dad's world. Of course, that meant she got pretty spoiled, but she never flaunted it. She was always a sweet, sweet girl," Brooke said staring off into nothingness.

Despite herself, Hayley gently squeezed her knee. "It's okay. She's in a better place now."

Tears began to run down Brooke's face. "I know. I just miss her so much." She turned to look at Hayley. "I loved her."

Hayley hugged the crying girl. They sat in silence for a while before Brooke said, "Sorry. We can keep going."

They straightened up, and she wiped her eyes.

"Okay. Well, she was used to living in a bigger town. Do you think that could have led to this happening?" Hayley asked.

Brooke shook her head. "No. She was nice to everyone. It didn't matter where they came from. Deep down she was a Catholic who knew it was wrong to treat different people differently, even if she didn't follow all the rules concerning being with boys."

"Did she have any bad habits she might have picked up from a larger city then? Like . . . drugs?"

"No." Brooke's eyes went wide. "Why? Is that what you've heard?"

"No," Hayley said. "I'm just trying to cover all the bases. I don't want to write about how great a person she was if she was making such poor choices."

"Oh. But no. The worst drug she ever touched was booze. She'd never touch anything else. I couldn't even convince her to try pot with me. She just wouldn't do it."

"And there's no way she could have hid it from you even if she was?"

"Nope. We were too close. I would have known."

Hayley thought for a moment. This wasn't going anywhere. But she still had a few bases to cover. "What about jealousy? You said she was spoiled. Even if she didn't show it, people surely knew. Do you think anyone could have been jealous enough to kill her?"

Brooke looked at the floor. "I suppose people were jealous all the time, but no one really said anything. Except for Bethany Laureth. She was all sorts of pissed when Alison got that Presidential Scholarship and she didn't."

"Bethany Laureth?" Hayley repeated. "As in Dr. Laureth's daughter?"

"Yeah. Bethany was saying how the whole thing was rigged because Alison was the president's daughter and all."

Hayley's mind began to spin. Charlie and his fucking scholarship theory, she thought. She wanted to run out of the room and go talk to Tyler about what she had just heard, but she still needed to probe about Robert Ray.

"Really? That's strange, isn't it?"

"I think so," Brooke said. "Kind of fishy, isn't it?"

"Maybe. I will definitely look into it. Thanks for the lead."

Brooke smiled at Hayley. "Anytime. That's why we're here, right?"

"Yes it is," Hayley said, flirting as much with her eyes as she could. "I was also wondering about Robert Ray."

"What about him?" Brooke asked.

"Well, you said Alison didn't have a temper, but what about Robert Ray? Did he ever hurt her?"

Brooke shook her head. "No. Like I told you last time, he worshiped that girl. As far as he was concerned, she could do no wrong. He believed her almost to a fault."

"What do you mean?"

"Well, one time she just tried to pick a fight with him. She made up some bullshit about some guy, and instead of even getting kind of mad at her, he went and found the dude and beat the shit out of him."

"Was he a fighter?"

"Yeah. He was always in fights at the bar, but he would never hit a girl. He got into more fights over how other guys were treating their girls than anything."

Hayley stopped for a moment to let it all sink in. "So there's no way he could have done this?"

"No," Brooke said, eyes wide. "Like I've told you, he struck gold when he hooked up with Alison. He wouldn't do anything to screw it up."

"How well did you know him?"

"Once he and Alison became a thing—she was still in high school, of course—he and I became pretty good friends. We'd go out to eat every now and then."

"I know you said you and him didn't ever do anything, but was there anything there that you wanted to pursue?"

"No," Brooke said, shaking her head. "He was cute, but once I saw how madly in love he was, he became more like a big brother to me. I helped him make all the right moves with Alison."

"So have you talked to him since the murder?"

"Of course," Brooke said with a shrug. "Not very much, though. He's changed. He's not his old self. He's distant. The only people he really talks to are his lawyer and Irene. He doesn't even go to the bar anymore. He just sits at home. Drinking."

Brooke trailed off and seemed to be watching a distant memory on the wall. She finished her wine cooler in one long drink.

"Wait," Hayley said, leaning closer. "A lawyer? I haven't heard anything about a lawyer."

Brooke shook herself from her trance. "You're writing a story about him, and you didn't know he had a lawyer?"

Hayley blushed and looked down. "Not much of a reporter, huh?"

Brooke smiled sweetly and slid right next to Hayley, draping an arm around her shoulders. "Don't worry. I mean, it's been kept pretty quiet. But it makes sense, doesn't it? If he's being accused of killing someone, he'd be stupid not to get a lawyer."

Hayley looked at Brooke, whose face was inches from hers. "I guess so. Do you know his name?"

"Yeah. It's Newton. Chris Newton. He lives in New Boston. Irene's used him before for whatever reason."

Hayley nodded. "Do you think I could talk to him?"

Brooke smiled sadly and shrugged. "I don't know. Robert Ray's pretty withdrawn, so Chris might not be willing to."

Hayley wasn't sure if it was the wine cooler or the incredible information she had just heard, but she felt dizzy. Bethany Laureth? A lawyer? What's next? she thought.

Sitting her wine cooler on the floor out of the way, Hayley stood up. "Well, Brooke. I think I've taken enough of your time. I should probably go."

Brooke hurried to her feet and put her hands on Hayley's hips. "So soon? I thought we were going to spend some time together? This wasn't just about your story, was it?" He face carried a look of sad confusion.

Hayley shook her head. "No. No," she lied. "I'm just not feeling well. Thinking about Alison's death kind of made me sick, I guess."

Brooke's face softened into a slight smile. "I could make you feel better."

Hayley forced a smile to her lips and slowly backed to the door, Brooke following closely. "I'm sure you could. Next time? I need to lie down."

Closing the gap between them so their bodies were touching, Brooke said, "You could do that here. With me."

Hayley felt panic rising inside her. "Uh, not this time. Can I have a rain check?"

Brooke smiled and whispered, "Any time you want." Then she kissed Hayley on the corner of her mouth.

Without saying a word, Hayley turned and pushed open the door and left without looking back. As she hurried down the hall, she could feel Brooke's eyes following her.

When she arrived back at Tyler's room, she found he was gone.

She yanked her phone out of her pocket and tossed the digital recorder onto his pillow. She dialed his number. He answered on the fourth ring.

"Hello?" he asked.

"Ty! She fucking kissed me!" she blurted out.

Tyler was silent for a moment. Then asked, "Did you like it?"

"What!"

He laughed into the phone. "I'm just kidding. Why did she kiss you?"

"Because she's apparently a bi-sexual sex addict, that's why."

"Oh. At least you know."

"Shut up."

Tyler chuckled some more. "So is that all that happened?"

"No. I found out that Bethany Laureth was pissed she didn't get a scholarship that Alison got. Maybe Charlie was right with his little idea of the murder being about money."

"Wow!" Tyler exclaimed. "That's crazy!"

"I know. And did you know Robert Ray has a lawyer?"

Tyler thought for a moment. "No. That's weird. How didn't we know about that?"

"I don't know, but Robert Ray is your angle. Thought you might want to know."

"Yeah. Thanks."

"So where are you anyway?" she asked.

"I'm out on the golf course. Practicing. The last tournament before the winter break—the Alfanus Invitational—is just a few weeks away. I've got to get ready," he said.

"Oh. That's right. I forgot. Sorry," Hayley said. "You still avoiding number fourteen?"

"Yeah," Tyler said, despair in his voice. "Every time I play it I see Alison dying in Robert Ray's arms. It almost makes me sick, and then the dreams get worse."

"Sorry, babe," she said.

"It's okay."

"Well, I'll let you get back to your game. I'm going to write up the interview and start working on my story."

"Okay. Good luck. Oh, and give Charlie a call. Fill him in."

"Okay. Will do," she said, hanging up.

She dialed Charlie's number and quickly filled him in on what was going on, leaving out the kiss because she didn't want to catch a bunch of crap from him about it.

"Holy shit, Ginger!" he said when she'd finished her summary. "Dr. Laureth's daughter! I can't believe her name didn't jump out at me when I looked over the list of scholarship finalists! Damn!"

"At least we know now," Hayley said.

"True, and maybe I was right about the scholarship theory."

"Looks like you might be on the right track."

"I'll check out if she has a criminal record or anything. God, I hope she does. That would make things so much easier," Charlie said.

Hayley shook her head. "Good luck with that. So is Joni still pissed at you?"

"Nah. I smoothed that shit out."

"What did you do in the first place?"

"Don't know. Don't care," Charlie said.

"You're an A-class guy," Hayley said with thick sarcasm.

"Don't start flirting with me. You're dating my best friend."

"Good-bye, Charlie," Hayley said with frustration.

"See ya."

Hayley grabbed her laptop and fired it up. Listening to the digital recorder, she began to transcribe the interview.

On the golf course, Tyler stopped on the No. 15 green. He had skipped No. 14, which should have meant he'd feel fine, but thinking about what Hayley had told him worried him. A lawyer? Tyler had never spoken with a lawyer before. It frightened him. And just the thought of a student killing Alison over a stupid scholarship sent chills down his spine.

As best as he could, Tyler pushed the thoughts from his mind and went to the No. 16 tee box to finish his round. He needed to hurry because it was getting dark.

Charlie stood on his porch. Inside his house he could hear the shower running as Joni shaved her legs or whatever.

"Dr. Laureth's daughter," he said to the still air. "Holy fucking shit."

Charlie knew he had some work to do. He had to look into the past of Bethany Laureth. Sure, he knew she was a freshman and the daughter of a professor, but that was it. He had to know more.

And the lawyer. Chris Newton. He'd heard the name before. He'd have to look into him as well, so he could help Tyler tackle his Robert Ray story.

"Holy fucking shit," he said again.

Charlie felt like he was close to uncovering the identity of the killer. All he needed was the murder weapon, and the case would be wrapped up. Then all the journalistic awards he wanted were his.

Chapter Twenty

Sheriff Giles stood at the window of his office in the New Boston-Bowie County Courthouse. His large belt buckle clanged loudly against itself as he tucked his shirt back in and zipped his pants back up.

In the reflection of the window, he could see Bowie County's attorney, Leslie Black, pulling her dress back down over her slender, tanned thighs and smoothing her jet black hair.

Sheriff Giles turned around. With a crooked smile, he said, "This overtime business is tough, but someone's got to do it."

Leslie Black walked up to him and kissed him on the cheek. "It is tough. Hopefully it doesn't end any time soon."

Sheriff Giles pinched her on the butt and sat on the edge of the desk. "Me too, hot stuff. It will be hard to explain to my wife why I have to work late if I don't have a fucking job. I have to get reelected next fall."

"Yes you do," Leslie said, pointing a long finger at him. The soft light from the desk lamp made her red fingernail polish glimmer.

Sheriff Giles nodded his head. "I do, but it ain't gonna happen if I don't catch that fucking killer up in Hooks."

"Are you even close?"

"You know how close we are," Sheriff Giles said with a terse look toward his mistress. "You're the prosecutor on this whole mess."

"You're right. You need to get a whole lot closer."

"Closer?" he said, raising his voice. "Closer? We need to get a goddamned clue. We can't find the fucking gun, and no

matter what I do, we won't be able to make anything stick on
that fuckstick Robert Ray."

Leslie considered this a moment. "True. I can't push for
more search warrants on Robert Ray. The judge will start to
get suspicious. We've got to find someone else."

Sheriff Giles narrowed his eyes at Leslie. "What are you
saying?"

She rolled her eyes. "Don't play stupid, Bill. We've done
it before. We'll have to just pin it on someone. We've got to
come up with an arrest and conviction, or we'll both be out
on our asses. Think about it. President Alcott is your biggest
donor. If we don't put someone behind bars for killing his
daughter, well, you can kiss that money good-bye."

"Ah shit," Sheriff Giles said, rubbing a hand over his face.
"How in the hell are we going to pull it off?"

Leslie patted Sheriff Giles on the chest. "Figure it out.
Hooks is such a shit hole it shouldn't be hard to drop a few
.45-caliber bullets under their couch and then miraculously
find them during a search. You'll be a hero. Everyone will
feel safer, and we'll keep our cushy spots here in the courthouse."

Sheriff Giles nodded. "Okay," he said, exhaling loudly.
"I'll think about who we could pick."

"That's a good boy," Leslie said, gently squeezing his
cheeks.

Leslie turned and began to walk out of the office. "Oh, by
the way, the coroner is finally releasing Alison's body this
week."

"What the fuck took so long?"

She shrugged. "Those assholes in Dallas don't give two
fucks about us country bumpkins here in Bowie County.
They took their time. We should have a full report in a few
days. Expect a funeral. Maybe that would be a good time to
raid someone's home since I'm sure you'll choose someone
who will attend the funeral," she said as an order.

Sheriff Giles nodded.

"How about we have a special meeting again tomorrow night?" Leslie asked, changing the subject.

"You want more already? I could give it to you now."

Leslie shook her head. "No. I told my husband we would have sex tonight. I'll need something to forget about him sweating all over me. How does 8:45 sound?"

Sheriff Giles smiled. "Sure. Wear something nice and slutty."

"You first," she said and disappeared through the doorway.

Sheriff Giles stood up and went behind his desk. He sat down, and his wooden chair creaked. He looked around his office.

"What poor bastard is about to become a killer?" he asked the empty room as he began to contemplate his options.

Chapter Twenty-one

Charlie woke up early the morning after Hayley's fateful interview with Brooke. He quickly and quietly dressed, leaving Joni sleeping soundly in his bed.

On his way to the office, he knew he had to make a stop. He had to set his plan in motion. Talking to President Alcott wouldn't be an easy task, but he had an idea how to make it happen.

Pulling up to Salerno Hall, named after the Italian city where St. Alfanus was the archbishop, Charlie hopped out of his car. This was the building that housed the president's office, as well as Admissions, all the school records, and the offices of the deans.

He quickly mounted the steps and went inside. The doors were already unlocked even though it was 6:00 a.m. Inside, he stopped and listened intently. He heard the squeak of wheels come from down the hall, so he followed the sound. As he neared, he saw the janitorial cart parked outside of the men's room.

Charlie went up to the cart and looked inside. The janitor, Delvin Pratt, was on his knees scrubbing a urinal.

"Delvin," Charlie said.

The old man looked up. His lip protruded outward like he was a member of some African tribe whose members used stones to stretch their lips. A stone wasn't the reason Delvin's lip stuck out. For him, it was because he always had a huge wad of Skoal tucked there.

"What?" Delvin asked, though it was barely understandable due to the tobacco and his habit of mumbling constantly.

"I need your help," Charlie said.

Delvin spat into the urinal and stood up. A string of saliva hung from his chin. His small eyes stared at Charlie through spotted and dirty glasses. "What?"

Charlie flashed his best disarming smile. "I need to talk to President Alcott. Is he in yet?"

Delvin shook his head. "He hasn't been coming in until around nine most mornings," he mumbled.

"Oh. Okay. Well, I can't wait around that long. Can you just let me in so I can leave him a note?"

Delvin mumbled something.

"What?" Charlie asked.

Delvin, who had walked to his janitorial cart, spat into the attached trashcan. "I'm not supposed to open people's offices for students."

"Oh. Well, I talked to Nick . . . I mean Officer Jones, and he said it would be fine for you to do it this time," Charlie said, quickly coming up with a lie.

Delvin eyed him. "I don't know . . ."

"Come on, Delvin. Jonesey said it was okay."

"He didn't tell me."

Charlie sighed. "He said he would come do it himself, but he was busy. Can't you just help me out this one time?"

Delvin mumbled something laced with profanity.

Charlie locked his fingers behind his head. "Please," he said, putting on his most desperate face possible.

Delvin stared at him with cold eyes. Then he suddenly softened. "You just make damn sure you get out of there right away. Don't touch any of his shit. Promise?"

Charlie smiled. "Promise."

"Sonofabitch," Delvin said as he slowly began to walk toward President Alcott's office.

Charlie followed.

Delvin unlocked the door and pointed an arthritis-ridden finger at Charlie. "Make it quick. Don't touch any of his fucking stuff," he mumbled before walking back to the men's room.

Charlie went inside and closed the door behind him. He could always count on Delvin to come through for him. He always put up a little bit of a fight, but he always caved in.

Charlie went to President Alcott's desk and looked around. Without too much searching, he found the schedule for President Alcott's day in a leather-bound folder. It looked like it had been typed by his secretary and left in the binder after President Alcott had left the previous day. A couple of appointments had already been changed with a red pen, so Charlie grabbed a similar pen from a coffee mug filled with pens and pencils.

Pulling the cap off, he looked at the times listed on the agenda. President Alcott has some free time right before lunch, so Charlie drew a red line from that gap to the margin of the page. There he wrote: "11:45 a.m.—Charlie Harrison"

The other appointments had descriptions, but Charlie figured it would be best not to put why he needed to talk to the head of the college. Knowing it was a discussion about his murdered daughter would probably make President Alcott cancel the appointment.

"I've got to give a reason, though," Charlie said to himself.

Beneath the appointment he had forged, he wrote: "Newspaper travel for coverage of football team."

Charlie laughed at his own joke. The St. Alfanus football team wouldn't be traveling anywhere. They only had two games left, and they were so bad they wouldn't be extending their season. However, Charlie figured that seeming like a hopeful sports fan wouldn't hurt to get himself inside and sitting across from the president.

He recapped the pen and placed it back into the coffee mug.

As he began to leave the office, he saw a few pictures of Alison hanging on the wall. One was a family portrait with the president, his wife, and Alison smiling broadly. The other was what appeared to Alison's senior portrait. It was a black and white print, and she had a serious look on her face, which peeked out over the collar of a leather jacket. The other picture was a picture of Alison standing in front of the St. Alfanus fountain. It was a candid shot. She was laughing at something. She seemed so carefree and full of life, clearly with no knowledge she would be killed. It made Charlie sad, and suddenly he felt a small twinge of guilty for breaking into the president's office. He left, pulling the door closed behind him and making sure it was locked.

Delvin was no longer in the hallway.

Charlie went outside and pulled his car into a different parking lot closer to the newspaper offices. He went inside and turned on his computer.

He pulled up a search engine and typed in Bethany Laureth's name.

She came up on the first few hits. Most of them were about her excelling at volleyball and academically.

The rest of the results didn't talk about Bethany. Instead, they talked about Dr. Arthur Laureth.

"What the hell?" Charlie asked as he skimmed the results.

He chose one link from a newspaper in Missouri.

As Charlie read the article, his jaw dropped. It seemed Dr. Laureth didn't have a sterling history. Before coming to St. Alfanus, he had taught English at another small college in southern Missouri. He had been unceremoniously let go because he had gotten into a fight with the college president over his salary. The college president ended up with a broken nose, and Dr. Laureth earned himself assault charges.

"No. Fucking. Way," Charlie said.

He printed the article and went back to the search results page. He clicked on another link. It was another newspaper article about the assault trial. Apparently Dr. Laureth had a temper. During the trial, a profane outburst and shattered water glass got him held in contempt.

According to the article, Dr. Laureth served little time behind bars for his actions. The article didn't say it, but Charlie could read between the lines that Dr. Laureth had paid for his freedom. Part of the settlement clearly meant leaving the college without any severance package and, most likely, a sizeable donation to the school.

Charlie began to salivate. A hothead father and a daughter pissed about a scholarship competition she viewed as rigged sounded like a great scenario for a murder.

He printed the second article as well before going back to the search results page.

None of the other results really caught Charlie's attention. There was a press release about Dr. Laureth's hiring from the St. Alfanus website, but it said nothing about his past transgressions.

Charlie closed the internet browser and sat back in his chair to think. His idea that maybe, just maybe, the murder had been based on money had been a long shot. Even he could admit that, but now it seemed more plausible.

He wanted to run something in the week's paper, but how could he do it without the police officially naming Bethany and Arthur Laureth as suspects?

Charlie picked up an old soft drink cup and yanked the straw out of the lid. He began chomping on the plastic as he thought.

Slowly a plan emerged. He would just have Ginger include Brooke's comments about what Bethany had said. That would set the stage. Then Charlie could write a story about Dr. Laureth's past to begin to plant an idea in the minds of everyone.

The only problem was what reason was there to bring up what Dr. Laureth had done? It wasn't enough, Charlie reasoned, that he was probably guilty as sin. There had to be some reason to bring the story up now, other than the fact Charlie was becoming more and more convinced of Dr. Laureth's guilt by the second.

How could he bring this up?

Then the idea struck him. If Dr. Laureth truly was such a high-tempered guy, the story casting his daughter in a poor light would probably set him off. Some angry outburst would warrant a story, and then Charlie could bring up his past, which combined with his daughter's statements would create a cloud of suspicion that would hopefully result in an arrest.

"Yes!" Charlie shouted to what he thought was an empty office.

"Yes, what?" Tyler asked from his desk.

Startled, Charlie turned around and saw his friend sitting at his computer wearing workout clothes. "What the hell are you doing up so early for?"

"Early? It's almost eight o'clock. I went for a jog and swung by here to check my e-mail. Why were you here so early?" Tyler asked.

Charlie walked over to Tyler's desk, glancing at a wall clock. He'd lost track of time, but it was for a good reason. He pulled up a chair and started to sit down when he noticed something sitting on Tyler's desk.

"What's this?" he asked, pointing at the glass bottle with a miniature boat trapped inside by a piece of cork.

"It is what it looks like, I guess. A boat in a bottle. I found it when Hayley and I were at the Ozarks. It was buried in the mud under the dock. Who knows how long it had been there, but I thought it was pretty neat. So I brought it home. Figured it would look nice here on my desk."

Charlie nodded. "Right. That's not gay at all."

Tyler frowned at him and turned back to his computer.

Undeterred, Charlie said, "Listen, I think we might be on the trail of the killer. I think I might know who it is."

This got Tyler's attention. He turned back toward Charlie. "What? Who? How?"

Charlie smiled and launched into his explanation, showing Tyler the news articles he had printed out. When he had finished, he leaned back and looked at Tyler. "See, Ty, we're going to be heroes."

Tyler nodded slowly, his face still covered with shock and surprise. "Wow. I guess so. I mean, are you sure it was Dr. Laureth, though?"

Shrugging, Charlie said, "Not yet, but I will be. We just have to set the trap like I said. I've got an appointment with President Alcott today. I'll just casually bring up Dr. Laureth's past with him to feel things out."

"Wait. How did you get an appointment with President Alcott? He has refused to speak to anyone even remotely connected to the press."

Charlie smiled a sly grin. "Don't worry about it, Ty. I'm good. Don't forget that."

Tyler had heard this type of speech too often, and he knew it generally meant Charlie was up to some sort of under-handedness.

"Did you break any laws to get this appointment?"

Charlie thought for a moment. "I don't know. Not really."

Shaking his head, Tyler said, "You know, in our reporting class we're covering a chapter on ethics. You might want to come and sit in for a while. Kind of as a refresher for you."

Charlie's smile broadened. "But going to a class I didn't pay for would be unethical itself. I can't do that, Ty."

"Whatever," Tyler said, logging off his computer and standing. "I have to go get ready for class."

"See ya later," Charlie said as the two exchanged a high-five, handshake combination they always performed when saying good-bye.

"Later," Tyler said, leaving the office.

Charlie went back to his office and began typing up his plan. He just knew Dr. Laureth was behind this. It fit together too perfectly.

When he had it finished, he included it in an e-mail, along with links to the stories he found and a synopsis of what he was thinking. He fired the message off to Hayley and copied Tyler in on it.

Charlie was so proud of himself, he decided to go treat himself to a Coke, so he left the office and went up to the main floor of Cormac Hall to the vending machine.

As he fished the cold can of soda out of the machine, he saw Officer Jones walking toward him.

"Nick," Charlie said with a smile and wave.

Officer Jones nodded at him. "Dammit, Charlie. Don't call me that, especially when people could hear you. It makes me look bad."

"Sorry, Officer Jones," Charlie said sarcastically. "Anything new to report? We haven't been keeping up with our daily meetings."

Officer Jones shook his head. "No. Things have been pretty quiet. I was pretty surprised. I figured all hell would break loose here on campus with Fall Break and all, but it was nice and quiet. Even got to go home a little early."

"Oh yeah? How'd you swing that?" Charlie asked as the two walked outside and took a seat on a bench near the entrance.

Officer Jones said, "Well, President Alcott said on account of the break I could go home early if I wanted. Usually that really meant 'stay until things have quieted down,' which was never early. But this year things worked out nice."

"Cool," Charlie said, taking a drink from his soda. "I need to ask you something, Nick. I mean, Officer Jones."

"What's that?"

"Well, you know this whole murder business? What if I've come up with a suspect? If I asked you about him, would you tell me what you know about him?"

Officer Jones narrowed his eyes at Charlie. "What are you saying? Are you trying to lone-wolf the investigation? That will only get you hurt. Go to the cops."

Charlie cocked his head to one side. "I am. You. Your name is Officer Jones, isn't it?"

"Oh sure. Now you call me a cop," Officer Jones said, shaking his head and clapping his hands on his knees. "This is above me. I'm just a lowly security guard who does what he is told."

"No. Bullshit, Nick!" Charlie said in a tense whisper. "You can help me. We've got a good relationship. We've known each other for a while now. You can help me. Besides, you've worked for Alcott for a long time. Wouldn't it be nice to help solve his daughter's murder? Help give him closure?"

Officer Jones thought about this for a moment and sighed. "You're right, I guess. It sure would be nice to be recognized around here. You know, most people just overlook campus security."

Charlie patted Officer Jones on the shoulder. "I don't overlook ya, Nick. I know you are an important part of this campus."

Smiling sadly, Officer Jones said, "I know you do. You're a good kid . . . Shit. Fine. I will help you if I can. But I don't want to be too involved here. It might not always feel good to be ignored, but in a deal like this, keeping my head down doesn't seem like a bad idea."

Charlie smiled and nodded. "I hear ya."

"So who do you want to know about, Charlie?"

Charlie looked around. "Dr. Laureth," he finally said in a whisper.

Officer Jones seemed puzzled. "You think he killed Alison?"

Charlie shrugged. "Maybe. See, I found out that at the last college he worked at, he got fired for punching the college president. Then, Alison's roommate tells one of my reporters that Bethany Laureth was pissed she didn't get the scholarship money Alison did. She started claiming the whole thing was rigged. Not to mention the fact how Dr. Laureth himself told me money meant everything at this place. So here's what I was thinking. He's a hothead, and his little girl feels cheated. Maybe he gets mad, and since Bethany called out Alison for maybe getting special treatment, Laureth takes aim, excuse the pun, at Alison."

Charlie sat back and looked at Officer Jones with a quizzical look.

Officer Jones swallowed hard. "Seems like you've given this some thought."

"Yep," Charlie said. "What do you think?"

"Well," Officer Jones started slowly. "It seems like it could be. You make a pretty good case."

Charlie started to smile. "Thanks. So, what do you know about Dr. Laureth? You think he'd be capable of this?"

Officer Jones looked straight ahead and started to drum his fingers on his thighs. "I suppose. He does have a temper. I saw him screaming at the English Department's secretary once because she lost something he needed. I suppose he might have done it."

Charlie nodded. "That's what I needed to hear."

Finally turning to look at Charlie again, Officer Jones said, "But please. For the love of God. Don't bring me up in this. Just use the articles you found."

"Okay. Will do. I will see what President Alcott has to say about him later this morning."

"What?" Officer Jones said, alarm in his eyes. "You can't go talk to him about this. It's his daughter that got killed, for Christ sake!"

Charlie put his hands up. "Whoa, whoa. Calm down. I've already got the appointment. It's fine."

"How did you get that appointment? There's no way he'd agree to talk to you of all people."

"I didn't make the appointment with him. I went through . . . his secretary. Can't remember her name. I'm going to talk to him about traveling expenses for the paper. I'll just bring up some of this other stuff if I get the chance. No worries."

Officer Jones shook his head and eyed Charlie with suspicion. "You better not have fucking done anything you shouldn't have. And you better not do anything you shouldn't once you get into that office. If you do, I'll personally escort your sorry ass to New Boston and lock you up in the shittiest cell they got."

The smile vanished from Charlie's face. "Okay. Okay. I'll be careful. You can trust me, though. I'll handle this delicately. I know you feel close to President Alcott and you want to protect him. I understand, and I'll be careful."

Officer Jones narrowed his eyes at Charlie. "Don't bring me into this, you understand?"

Charlie nodded.

Officer Jones stood up and said, "You better." He walked away.

Charlie watched him go. He finished his Coke and tossed the can into a nearby wastebasket. He leaned back on the bench and stretched his arms across the top.

That went better than I figured it would, he thought to himself. He was actually helpful. I just hope he doesn't interfere with my appointment.

Charlie pulled his cell phone out of his pocket and checked the time. It was 11:37 a.m.

"Shit," he said under his breath.

He jumped up off the bench and began to run across campus toward Salerno Hall.

Charlie arrived at the president's office right at 11:45 a.m. He rushed through the door and saw President Alcott talking to his secretary. They both looked at him.

"Mr. Harrison," President Alcott said, a stern look on his face.

Flashing a disarming grin, Charlie said, "The one and only. Sorry if I'm a bit late. I had class and whatnot."

The secretary looked at Charlie and then back at President Alcott with her lips pursed. She tapped the appointment sheet.

President Alcott nodded and said in a gravelly voice, "My secretary says you never made this appointment with her. How did you get it?"

Charlie continued to smile and shrugged. "I just called in. Whoever answered said she'd put me down. I never asked for her name. Maybe it was someone who shouldn't have been answering that line. I don't know."

President Alcott's stare didn't waver.

"Listen," Charlie said, feeling beads of sweat form on his brow. "I'm already here. Can I just have a moment of your time? It won't take long."

The secretary and president exchanged another long look. Then she gathered her things and left.

"Have a seat," President Alcott said, motioning toward an expensive looking chair across from his desk.

Charlie did as instructed.

"So what can I help you with?" President Alcott asked.

"First," Charlie said crossing his leg at his knee, "I wanted to talk to you about following the football team as they progress into postseason play."

President Alcott looked at him disbelievingly. "Nice try, Mr. Harrison. As much as I hate to admit it, you and I both know that won't be happening. Why are you here?"

Charlie swallowed hard and didn't say anything.

"Mr. Harrison, you're wasting my time."

Charlie dropped his leg to the floor and leaned forward on his knees. "Okay. I'll cut the crap, sir. You haven't spoken publicly about what happened concerning your daughter. Can I ask you a few questions since I am with the local paper?"

President Alcott stood up abruptly. "Get the hell out of my office!" he bellowed.

Charlie didn't move.

"I will call campus security, and Officer Jones will see to it that you are removed from this office."

Charlie slowly stood. "Please don't do that. I'll go. I just wanted to try and help catch Alison's killer. I thought if we talked to you and, you know, painted the right picture, it might flush something out. That's all."

President Alcott took a menacing step toward Charlie. "No."

Charlie gave ground. "Fine. I'm just trying to help."

"Leave. Now," President Alcott growled, his hands clenching into fists and his face turning red.

Charlie was in the doorway when he said with a hint of indignation, "You know. I know about Dr. Laureth's past. Seems like he has a temper. He was probably pissed his daughter didn't get the scholarship that Alison did. Ever think of that?"

President Alcott said nothing and closed the door in Charlie's face.

Charlie let out a long breath. He realized he'd forgotten to breathe during the encounter.

He turned away from the office door and left Salerno Hall.

Suddenly he felt exhausted. It was a Tuesday. Charlie had classes he should go to, but he didn't feel like it. His plan had totally blown up in his face, and he worried he'd said too much and maybe blew any chance of ever again having a working relationship with President Alcott.

"Fuck me," he said.

Production of the paper was a couple days away, so Charlie decided he could afford some time away from the office. He got into his car and drove home.

He poured a large glass of whiskey and water, turned off all the lights and sat in his living room, sulking and thinking what he could do next. All the while, the Texas Intercollegiate Press Association awards felt like they were slipping through his fingers because things weren't going as he had thought.

Chapter Twenty-two

Getting out of class around 3:00 p.m., Tyler decided to swing by the *Clarion* to see what Charlie was doing, but the office was dark, and no one was nearby.

"That's weird," Tyler said to himself as he left Cormac Hall.

It didn't really bother him though. He needed to practice his game. The Alfanus Invitational was getting closer by the day. Three weeks to be exact. Tyler had to get back to his old game. If he won the Alfanus Invitational, it would mean good things for him. It meant he'd be leading the pack as he strove for the NAIA title.

Tyler didn't care. Golf wasn't as all consuming anymore. Ever since he had stumbled upon the murder scene of Alison Alcott, Tyler didn't care about the same things he used to. Golf was taking a backseat to the newspaper and becoming a journalist, and Hayley was becoming more important to him every day, which was possibly the strangest thing to Tyler because he'd never taken the time to develop a relationship with a girl before.

Walking past the clubhouse, Tyler suddenly wondered if Brooke was working the equipment desk. He hoped she wasn't. An encounter with her after what Hayley had described happening would be awkward, even if she didn't know he and Hayley were a couple.

As luck would have it, Brooke wasn't at her usual post. However, the alternative wasn't the greatest. It was Mark Grower, Tyler's golf coach.

"Tyler!" he said cheerily. "Glad you came out today! The invitational is getting close. How're you playing?"

Tyler shrugged. "Okay, I guess. A little rough on parts of the back nine."

"Well, work on that today. In fact, skip the front and just play the back twice. At least twice. If you can win the invitational, it will put you in great standing for the title, but I'm sure you know that. More importantly though, we need to do well at our own tournament, and you're the guy that can carry us there," Coach Grower said.

"Okay," Tyler said with a nod. "I'll do my best."

Coach Grower grinned. "That's my star!"

Tyler grabbed his clubs and turned to walk away when Coach Grower called after him. "Tyler."

Tyler turned around and saw the grin was gone from his coach's face. "Yeah?"

"How are you? I mean, I've see the stuff you're working on for the paper, and I know you, uh, found her. Are you okay?"

Tyler managed a weak smile. "I guess. As good as I can be."

Coach Grower nodded. "That's good. Real good. Maybe it would help if you laid off the newspaper for a bit. You know, until after the tourney. Keep your mind clear."

Tyler stared at his coach blankly. "I'll think about that."

Coach Grower smiled again. "Great. And don't forget to only play the back since you're struggling with it."

"Right," Tyler said flatly and walked away.

Teeing up on the No. 10 tee box, Tyler felt anger swelling inside of him. He crushed the ball down the fairway.

He couldn't believe his coach was suggesting not working for the paper in order to protect the golf team. Who really cared? How many NAIA golfers moved on to play in the PGA? Tyler didn't know for sure, but he was willing to bet it wasn't many.

"Asshole," he said of his coach to no one but himself.

The word shocked him. He didn't normally use swear words. Never had really.

"I guess Charlie's starting to rub off on me," he said to himself as he prepared to hit his second shot.

As he progressed through the holes, he had moderate success. He finished a round of eighteen just above par. It wasn't great, but it wasn't too bad. Of course, that wasn't a true score. He skipped No. 14 both times around.

For fun, Tyler went to the front nine and began to play it. He wasn't doing it because he needed practice on these holes. Instead, he was doing it so he could think and let his body lead him through the holes.

He knew Hayley had already begun her assignment by talking to Brooke. He wasn't sure where Charlie stood, but he doubted it would take his friend long to spring into action.

That meant Tyler needed to get going as well.

The lawyer. That's where Tyler figured he'd have to start. Still, he was apprehensive about speaking with such a person. He'd never done it. Talking to the police had been bad enough. But now a lawyer? Tyler wasn't sure he could handle it.

"I've got to, though," he said out loud, hoping his clubs would take the hint and give him a quick pep talk.

The clubs didn't respond, so Tyler just kept playing and thinking about the task before him.

By the time he was finished with his twenty-seventh hole of golf for the day, it was getting dark. He returned his clubs. Brooke was working the desk. Oddly, she didn't say much. She was reading a book and had tears glistening on her cheeks.

Tyler felt like he should have asked her if she was okay, but he didn't want to risk kicking up a conversation. Brooke had to know at the very least, he worked on the paper with Hayley. The breeding ground for uncomfortable questions was too great.

Instead, she silently checked his clubs back in, gave him a soft smile and went back to her book.

Hayley had a night class on Tuesdays, so Tyler went back to his dorm room. First, he tried calling Charlie to see what he was up to. Charlie didn't answer. He then turned on the television and his laptop, meaning to do some research on Robert Ray's lawyer. Instead, he fell asleep as the evening newscast came on.

Chapter Twenty-three

Darkness had settled over the campus of St. Alfanus. Gerald Alcott still sat in his office, though. He hadn't gone home to his wife like usual. Instead, he was sitting in his special part of Salerno Hall with no lights on. The only illumination came from the computer screen and the glow of the moon streaming through the large window behind his desk.

President Alcott had been sitting like that since he had spoken with the editor of the campus newspaper, Charlie Harrison. The conversation between them had unnerved him a great deal, so badly he had canceled all his appointments for the remainder of the day, claiming he wasn't feeling well. In light of what had happened to his family, everyone accepted this without question.

Truth be told, he didn't feel very well at all. His stomach felt twisted and he a little nauseous, but it wasn't the flu or a bug or even a bit of indigestion. What Charlie had said to him right before he left earlier that day was the source of his ailment.

Dr. Laureth did have a violent past. President Alcott had known all of this prior to hiring him, of course, but he felt it was the Christian thing to do to hire him and give him another chance.

Most of Dr. Laureth's problems probably stemmed from his time in the military, President Alcott figured. Dr. Laureth had never come out and said exactly what he had experienced, but President Alcott had been told enough to know Dr. Laureth had gone through some difficult, blood-splattered times that inevitably changed him forever.

None of this had ever seemed too pertinent, though. Not until Charlie had made the devastating suggestions that had President Alcott still struggling to keep his breakfast down.

Could someone whom he considered a friend have killed his beautiful baby girl over a scholarship?

President Alcott didn't even want to consider the idea, but he knew he had to. It made some sort of strange sense. He should probably thank Charlie for even coming up with the idea, but he knew he could never do that. Even if it helped catch his daughter's murderer, he couldn't thank Charlie because of the way he had approached the situation.

Charlie Harrison wasn't someone President Alcott knew even remotely well, but he knew enough to know Charlie was slimy and only worried about himself. Coming into his office, most likely through a web of lies unnoticed until it was too late, proved it. All Charlie wanted was a good story. President Alcott refused to give it to him.

Even so, something had to be done. As tears began to roll down his cheeks, President Alcott picked up the phone and dialed the personal line of Sheriff William Giles.

"Hello?" Sheriff Giles answered, clearly short of breath.

"Uh, Sheriff Giles, are you okay?" President Alcott asked.

"Yeah. Yeah," Sheriff Giles said. "Was just, uh, outside of the office. Heard the phone ringing. Had to run to catch ya in time. You know me. I'm no sprinter."

"Right. Okay. Well, this is Gerald Alcott from St. Alfanus."

"Oh. Hello, sir," Sheriff Giles responded, suddenly putting on a more official tone. "What can I do ya for this evening?"

President Alcott swallowed hard. "It's. It's about my daughter."

"We're working on it, sir. I'm confident we'll have a suspect in custody soon," Sheriff Giles jumped in.

"That's actually what I wanted to talk to you about. I think I know who might have done it. At least he could have, though I hope he didn't."

This caught Sheriff Giles' attention. "And who might that be, sir?"

A long pause.

"Sir? You there?"

"Y-yes," President Alcott answered as tears streamed down his face and his voice became thick with emotion. "It's just . . . I thought he and I were friends. I thought with our daughters going to school together that we'd become closer friends. It's hard to have friends in this position. Everyone just pretends so they can get what they want. I thought he was different. I guess I might have been wrong."

"Sir, I understand this is tough," Sheriff Giles said, excitement rising in his voice. "But I need you to tell me who this guy is."

"It's. It's Dr. Arthur Laureth. He teaches English here. His daughter didn't get the Presidential Scholarship like my Ali did. I think maybe his daughter thought it was rigged to favor Ali. Arthur has a temper and history of violence and a military background. I . . ." President Alcott trailed off and began to sob into the phone.

Sheriff Giles attempted to comfort the man, and after a while, he calmed him down enough for him to listen. "Sir, I want you to know how much I truly appreciate this. I will look into, and if we find evidence that bastard did this, we'll hang him up by his balls."

Normally President Alcott wouldn't have approved of such language, but he said nothing about it. "Thank you, Sheriff. Thank you so much for all your work on this. I just hope it can come to a close soon."

"Yes sir."

"I've got to go home and talk to my wife," President Alcott said with desperation in his voice.

"Okay. You take care this evening, you hear?"

"Yes. Yes, I will. Good-bye, Sheriff."

"Good-bye."

President Alcott hung up the phone and put his face in his hands on his desk. He cried for nearly fifteen minutes before he was able to compose himself enough to go home.

In his office, Sheriff Giles was not crying. He was dancing.

"Hot damn!" he shouted.

Leslie Black was sitting naked on his desk. "What?" she asked, hopping down and walking over to the half-clothed sheriff.

"That was Alcott!" Sheriff Giles said with excitement. "He thinks one of his fucking professors shot his daughter, and Alcott laid out the motive for me. This couldn't be any sweeter!"

Leslie smiled slyly. "Excellent. We should celebrate," she said as she yanked his pants to his ankles.

Gathering her up in his arms, Sheriff Giles said, "Yes indeed. Tonight we celebrate. Tomorrow we investigate, and by the end of the month, we've got that motherfucker locked up. Just like the election."

Leslie nodded and kissed Sheriff Giles deeply before pulling him to the floor with her.

Chapter Twenty-four

By mid-day Wednesday, Tyler still hadn't tried to call Robert Ray's lawyer, Chris Newton, even though he had found a phone number for him. Production would start the next day, and the biggest piece the paper had going was Hayley's story about Brooke. Charlie wouldn't be happy about that. He really wanted the stories about the murder so the paper could prove the sheriff's department was worthless.

Tyler didn't like Charlie's reasons, but he too wanted to solve the murder, for Alison's family.

Leaving Maier Science Center from his biology class, Tyler slowly headed toward the *Clarion*'s offices. He worried how Charlie would react to his lack of progress, but when he got inside, Charlie wasn't there.

Tyler found it odd, but he didn't think too much about it. Besides, he figured this gave him the chance to call Mr. Newton.

Picking up the phone at his desk, he pulled the slip of paper with the phone number on it out of his pocket. He'd been carrying it with him since he had found it, in hopes he'd work up the nerve to make the call.

Tyler swallowed hard and took a deep breath. He dialed the number and listened to the ringing on the other end.

"Hello?" came a male voice, which shocked Tyler because he was expecting a secretary.

"Uh. Hi. Can I speak with Mr. Newton please?"

"This is he," the man said.

"Oh. Okay. Hello, Mr. Newton."

"Hello. What can I help with you?"

"Well, my name is Tyler Fox, and I work at the *Clarion*, The student newspaper at St. Alfanus, and I was wondering if I could talk to you about the Alison Alcott murder, since I was told you were representing Robert Ray."

"I see," Newton said. "We'll, Mr. Fox, why do you want to do that exactly? Going to try and make my client look worse? Just like that picture of him sitting in the back of the police cruiser?"

Damn it Charlie, Tyler thought.

"No, sir," Tyler said instead. "I honestly don't believe Robert Ray did it, and I was hoping to speak with him to, uh, really show people how good of a guy he is. How he really cared for Alison and would never have done this. I mean, he was the only witness, so him talking about it would probably help paint a better picture for him."

"Mr. Fox, I appreciate what you are claiming to be attempting to do, but though my client has been released, there is no doubt in my mind he is still being considered as a suspect since, as you pointed out, he was the only witness to the event in question. Therefore, I believe it would be in the best interest of my client to simply say no. I would be doing him an injustice to allow him to speak with you and possibly damage his case," Newton said.

Tyler sighed. "Okay. I guess that makes sense. But what about you? Can you say anything? I have a story I need to write, and it would really help if I could get some sort of quote or something."

Newton thought for a moment. "Okay. I'll give you a quote you can use. Get a pen and paper ready because I'm only going to say it once."

"I'm ready when you are, sir."

"Good. Here it goes. My client, one Robert Ray Turner, is innocent of any wrongdoing. The heinous crime he is alleged to have committed did not happen at his hands. This should be painfully obvious since the police report clearly spells out how my client was assaulted during the incident. However, Bowie County Attorney Leslie Black and County

Sheriff William Giles seem to have it out for my client, as is evident by the longer than necessary holding of him and the continued scrutiny he is being subjected to. Until the true culprit is apprehended, I fear my client will continue to feel harassed, which we will continue to fight until his name is cleared and adequate compensation is made for the distress he has been forced to endure," Newton said.

Tyler was still frantically jotting down the last part of the quote.

"You still there, Mr. Fox?" Newton asked.

"Yeah. I'm just finishing up my notes. Sorry."

"Not a problem. Will that work for you?"

"Uh. Yeah. I guess. Do you think the cops have it out for Robert Ray, though? It kind of sounded like it."

"I have no further comment to make," Newton said quickly, "but you can read whatever you like into what I said. Just know this. Robert Ray Turner did not kill that girl. I've never been so sure of anything in my life."

"How can you be so sure?" Tyler asked.

"Listen, kid. Off the record, I've represented a lot of bad people and defended them knowing good and well they were guilty as sin. There's no way Robert Ray did this. The whole thing has really messed up his head. He's depressed. Won't talk to anyone. Even when I try to contact him, it's like pulling teeth. I'm married, but until I met Robert Ray, I still didn't believe in true love. That guy loved Alison Alcott. He might have killed someone for hurting her, but he'd never harm a hair on her head."

"Wow," Tyler said, clearly impressed.

"Don't use any of that, understood?" Newton asked with a softer tone than the rest of the conversation had carried.

Tyler nodded as if Newton could see him. "I promise I won't. Thanks for your time."

"You bet. Thanks for calling. No one else has taken the time to do so."

"I hope Robert Ray gets proven innocent."

"He will. Believe you me, he will," Newton said as he hung up.

Tyler hung his phone up and looked at the quote he had scrawled on his notepad. It said a lot without really saying anything, except clearly accusing the local law enforcement of not doing its job properly.

He shut the notepad and stood up, shoving the pad into his back pocket and the pencil he had used behind his ear. He started to leave when Charlie came into the office. He smiled.

"Hey. How's it going?" Tyler asked.

Charlie smiled back, and Tyler saw his eyes were bloodshot. "Pretty good."

"You okay?" Tyler asked. "You don't look so good."

Charlie shrugged. "It was a long night. Lots of booze."

"You and Joni again?"

Charlie shook his head. "Nope. We're just fine for now."

"So what was it?" Tyler prodded.

"Well," Charlie said. "I went and talked to President Alcott yesterday."

"That's right! How'd it go?" Tyler asked excitedly.

"Yeah, it didn't go so well. He refused to talk to me really. Basically shoved me out of his office. He was pretty pissed I was there."

Tyler shook his head. "See? However you got that appointment backfired, didn't it? Do you want to borrow my ethics book? The offer is still on the table."

Charlie chuckled and shoved Tyler in the chest. "Shut up. I don't need your damn ethics book. Hell, I probably have mine somewhere still safely wrapped in its plastic."

"Probably. You really seem to have learned a lot in that class."

Charlie dismissed this. "Anyway, I was pretty bummed about how it went down, so I just went home and spent the day drinking. I was just convinced we were screwed on this whole deal. I figured without an interview with President Alcott the story would just be fucked. But then I had a moment of clarity while I was spewing whiskey onto Joni's flower bed next to the porch," Charlie said, his eyes lighting up.

"We don't need President Alcott. If he doesn't want to help us catch his daughter's killer, fuck him. We'll do it without him. Without the cops. Without anyone. We'll do it our fucking selves."

Charlie poked Tyler in the chest again. His eyes had a strange glimmer that made Tyler feel uneasy.

"How?" Tyler asked.

"However we want. It doesn't matter. We're going to do it, and we're going to be heroes. The journalistic community will praise us. This fucking school will bow down to us. We will be gods among men."

Tyler was a little worried by the words being spewed from his friend's mouth. "You sound crazy, Charlie."

The look vanished from Charlie's eyes, and he just smiled at Tyler. "No worries, Ty. I'm just saying I think we can do it. We have to because it looks like no one else is."

Tyler eyed Charlie skeptically. "Okay."

Charlie patted Tyler on the shoulder and went into his office. From his chair he yelled, "So, how's the Robert Ray angle coming?"

Walking into Charlie's office, Tyler said, "Well, I just talked to his lawyer, Chris Newton. He told me I couldn't talk to Robert Ray, but he gave me a pretty good quote."

Tyler handed his notepad to Charlie so he could read it.

"Cool," Charlie said, handing it back when he was finished. "Now you just have to talk to Robert Ray."

"But Mr. Newton said I couldn't."

"Fuck him," Charlie said with shrug. "We can talk to Robert Ray. We just have to do it without the lawyer finding out."

"And how are we going to do that?

Charlie smiled. "Not we. You. Go to see Irene. See if she can get you in. If not, just drive out to his house. Storm him."

Tyler shook his head. "I don't think I can do that, Charlie. The lawyer said it could jeopardize his case. We know he's innocent, but the courts don't. If doing something hurts his case, it wouldn't be a good idea."

Charlie stood up and stepped closer to Tyler. "No. Fuck that. You're a journalist. When I hired you, you said you wanted to learn. I said I'd do that. This is how it's done. You want something, go get it. If you get caught, play dumb. Act like you didn't know you weren't supposed to be there. It's always easier to ask for forgiveness than permission."

Tyler took a step back. "But . . ."

"No. Don't give me any buts. You want to be a journalist? You've got the talent, but do you have the drive? You'll have to drop this innocent, good-boy shit and nut up. That make sense? Do you want to be a journalist?"

Tyler nodded slowly. "Yes. I do. I just didn't know it meant breaking the law. I thought journalists did good for their communities and country."

"They do. They report important things that others want to keep quiet. This is one of those things. Sometimes extreme measures have to be taken. You shouldn't ever knowingly break the law, but sometimes you have to bend the rules and blur the lines. And for the record, what I'm telling you to do isn't illegal. I'm just telling you to ignore the lawyer because what Robert Ray has to say might be vitally important. So you tell me, Tyler Fox, what is more important? Following the rules to a T, or helping clear a guy of murder for good and basically save his life?"

Tyler thought about this. "I guess you're right."

"You're damn right I am," Charlie said, sitting back down.

"I guess I'll go see Irene," Tyler said, turning to go.

"Not right now. We won't be able to get the story by the deadline. Let's tackle it Sunday. I'll even go with you. For now, let's go over the other, non-murder stories and get them ready. Cool?" Charlie asked.

Tyler shrugged. "Okay."

The rest of the day the two prepared the final budget, and the next day, with the help of Hayley, the paper was published.

On the front page, stripped across the top, was the story Hayley wrote. The headline—which read, "Alcott's roommate tells of jealous students over scholarship as murder investigation continues"—was a little sensationalist, but Charlie said he didn't care. He wanted people to read it.

Friday morning when Dr. Laureth picked up a copy and read the lead story in his office, his face turned bright red, and he slammed his coffee cup down on his desk, sending pieces of ceramic and drops of coffee everywhere.

He stormed out of his office.

Chapter Twenty-five

Sheriff Giles sat back in his chair and laughed. Lying on his desk was the latest copy of the *Clarion*, and on the front page was a story in which the dead Alcott girl's roommate had basically accused the daughter of his new murder suspect of committing the crime.

"This is fucking great!" he said cheerily. "Those dumb fucking kids are just laying it all out for us! How great is this?"

He grabbed the phone receiver and dialed Deputy Bonner.

"Randall, what are you doing?" he asked when the deputy picked up.

"Shaving, Sheriff. Why are you calling so early?" Deputy Bonner asked.

"Early? It's just after eight. You're on the clock."

"No. Not today. Got a doctor's appointment this morning. Took half a personal day."

Sheriff Giles chuckled. "Not any more. We got some shit to do. We have a new suspect in the case. He's a professor at the college, and that shitty newspaper those kids run just called out his fucking daughter as the killer."

"What?" Deputy Bonner asked. "That little shit Charlie Harrison is actually on the right track?"

"I wouldn't say that. He's in the ballpark. Right family."

"Okay," Deputy Bonner said with confusion. "But why is this guy a suspect? And who is it?"

"It's Dr. Laureth. An English guy. He's the suspect because . . . well, President Alcott thought maybe he might have done it. Seems he's got a history of sorts. Got fired from the last college for punching out the president there. Also, he's ex-military. Alcott said he's got a temper. Said he thought he might be pissed because his daughter didn't get some stupid-ass scholarship."

"Really?"

"Yep."

"And you think Harrison's got this figured out?"

"No," Sheriff Giles said shortly. "He's just going after what the dead girl's roommate said. There's no way he's so close to the answer. But he'll get there, especially when we arrest Laureth."

Deputy Bonner was silent for a moment. Then he said, "Okay. But I still don't understand how you know this."

Sheriff Giles frowned. "No, dumbass. Pay attention. I said he printed an article that called her out."

"So in the paper he said this Laureth's daughter was the killer?"

"No," Sheriff Giles said with a frustrated sigh. "He quoted the dead girl's roommate as saying something about Bethany Laureth, Doc Laureth's daughter, being pissed about not getting a scholarship that Alcott's daughter got. The roommate said this Bethany was claiming the whole deal was rigged. And the other night Alcott himself called me and said he suspected Doc Laureth. You follow me?"

"I guess," Deputy Bonner said. "Basically, Harrison thinks he's pretty smart and has it figured out, but he doesn't."

"Yep. Ran a big-ass story about the roommate and everything she said. The title of the story says, 'Alcott's roommate tells of jealous students over scholarship as murder investigation continues.'"

Deputy Bonner scoffed into the phone. "Sounds like he's blowing that sucker up quite a bit."

"Yep. I've been reading the paper since the murder happened. He's been reporting on it every week, but he ain't had shit. He's probably got a fucking boner over what this girl said. Probably thinks he's blowing the case wide open."

"Jesus," Deputy Bonner blew into the phone. "I hate that kid. He's the one that violated my daughter."

Sheriff Giles stifled a laugh. "That so?"

"Yeah. Little douche bag. It will put a smile on my face when he realizes he didn't have it right."

"That's right, so you need to get your personal shit done so we can get to work on bringing Laureth in before we have a bunch of fireworks up there. If he's a hotheaded sonofabitch, anything could happen," Sheriff Giles said.

As soon as the words left his mouth, his radio squawked, and the dispatcher said there was a fight between a professor and student at St. Alfanus.

"Holy shit!" Sheriff Giles said. "You have your radio on?"

"Yes sir," Deputy Bonner said. "Looks like the fireworks are lighting off early."

"See at the college," Sheriff Giles said, slamming the receiver down and running out the door of his office.

On his way to Hooks he called Leslie Black and filled her in. They agreed to meet later to finish planning how to hang the murder on Dr. Laureth.

Chapter Twenty-six

Dr. Laureth's office was on the second floor of Cormac Hall, but his feet barely touched the steps on the two flights leading to the basement.

From the basement landing, he could see the front door of the *Clarion*, and his fist got tighter around the copy of the latest edition of the newspaper. With long strides, he bounded to the door and flung it open. Charlie was at his desk, and he looked up to see who had come in.

Dr. Laureth started toward him. "You sonofabitch!" he shouted. "How dare you put that shit in the paper about my daughter!"

Charlie stood up and stepped out of his office. "Calm down!" he said loudly.

"Fuck you, Harrison!"

Charlie's hackles rose. "Listen, I'm not a college president, so you shouldn't break my nose. It's just not your style," he retorted smartly.

Dr. Laureth's face turned a darker shade of red as his anger increased, but he stopped going forward. Breathing heavily, he asked, "What the hell do you know about that?"

Charlie smiled a wide grin. "I know assault charges follow you."

Dr. Laureth nodded and smiled an evil grin. "I'll show you assault charges, you little motherfucker," he said angrily in a scarily soft voice. "You basically claimed my daughter was Alison Alcott's fucking murderer. I'll make you pay."

Charlie looked over to his right. Tyler and Hayley were standing behind a partition, so Dr. Laureth didn't see them. Hayley had a camera in her hand because she'd been just about to go outside to take fall pictures in case the paper needed wild art next week. Charlie locked eyes with her, lowered his to the camera and then raised them back to hers. She understood and nodded slowly.

"Make me pay? That sounds like a threat, sir," Charlie said sarcastically but not giving any ground.

Dr. Laureth stepped forward and flung the paper at Charlie. "It's not a threat. It's a promise."

"How clichéd," Charlie said wryly.

This set Dr. Laureth off. He let out a scream and lunged at Charlie, who didn't attempt to move. One punch landed squarely on Charlie's nose, shattering it. Blood spewed from his nostrils and mouth as he stumbled back. Hayley began firing pictures, but she wasn't using the flash, which meant Dr. Laureth didn't notice. Tyler called 9-1-1.

As Charlie stumbled backward toward the wall, Dr. Laureth continued to advance. He and Charlie slammed into the wall together. Dr. Laureth grabbed Charlie by the hair and punched him in the mouth again. Then he pulled back and punched him in the stomach once, twice, three times. Charlie made no attempt to fight back.

Getting off the phone with the police, Tyler rushed to his friend's aid. He grabbed Dr. Laureth by the back of the shirt and pulled, but the professor was stronger than he appeared. He shrugged Tyler off and went back at Charlie.

Tyler regrouped and jumped on his back, slipping one arm around Dr. Laureth's neck and pulling on his wrist with his other hand for leverage. It wasn't a sleeper hold, but it got Dr. Laureth's attention.

With Tyler dangling from his back, Dr. Laureth stumbled away from Charlie, who appeared to be on the brink of unconsciousness as blood covered his face and pooled on his chest since he had slid down the wall and was slumped over on the floor.

Dr. Laureth began to struggle for breath, but his strength didn't seem to decrease. He began to swing back and forth so Tyler began to slide around behind him. Soon Dr. Laureth picked up enough momentum that he flung Tyler into the glass window that made up part of Charlie's office. Tyler's hips and legs crashed into the glass, sending a thick crack snaking its way across the pane.

Tyler didn't let go, so Laureth slammed him into the glass again, causing more cracks to appear.

He was just about to throw Tyler against the glass again when Officer Jones burst into the room.

"Put him down!" he bellowed.

Dr. Laureth stopped in mid-swing and looked at Officer Jones. He flipped him off and began to swing back and forth again.

Officer Jones reached to his holster and pulled out a Taser stun gun. "Let go of him, Tyler!" he shouted as he squeezed the trigger.

Tyler released his grip and slid down Dr. Laureth's back as the barbed darts from the stun gun flew through the air and sank into the flesh of the professor's arm and chest. Instantly the high-voltage charge traveled through the copper wires attached to the ends of the darts and the gun itself, dropping Dr. Laureth to the floor in a convulsing pile of moans and groans.

Tyler scampered to his feet and went to Charlie's side. He put a hand on his shoulder.

"Are you okay?" Tyler asked.

Charlie gave a struggling smile. "I look like a million bucks, don't I?"

Tyler shook his head. "Don't joke. I'll call an ambulance."

Charlie nodded.

"I'm already on it," Hayley said from behind them.

Behind them, Officer Jones was standing over Dr. Laureth with his cell phone to his ear. He hung up and looked at Tyler.

"Sheriff Giles said he and Deputy Bonner are on their way. Is the ambulance coming too?" he asked Hayley.

"Yes," she said, going to Tyler's side and hugging him. "Are you okay, Ty?"

Tyler nodded and looked at Charlie. "Help's on the way, buddy."

"Great," Charlie moaned as he slipped out of consciousness.

Sheriff Giles, Deputy Bonner, and the Hooks EMS Service arrived shortly thereafter. The officers handcuffed Dr. Laureth as paramedics tended to Charlie, who they loaded into an ambulance.

As he waited for the ambulance to drive away, Charlie woke up enough to say, "Get pictures of Laureth in the cop car."

Hayley looked at him in disbelief. "Are you serious?"

Charlie nodded as the paramedics closed the ambulance doors.

Hayley looked at Tyler. He shrugged. She ran back down into the *Clarion* office and grabbed the camera. She ran up to the police cruiser and fired a series of shots of Dr. Laureth sitting in the back seat. Before she could get too many pictures, Sheriff Giles ran her off.

"Now now, little lady. No more pictures," he said stepping between Hayley and the car.

Hayley looked at the large man and stepped back without saying a word.

Tyler took her place and asked, "So what's going to happen to him?"

"He's going to jail, assuming that old boy who got his ass kicked wants to press charges."

Tyler nodded. "I'm sure he does."

Sheriff Giles nodded, and Tyler started to walk away. Then he stopped. He remembered what Charlie had said about either being a journalist or not.

"Uh, Sheriff Giles. Dr. Laureth was ranting about the story Charlie wrote that talked about the murder. Does this have anything to do with that?"

Sheriff Giles stared at Tyler with narrow eyes. "What are you getting at?"

"Well, uh, Charlie thought maybe Dr. Laureth might have done it, and he was pretty mad. I don't know. Just thought I should ask."

Sheriff Giles sneered and thought, holy shit, they really were onto something. Maybe I can use this. "Well," he said. "I don't know what happened here today. I wasn't here. As for the murder, I'll just say this professor is now a person of interest."

Sheriff Giles smiled to himself and thought: that ought to move things in the right direction.

Tyler nodded. "Oh. Okay."

Sheriff Giles walked away and joined Deputy Bonner, who was interviewing Hayley. Tyler found Officer Jones and nodded a hello. "You think Charlie will be okay?"

Officer Jones nodded. "I think so."

"That's good," Tyler said. Silence spun out between them for a bit before Tyler said, "Charlie thought Dr. Laureth killed Alison. That's why we ran the story about Alison's roommate saying what she said. Charlie thought it would flush him out. We got a reaction, I guess. You think he did it?"

Officer Jones took a deep breath and slowly let it out. "I don't know, Tyler. It sure looks like he has a guilty conscious, doesn't it?"

Tyler nodded. "Sure does."

"But don't say I said that," Officer Jones said quickly. "I don't want to be involved in this."

"Okay," Tyler said.

"Well, looks like the deputy is done with your friend there. Better go see how she's doing."

"Yeah. Okay."

Before Tyler walked off, Officer Jones said, "How about you? You okay?"

"I suppose," Tyler said. "He slammed me into that window pretty good while I was pulling him off of Charlie."

"Did you get looked over by the medics?"

"No," Tyler said with a shake of his head. "I figure I'll go see Charlie at the hospital. I'll get looked over then."

"Good," Officer Jones said, patting him on the back and walking toward Sheriff Giles and Deputy Bonner.

Hayley came up to Tyler and hugged him tight. "That was terrifying."

Tyler hugged her back and smoothed her hair with one hand. "I know. I know. But it's over. And Charlie is going to be fine."

"I hope so," Hayley said from his chest.

"He will," Tyler said. "Want to go to the hospital and see if he's okay?"

Hayley nodded, and the two let go of each other. Looking around, they realized how many students had gathered to see what was going on.

"Wow," Hayley said.

Tyler didn't say anything and hustled Hayley away from the crowd.

Sheriff Giles watched the two leave. "Reckon they'll go fuck now?"

Deputy Bonner chuckled. "Probably so. Redheads like her probably love the sight of boys fighting."

"Ha. Probably right," Sheriff Giles said. "What about you, Nick? Think they'll do it? You see everything around here. You caught them fuckin'?"

Officer Jones shook his head. "No, I haven't."

Sheriff Giles laughed. "You will. They've got a thing going. I can tell."

The three stood in silence for a moment thinking about the two young lovers. Deputy Bonner broke the silence. "So you going to charge him with the murder too?"

Shrugging, Sheriff Giles said, "Not right away. We'll have to get a warrant and search his place." With a smile, he continued, "I figure we'll find something, though."

Deputy Bonner nodded, and Officer Jones looked at the ground.

"Well, boys, guess we better take this sorry bag of shit to New Boston," Sheriff Giles said, patting his stomach with both hands.

He and Deputy Bonner got into their police cruisers and drove off while Officer Jones broke up the crowd of on-lookers.

At the Hooks hospital, Tyler and Hayley sat in the only waiting room in the entire facility. The nurse said they couldn't see Charlie until the doctor was sure surgery wasn't needed. While they waited, they talked little, and the nurse looked Tyler over and deemed him okay, just bruised.

It was almost noon before they were allowed into Charlie's room. He had a splint on his nose, and bruises were already appearing below his eyes. His lips were swollen and split, and his teeth had blood on them. He was smiling, though.

"Glad you two could make it," he said.

Tyler grabbed his friend's hand. "Wouldn't have missed it for the world."

"How are you feeling?" Hayley asked.

"Okay," Charlie said. "The doc's got me on some good drugs. I barely feel anything."

Hayley smiled.

"So did they arrest Dr. Laureth?" Charlie asked.

"Yep, and Sheriff Giles said he was a person of interest in Alison's murder," Tyler said.

Charlie's smile widened, though it instantly shrank as he winced with pain. "I knew it. I fucking knew it."

Hayley and Tyler nodded.

"How about pictures? You get any?"

Hayley shrugged. "I think so. I haven't looked at them yet, but I'm sure we did."

"Good," Charlie said.

"Has anyone called Joni?" Hayley asked.

Charlie nodded. "Yeah. I had the nurse call. She's on her way."

"Good," Hayley said.

The doctor then came in and told them they needed to let Charlie rest.

Hayley and Tyler left. They rode back to campus in silence. They didn't go to any of their classes that day and did little over the weekend. Tyler didn't go talk to Irene.

Chapter Twenty-seven

The next few weeks were quiet on the campus of St. Alfanus. Students and faculty were quietly discussing Dr. Laureth's attack on a student and his subsequent arrest. The *Clarion* ran a story about the incident and mentioned that the sheriff had said Dr. Laureth was a suspect in the murder of Alison Alcott. This fed the fodder on campus, and knowing he was behind bars, though not convicted of anything but an assault, put everyone at ease.

A funeral for Alison was held, and though the *Clarion* covered it, it was rather uneventful.

Charlie went back to work a couple weeks after he was attacked and took the paper back over. Tyler, Hayley, and Joni managed to keep it publishing in his absence.

One of the first things out of Charlie's mouth when he got back to the office was, "Tyler, did you talk to Robert Ray yet?"

Tyler shook his head. "No."

"Then we are tonight," Charlie said.

"Why?" Tyler asked. "Dr. Laureth is already behind bars. What's the point?"

Charlie starred at his friend through swollen and blackened eyes. "Are you serious right now? We have to be complete. This interview helps seal everything up so that when Laureth is charged with the murder, we'll have covered every angle of the story. This interview is a must-have."

"Fine," Tyler said, defeated. "I'm just worried about that lawyer."

"Fuck him," Charlie said. "Now, I've got to go get a few back assignments to make up. I'll see you after bit."

That evening Charlie picked Tyler up and then went to Irene's. Stepping inside the bar, Charlie and Tyler were both impressed with how quiet the place was. Only a handful of people were inside, sipping on frosty glasses of beer.

Behind the bar, they could see Irene doing dishes and puffing on a cigarette between taking shots of whiskey.

"There she is," Charlie said as they walked in. "All we have to do is go ask her, that's all. Don't worry. It'll be fine."

Tyler nodded as they reached the bar. Each took a seat on a barstool.

"What can I get ya?" Irene asked, cigarette dangling from her lip.

"I'll take a beer," Charlie said.

"What flavor?" she asked.

Charlie shrugged. "Coors?"

She nodded and looked at Tyler. "And for you?"

"Uh, I'll have the same," he said, worried as usual he would get carded.

Irene nodded again and went to fetch their drinks. Charlie nudged Tyler. "When she gets back, just ask her. I'm sure she remembers you from last time."

"Okay," Tyler said uneasily.

Irene set their beers down in front of them, and each took a sip. Irene started to walk away, but Tyler stopped her.

"Hey, Irene. Can I talk to you?" he asked.

She turned to look at him, eyebrows raised. "What about?"

"Well, do you remember me? I'm the one who talked you about Robert Ray. My name is Tyler."

"Yeah," she responded skeptically.

"Well, I need to talk to him now. We know he didn't do it, and we just wanted to talk to him about everything. Give him a chance to . . . speak his piece, I guess. I mean, everyone has to be wondering what he's thinking, especially since Dr. Laureth's now the primary suspect. You think he'd talk to us?" Tyler rambled nervously.

Irene took a long drag on her cigarette and slowly blew out the smoke. "I don't know. I talked about the last one you wrote with Robert Ray. He appreciated it. Said you made him sound like a human when everyone else was making him out like a damned animal."

"Thank you," Tyler said.

"But, the lawyer we got doesn't want us talking to anybody until he's off free and clear," Irene said.

Tyler nodded. "Okay, but it sure would be really helpful if we could talk to him."

Irene smiled softly. "I bet it would. So what exactly would you ask him?"

"I don't know for sure. I just want to talk to him about how much he misses Alison and what it was like to go through what he's been through. Most importantly, though, I want to know what it was like to be a suspect in the murder case of someone he loved. I just want to show people he's a good guy to get rid of any notions he is a killer," Tyler explained.

Irene considered this for a moment and snuffed out her cigarette in an empty beer bottle sitting on the bar. She eyed Tyler. "I think you're an honest kid. Some of the other reporters who have come in here . . ."

"Other reporters have been in here?" Charlie interrupted.

"Yes," Irene said, "and they're just vultures. They always were just trying to get some negative stuff. Never even pretending to want to tell a good story. But you, Tyler, you seem to be one of the good ones."

Tyler smiled and blushed. "Thanks," he said with embarrassment.

"I'll tell you what. Let me call him and see if he's willing. I can't promise anything, but I can try," she said.

"That would be great!" Charlie blurted out.

Irene ignored him and walked over to a phone hanging on the wall next to a picture of horses playing poker.

Tyler watched her walk over to the phone and saw the picture. "Horses?" he asked Charlie as he pointed at the picture.

Charlie shrugged. "Whatever. It's Texas. Besides, who gives a shit? We're about to get to talk to Robert Ray! This is great!"

"I still don't understand why, though," Tyler said, taking a drink. "Why do we need to talk to Robert Ray so bad?"

Charlie hung his head in mock shame. "Have I taught you nothing? It is part of the story. We have to talk to him for the reasons you babbled to Irene and because he was an accused person. That's too juicy not to cover."

Tyler nodded. "Okay. I guess, but . . ."

"Shut up," Charlie hissed. "She's coming back."

Tyler looked over and saw Irene walking toward them. Her face carried no expression.

"Well," she said, reclaiming her post at the bar. "I talked to him. He didn't sound too interested."

Tyler hung his head. "Damn. Well, thanks for trying, I guess," he said, turning to walk away.

"Wait," Irene said. "All I said was he wasn't too interested. Did I say he wouldn't talk to you?"

"Fuck yeah!" Charlie shouted and slapped the bar.

Tyler slowly turned around and looked at Irene with a smile. "That's great! Thanks so much!"

She nodded. "Glad I could help."

The two started to leave when she shouted, "Wait! You two little peckerheads going to pay for your drinks?"

Charlie rolled his eyes. "Shit," he said before he jogged back to the bar and tossed money to Irene.

He rejoined Tyler outside, and they climbed into Charlie's car.

"Do you know where we're going?" Tyler asked uncertainly.

Charlie smiled. "Yep. I looked up this address quite a while ago. I knew I'd be making this drive one way or the other. Whether I was welcome or not."

Tyler shook his head and cranked the radio volume up. Charlie's stereo was tuned to a country music station. Garth Brooks was singing "Friends In Low Places," so Charlie and Tyler sang with him as they drove.

As they pulled into Robert Ray Turner's driveway, Tyler turned the radio down and took in what he was seeing. The farm where Robert Ray lived seemed to be in exceptional state. The average-sized house looked like it had been painted within the last few months; the grass of the lawn looked as though it was carefully cut; and all the outbuildings showed little age or wear and tear.

"Farming must be treating him okay," Charlie said, noticing the same things Tyler had.

Tyler nodded as the car rolled to a stop. They got out. Dusk was settling over the landscape, casting deep shadows. From the porch a single light burned, marking the entrance to the house.

Charlie and Tyler headed for the doorway, but just as they were about to ring the doorbell, they heard the unmistakable click of a shotgun being cocked.

Slowly they turned and looked to their right toward the source of the sound. Robert Ray was standing there, the gun leveled at them. Hanging from the fingers of the hand pointing the barrel of the gun at them was a half-full bottle of Jim Beam whiskey.

"Who the fuck are you two?" he asked in a slightly slurred voice.

"Shit. First a fist fight, now a shotgun. I'm such a shit magnet," Charlie said quietly to himself.

Tyler heard him but didn't respond. Instead, he raised his hands and said, "Robert Ray, my name is Tyler Fox, and this guy with me is Charlie Harrison. We work for the paper at the college. Irene said she just called to make sure it was okay for us to come see you. She said you told her it was fine."

Robert Ray stared at them through bloodshot eyes. "What if I changed my mind?"

"You've got to be fucking kidding me," Charlie said, again speaking to himself. At least, Tyler hoped he was talking to himself.

"Why would you do that, Robert Ray?" Tyler asked.

He shrugged. "Why not? What's in it for me?"

"Closure," Tyler blurted out without thinking. Charlie looked at him with a strange glance. Tyler continued, "All we want to do is talk to you about how much you miss Alison and never would have hurt her. And maybe we could talk about what it has been like to be accused of murder and what you can remember about the real killer."

Robert Ray seemed to consider all this, though the shotgun never lowered. Finally he said, "Fine. But only because Irene said I should. Of course, when I finish this bottle of whiskey, we're done. And if you don't leave, I'll start shooting."

"What? Why?" Charlie said, finally speaking loud enough for Robert Ray to hear.

"Why not? Ali's dead. I've got nothing to live for, except drinking and shooting. Fuck it. Nothing matters anymore," Robert Ray said, sinking into a lawn chair.

"That's not true," Tyler said. "Plenty still matters."

Robert Ray pointed the gun into Tyler's crotch. "Shut the fuck up. I don't want to hear it. That's all Irene and everybody says. They don't know. I know. And I know nothing matters anymore."

"Okay. Sorry," Tyler said with wide eyes.

Robert Ray nodded and brought the gun up. He sat the butt of it in his lap and let the barrel rest on his chest and over his shoulder. Leaning his face against the cool metal, he took a long drink from the bottle of whiskey. When he sat it back on his knee, a quarter of the liquid was gone.

Tyler and Charlie looked at each other.

"Okay," Charlie said. "First thing's first. Obviously you miss Alison, but can you tell us about why you feel that way? Why she meant so much to you?"

"She was gorgeous," Robert Ray said. "The sweetest girl I've ever met. She was so smart and pretty I thanked God every day for her deciding to slum it and be with a cowboy like me. I wish God would have killed me that night instead of her. She didn't deserve to go. I've done enough shit before that it would have made some sense. But not her."

Tyler was jotting notes down furiously. He looked up and said, "What kind of past do you have? What do you mean?"

Robert Ray giggled slightly at some joke only he could hear. "Me? I like to fight. A lot."

"Any issues with guns before?" Charlie asked.

"Nope. Just fights," Robert Ray said, taking another long drink.

The Jim Beam bottle now held only a quarter of the whiskey it had earlier.

"Okay," Tyler said. "Can you remember anything about the killer? Did you ever get a good look?"

Robert Ray slowly shook his head. "No. If I had, that sonofabitch would be dead. He killed my baby, so I'd kill him back."

"Was the guy big?" Charlie asked.

"No. Medium height. Not much taller than me. Fucker blindsided me while I was pissin'. Never saw him coming. Knew it was a dude though cuz there's no way a chick could have hit me that hard. Fuck me runnin'," Robert Ray said, beginning to slur his words more often.

Eyeing the rapidly lowering level of booze in the bottle, Charlie said, "So what's it been like being accused of murder? Having to spend time in jail?"

Robert Ray looked at Charlie. "How the fuck do you think?" he asked before taking another long drink, leaving only one more swallow in the bottle. "It sucked. All my friends stopped talking to me; people who saw me on the streets steered clear and . . . ," he said, trailing off. "Shit. People treated me like I was covered in shit or something. Kind of was, I guess. This is some shit storm. I didn't fucking kill her. Never would. But do people listen? Fuck no!"

Robert Ray began to sob and started to lift the bottle to his lips. Charlie looked at Tyler with panic, so Tyler spoke up.

"One more thing," Tyler said abruptly, causing Robert Ray's hand to freeze halfway to his mouth. "We know you didn't kill her, and you know you didn't kill her. But if there was one thing you'd say to people to convince them you didn't, what would it be?"

"I loved her," Robert Ray said. "I'd rather kill myself than even make her cry."

Robert Ray drained the last of the liquor from the bottle, and Tyler and Charlie sat up straight in their chairs.

"I'm empty," Robert Ray said staring at the bottle in his hand. "Damn it."

Then with sudden skill that belied his drunken state, Robert Ray tossed the bottle toward the grass. With incredible speed, he brought the shotgun to his shoulder and fired without leaving his seat. The wad of shotgun pellets shattered the glass bottle before it even got near the grass.

Robert Ray stood and looked at the two reporters. "Time to go, boys," he said.

Tyler and Charlie nodded and slowly stood. They quickly left the porch and got into the car.

From the porch, Robert Ray watched them leave. The gun at his hip but always pointed at Charlie's car.

As they drove back into Hooks, Charlie said, "Well, that was fun."

Tyler let out a long breath. "Right. Fun."

"At least we got enough to write a little story, and we're the only ones that have talked to him," Charlie said happily.

"Great. We almost got our asses shot off, but we got a story."

Ignoring Tyler's tone, Charlie said with a dose of his own sarcasm, "That's the spirit."

In the next issue of the *Clarion* they ran the story. For the first time, even counting the murder issue, every copy of the *Clarion* was picked up.

Chapter Twenty-eight

On the morning of November 12, Tyler woke up early and went to the golf course. It was the day of the Alfanus Invitational, and he wanted to get warmed up by doing some putting and chipping on the practice green. He was nervous about the tournament. His coach and teammates were putting a lot of pressure on him to do well. He wanted to, but he hadn't been focusing on his game very well. With Charlie getting bloodied by the paper's adviser and the murder still hanging over the campus, Tyler had found it hard to even think about golf.

Also, the *Clarion* nearly got shut down after Dr. Laureth attacked the editor because suddenly the paper was without a faculty adviser, since the previous adviser was behind bars. Luckily one of the other English professors agreed to sign on as adviser, in name only.

As Tyler was making his way to the driving range to hit a few buckets of balls, Charlie came running up to him.

"Ty!" he said breathlessly, his eyes still underlined with fading bruises. "How's it going?"

Tyler stopped and smiled. "I'm good, Charlie. As loose as I can be."

"That's great!" Charlie said, clapping him on the back. "You going to bring home the trophy for us?"

"I'm going to give it my best shot."

"That's great!" Charlie said excitedly. "I'm covering the story, and as I'm sure you know, Hayley is shooting the pictures.

Tyler nodded. "That's what I'd been told."

Charlie smiled. "Of course. Of course. Sorry. I'm just excited."

"It's just a golf game."

Charlie's smile widened. "It's not the golf game I'm excited about. You know how I've been calling the sheriff's department like every day to find out when they were going to formally charge Dr. Laureth with Alison's murder? Well, I talked to them this morning."

"On a Saturday?"

"Yes, but that's not the point. Focus," Charlie said. "They told me they were planning a press conference to announce the charges. The conference is going to be here at the clubhouse on Friday. Isn't that great? We're finally going to be proven right! The Texas Intercollegiate Press Association award is practically ours!"

"That's great, Charlie," Tyler said with a smile. "But Friday? It will be too late for this week's paper."

Charlie's smiled faded slightly. "Yeah. That sucks, but the important thing is we'll be right. We'll be famous!"

Tyler shook his head and smiled. "Whatever you say, Charlie."

Still smiling, Charlie looked around. "Okay. Well, knock 'em dead today. When do you tee off?"

"In about an hour," Tyler said.

"Awesome! Good luck!" Charlie said, trotting off.

Knowing the murder case was nearing its end put Tyler at ease. He drove the ball well while warming up on the range.

At the appointed time, Tyler teed off. The weather had become overcast and breezy, but people still turned out in droves to watch, most donning jackets to protect against the breeze.

Tyler played a stellar front nine. He was four strokes under par with his closest competitor at one under.

Teeing off on the back nine, Tyler felt good about his chances of winning. After shooting a birdie on No. 10, his coach came up to him.

"You're doing great, Tyler!" Coach Grower said happily as he walked beside Tyler toward the No. 11 tee box. "You're playing the best game I've seen you play! Keep it up!"

And Tyler did keep it up. When he got to the No. 14 tee box, he didn't feel his normal sense of dread come over him. It was once again another hole, not the scene of a horrible memory.

He laid up and put his tee shot at the bend of the dogleg. For his second shot, he took aim at the green. He pulled the face of his 7-iron back in his relaxed swing. He shifted his weight to his back leg. The club head arched over his head as his hips cocked. He straightened his right elbow and swung his hips forward. The club's shaft arched downward, and he shifted his weight to his front leg. The iron struck the ball with a powerful blow, sending the ball sailing down the fairway.

The gallery of onlookers clapped in approval, but Tyler instantly saw he had made a mistake. The ball was too high and still gaining speed. It flew over the green and disappeared into the thick trees behind the putting surface.

Tyler slammed his club into the fairway. "Damn," he said.

The gallery groaned, and Tyler shoved his club into his bag. Then he picked it up and trudged to where his playing partner's ball was. He watched in dismay as the player put his ball within three feet of the pin.

Knowing he wouldn't be able to find the ball in the trees and pond behind the green, Tyler took a drop and chipped on. He putted out, dropping two strokes and ending up only one stroke ahead of the pack.

Tyler rebounded on the next three holes, regaining one of his lost strokes. Coming into the final hole, Tyler was up by two strokes.

He teed off and hit the longest drive of his life. He ended up only one hundred yards from the green. He chipped on and one-putted to win the tournament.

After receiving his trophy and high praise from Coach Grower, Tyler went back to his dorm room where Hayley, Charlie, and Joni were waiting.

"Tyler! You the man!" Charlie exclaimed when he walked through the door.

Joni let out a scream, and Hayley came up and gave him a hug and kiss.

"You did great, Ty," she said.

Tyler was grinning from ear to ear.

The group spent the next few minutes discussing the round and congratulating Tyler. Charlie broke the pattern and asked a question.

"So on fourteen when you put it over the green, why didn't you just go find the ball instead of taking a drop?" he asked.

"Well," Tyler said. "The trees there are out of bounds. So I didn't have a choice. Besides, those trees are thick."

Charlie nodded. "Makes sense. Not to bring down the party, but I guess that is why the cops said they couldn't find a murder weapon. They said even that old deer trail they fig-ured the killer used, which is the only way a person could have quickly gotten away, was pretty overgrown."

Everyone looked at each other uneasily. "Can't you not bring that shit up, Charlie?" Joni asked.

"Sorry," Charlie said.

Tyler jumped in. "It's okay. He's right. That is what we were told. And I agree. It would be hard for anyone to run away through that crap. It's thick. I tried to look for a ball once and gave up in a hurry."

Everyone nodded.

"Besides," Tyler said. "That pond back there swallows anything that gets near it."

"Right," Charlie said dismissively. "Now enough of this talk. I shouldn't have started it. Let's head out to my place and party. I'm thirsty, and we've got a championship to cel-ebrate!"

Chapter Twenty-nine

The Tuesday following Tyler's Alfanus Invitational victory, Tyler and Charlie met in the *Clarion* offices to go over the budget for the week's edition of the newspaper. Charlie already had a majority of it mapped out, which he accomplished the day before while Tyler was busy with being the new athletic hero and his coach fawning over him.

"Okay," Charlie said after about thirty minutes. "We've accounted for everything, but Friday's press conference is still floating out there."

Tyler nodded. "True. What are we going to do?"

Charlie stood up from the chair he was sitting in next to Tyler and patted him on the shoulder. "Well, I was thinking this. We run a story announcing the press conference. In it, we say it is expected charges will be filed against the prime suspect. We won't use Dr. Laureth's name then. We'll hedge a bit. We'll bring up the fact Dr. Laureth is the primary suspect later in the story."

"Okay," Tyler said with a shrug of his shoulders. "Sounds good."

"That's not all," Charlie said, smiling and waving a finger at Tyler. "We'll also mention how we, the *Clarion*, brought Dr. Laureth to the surface by mentioning his daughter as a possible suspect by rehashing the previous stories. It will point everyone who reads it down the right path. They'll know we uncovered it all. An award is as good as ours!"

Tyler shook his head and stood up. "You're still hung up on that stupid award? Give me a break, Charlie," he said disgustedly. "You should be focused on the fact we exposed the killer. That we helped give closure to a family that's hurting. Jesus, Charlie, why can't you be human?"

Charlie smiled and shrugged. "I'll ask the Wizard for a heart. Right after we get honored in front of all the college journalists in Texas."

Tyler walked away and leaned against the wall. He stared at his friend. "You're a sick sonofabitch."

Charlie's eyes went wide and his jaw dropped. "What did you just call me?"

"You heard me," Tyler said with indignation.

"That's awesome!" Charlie said with a laugh.

Tyler was confused. "What?"

"You're finally using cuss words. Momma's so proud," Charlie said, hugging himself and pretending to wipe away tears.

"Screw you," Tyler said, trying not to smile.

"You're becoming a real journalist. As soon as you become more of an alcoholic, you'll be a true journo."

Tyler sat down in another chair and swiveled it away from Charlie.

Charlie laughed and began to aimlessly wander the office. "You know you're excited about the award. I don't give a shit why you wanted to solve the case; you know you won't turn down the award. That and the golf title you'll win later this year, you'll be on cloud nine."

"I don't know," Tyler said, still looking away from Charlie.

"What the fuck ever," Charlie said as he started to touch items on all the desks he walked by.

Tyler thawed a bit and turned around. "You really think we'll win it?"

"Of course," Charlie said. "No other paper is going to have anything as sweet as this. The only way it could have been better is if we'd found the gun."

"Yeah," Tyler said.

Charlie came to Tyler's desk and saw the corked bottle with the miniature boat in it. He ran his fingers over it and picked it up. He turned to Tyler with it in his hand. "Ty, you said you found this in the mud, right?"

"Yes," Tyler said. "I told you the whole story."

Charlie smiled. "Yeah. That schoolgirl outfit sounded hot."

Tyler frowned. "Anyway. Why do you ask?"

A slow smile spread across Charlie's lips. "And you said there was a pond back behind the green where Alison was killed, right?"

"Yes. What are you getting at, Charlie?"

"The cops never found the gun. You think those lazy fucks even bothered to drag the pond?"

Tyler's frown smoothed away as he realized what Charlie meant. "You think the gun could be in there?"

Charlie shrugged. His grin widened. "Well, if this bottle was in the bottom of that lake for who knows how long, why couldn't the murder weapon be in that pond?"

Tyler jumped to his feet. "Yes! Then we would be heroes!"

"Yep!" Charlie said, sitting the bottle back on Tyler's desk. "You're excited, aren't you?"

"Well hell yes!"

"I knew you wanted the award," Charlie said, lightly punching Tyler in the chest.

"Shut up," Tyler said, smiling as he deflected the punch. "So what do we do?"

Charlie slapped himself on the forehead. "Don't be so dumb, Ty. We go diving and find that motherfucker!"

"Now?"

"No," Charlie said with exasperation. "Not now. Tonight. We'll make it fun too. We'll get Joni and Hayley to help. They can wear bikinis. It will be great."

Tyler couldn't believe what he was hearing. "Bikinis? Why? Isn't the important thing we find the gun?"

"Sure," Charlie said. "But can't we have good scenery while we look?"

"Whatever. It's going to be really cold while we do this anyway. They probably won't wear bikinis."

Charlie shrugged. "A guy can dream."

Tyler dismissed this. "So what time should we meet?"

Considering this, Charlie said, "How about nine? At your dorm room?"

"Okay. I'll fill Hayley in, and you get Joni on board."

"Sounds good," Charlie said, picking his backpack up off the floor. "I better go to class for now, but I probably won't be able to focus. I'm stoked!"

"Me too," Tyler said, following Charlie out of the office. "Me too."

At 9:00 p.m. the group met in Tyler's dorm room. The girls were wearing long-sleeved T-shirts and gym shorts, not bikinis. Charlie and Tyler were wearing T-shirts and swimming trunks.

"Couldn't you girls have worn something else? Like, something with two pieces?" Charlie whined as they sat in the room.

"Charlie, shut the fuck up," Joni said. "It's going to be cold in the water, and you know it."

Charlie shrugged, and Tyler jumped in.

"Okay. Let's go over it again," he said holding a plastic bag up and tossing old golf gloves to everyone. "We will wear these in case we find it. We don't want to put our fingers on it."

"Right," Hayley said as she slipped her hands into the gloves. "Where did you get all these again?"

Tyler smiled. "Charlie convinced me to borrow them from the athletic department."

"Yeah," Charlie said. "Good thing I thought of it, huh?"

"Good job," Hayley said with mock admiration. "You're so smart."

"And what about when we find it?" Joni asked.

"What do you mean?" Tyler asked.

"Well, if we find it, what are we going to do? Just carry it back here?" Joni asked.

Charlie stood up. "She's right, Ty. What are we going to do?"

Tyler shrugged. "I don't know."

The group thought about it for a moment. Then Charlie snapped his fingers. "Ty! That bag! We'll take it with us and put it in there."

Tyler looked at the plastic sack dangling from his hand. "Yeah. Of course. That way we won't have to wear the gloves forever."

Charlie smiled. "Damn I'm good."

A groan escaped the group.

"Cram it, Charlie," Joni said as she stood up and looked at her friends. "Let's go do this."

Smiling but silent, they all left the dormitory and silently walked across the campus to the golf course. With Tyler leading the way, they cut across fairways and through tree rows to the No. 14 hole. They gathered at the edge of the trees standing behind the green.

"Okay," Tyler said. "The pond isn't too far in. All we have to do is walk in and start looking around."

"We aren't going to be able to see shit," Charlie said, looking around. "The moonlight isn't getting through these fucking trees at all."

"Yeah," Tyler said. "I guess we'll be doing it by touch."

Tyler stepped into the trees, and the rest followed. On the bank of the pond they flanked out around it with Tyler and Charlie on each end and the girls in the middle. Each stepped into the cool water.

"It's not too cold," Joni said.

"Wait until we go under," Hayley said as the water reached her midsection.

Soon all four of them were diving under and feeling around. When they came up for air, their hands were covered with mud, which was soon smeared on their faces as they attempted to wipe water out of their eyes. The girls' hair was also streaked with mud from when they pushed hair out of their faces.

After about thirty minutes of hunting, Charlie and Tyler came up at the same time. They could barley see each other across the pond.

"This sucks, dude," Charlie said breathlessly.

"Yep, but it has to be in here, right? I mean, the cops said they found no traces of the weapon in the trees. This is the only other place it could be," Tyler said.

"I don't know. Maybe that cocksucker still has it. Maybe Giles and his douche bags will find it in Laureth's house or something," Charlie said.

Tyler nodded, though Charlie couldn't see it. "Maybe. Damn it. This was dumb. What were we thinking?"

"Should we call it off?" Charlie asked.

"What?" Joni asked as she came out of the water. "We're giving up?"

"Maybe," Charlie said. "The killer probably still has the gun. That's why we can't find it."

Hayley had come up and heard this. "That would make sense, wouldn't it?"

"Probably. Damn," Tyler said, punching the water. "Why didn't we think of that before?"

"It's my fault," Charlie said. "I was the one who got all excited. I'm the one that wanted to find the gun so fucking bad so we'd be the ones who blew the case wide open. I'm sorry."

"We all agreed," Joni said. "It's no one's fault. Any one of us could have said no to this."

The group went silent for a moment. Then Charlie shouted.

"Fuck!" he said as he too slapped the water. "Let's get the fuck out of here. I need a beer."

They all agreed and started to make their ways to the pond's edge. As they went, Hayley stepped on something and let out a yelp.

"You okay?" Tyler asked with panic.

"I think so," Hayley said, her voice strained with pain. "I just stepped on something."

"Did it cut you?" Joni asked.

"No. I don't think so. Just hit me wrong, that's all," Hayley said.

"Was it a stick or something?" Charlie asked.

"I don't know. Let me check," Hayley said.

She quickly slipped below the surface of the water. Soon she exploded out of the water yelling.

"What is it?" Tyler asked.

Hayley was holding something in her hand. "I'm not sure! But I think it might be the gun!"

An excited holler came out of them all, and in a flurry of splashing, they scrambled out of the pond and the trees to the green. The moon was lighting the putting surface, and once they were all there, they huddled with Hayley in the middle.

"Let's see it!" Charlie said excitedly.

With trembling hands, Hayley held the object she had stepped on in the moonlight so everyone could see. She was holding a gun in her gloved hands.

"Holy shit!" Tyler said.

Charlie grabbed it from Hayley and studied it closely. "It's a Colt .45 with a damned silencer, and it's got a little bag tied to it."

Charlie squeezed the bag before opening it and picking out the contents.

"They're spent rounds," Tyler said in shock.

"This is the gun, isn't it? It's the motherfucking gun that killed Alison!" Joni exclaimed.

Charlie smiled, his teeth seeming to glow in the soft light. "Yes it is. Holy shit it is!"

"Well, what do we do with it?" Hayley asked.

"Give it to the cops," Tyler said.

"Eventually," Charlie said. "First we find out if it's Laureth's."

"How?" Hayley asked.

"We get the serial number and hope it's registered. Then it's simple," Charlie said.

"Shouldn't we just let the police handle that?" Tyler asked.

"We will. After we do it first," Charlie said. "Let's go back to the dorm and look it over."

Joni grabbed their plastic bag, and Charlie dropped the gun in. They then sprinted back to the dorms and dashed inside.

As they dripped muddy water on the carpet, Charlie pulled the gun out of the sack and looked at it again. Using his finger, he cleaned some of the mud off and searched for the serial number. When he found it, he held it up for everyone to see.

"Ladies and gentlemen," he said. "This might be the ticket right here."

"How are you going to find out?" Joni asked as she and Hayley used a couple of Tyler's towels to dry their hair.

Charlie bounced his eyebrows and grabbed his cell phone off of Tyler's dresser where he'd left it before going to the pond. He punched a few numbers and put the phone to his ear.

"Graham," Charlie said. "It's Charlie. I need something . . . Dammit, just listen . . . Yes, I will send you more for your book. I've already sent you some, haven't I? . . . Well then, why the fuck don't you think I'll send you more? . . . Fuck you . . . No. Fuck you . . . Are you done? This is kind of important . . . You wish. Now listen, do you still have any contacts with the New Orleans police department? . . . I know. I know. It's my fault, but can you just answer the question . . . Good. Can you call them, like now and ask to have a gun's serial number ran? . . . Why do you think? . . . Yes, you fucking idiot . . . So you can do it? . . . Okay. Here's the number."

Charlie read him the number and traded a few more words before hanging up. The group looked at him.

"He said he'd have a guy run the number. He said he'd tell him it was a gun he was going to buy off of the internet and wanted to make sure it was legit. Said he'd call back shortly," Charlie said.

"Who was that?" Tyler asked.

Charlie waved a hand at him. "Just an old friend. I'll tell you about him sometime."

Silence settled over the room as they waited for the phone to ring. After nearly twenty minutes, the phone began to play a song, which was Charlie's ringer.

Answering the call, Charlie said, "Took ya long enough . . . No. No. I'm sorry. I'm sorry. I do want the name . . . Yes. I need to watch my mouth . . . Yes. I will let you know about everything later. So who's the gun registered to? . . . What? No fuckin' way! . . . Okay. Thanks."

Charlie hung up and looked at his three friends.

"The gun is registered to N. A. Jones or, as we know him, Officer Nick Jones," Charlie said.

Chapter Thirty

Stunned silence settled over the group. They all looked back and forth at each other with wide eyes and slack jaws. Charlie was running his hands through his hair. Hayley was hugging herself. Joni had her hands on her knees. They could hear the sound of her nails scratching at her skin. Tyler had his fingers laced behind his head, his left foot bouncing up and down with nervous energy. He was the first one to break the silence.

"What the fuck?" he asked.

Everyone looked at him, slightly shocked by his word choice but too stunned from what Charlie had told them to say anything.

"Charlie, could Officer Jones have done this?" Tyler asked.

Charlie dropped his arms to his side and shrugged. "I don't know. I don't think so, but I don't know. It's his gun. It has a silencer. There were four shells in that stupid little bag, which is the same number of shots that killed Alison. Maybe he did do it."

Tyler nodded.

"But maybe the gun was stolen," Joni said. "Just because it is his gun doesn't mean he did it. And why was the gun registered? You don't have to do that in Texas. That isn't the law."

Charlie's face was pained. "Graham would have told me if the gun was reported stolen. And it wasn't registered technically, I guess. It was evidence or something the way Graham said it. Office Jones got caught with it during a DUI stop. The gun and serial number were temporarily entered into whatever system Graham used to track it down. I still shows up I guess. I don't know. I don't really understand either."

"Oh," Joni said quietly.

"Who's Graham?" Tyler asked.

"The guy I talked to on the phone," Charlie said. His eyes began to well up with tears. "I thought Nick and I were friends. I trusted him. How could he have done this? He seemed like such a good guy."

Joni went to Charlie's side, and Hayley said, "Maybe he didn't do it, Charlie. Maybe it was stolen like Joni said."

Charlie shook his head. "I don't know. Maybe," he said as tears rolled down his cheeks and Joni held him around the shoulders. "Maybe."

Tyler stood up. "So what are we going to do?"

Fighting back sobs, Charlie said, "I don't know. I don't know."

"Oh bullshit, Charlie!" Tyler shouted. "Don't quit now! You've been the one who's been all about solving this! The answer is staring us in the face, and you want to give up? You've taught me better than that, Charlie. You're better than that."

"Tyler," Hayley said softly, a scared look in her eye. "Calm down."

Tyler looked at Hayley and grimaced. "Sorry," he said to her. "Charlie, I'm sorry. It's just—It's just, you've been harping on me from day one about how to be a journalist, and you freezing up now goes against everything you've been preaching. You told me I had to decide if I wanted to be a journalist. I've decided. I wouldn't have gone swimming in that stupid fucking pond. Come on, Charlie. We're this close."

Charlie looked at Tyler through bleary eyes.

"Ty, knock off your shit," Joni said, defending Charlie. "Nick and Charlie were pretty close. How would you respond if you found out someone you knew might be a killer?"

Tyler began to say something, but Charlie cut him off. "If he'd listened to me at all, he'd go after him. Right, Ty?"

Joni and Hayley looked at Charlie with disbelief. Tyler smiled and said, "That's right. So how are we going to do that?"

Charlie stood up and hugged Joni around the waist. "We've got to find out if he did it or not."

"But how?" Hayley asked, going to Tyler's side.

Charlie was silent for a moment. Then he said, "We ask him."

Tyler cocked an eyebrow. "That seems like a bit of a stretch, even coming from you."

Charlie wiped his cheeks on the back of his hand. "True. I guess I can't just ask him."

"So what are you going to do?" Joni asked.

Sighing deeply, Charlie said, "I'll handle it. First, we have to get the rest of the paper ready." Charlie looked at the time on his cell phone. "It's getting late. Let's meet at the paper tomorrow afternoon and get to work. We've got three days. We can still go about business as usual. Nick is everywhere. He always knows what's going on around this campus."

"Like a girl and her boyfriend sneaking onto the golf course for a booty call?" Tyler asked.

"Probably," Charlie said. "So if he did this and thinks we know, he'll be able to tell we're up to something."

"Then why wouldn't he know we went for our little swim?" Hayley asked.

"Maybe we got lucky?" Tyler asked.

Charlie shrugged. "Maybe. I guess. If he knew and did it, he surely would have come after us by now."

The other three nodded in agreement.

"Well," Charlie said. "It's going to be a long couple of days. We just have to try to stay under the radar. Like I say, especially at a school as small as this, a security guard isn't going to miss a thing."

"Right. We just have to be careful," Tyler said.

"Go to all our classes—well, the ones we normally go to. And only hang around each other as much as normal," Charlie said.

"Okay," Hayley and Joni said in unison.

Charlie and Joni walked to the door. As they stepped out, Charlie turned and said, "Ginger, protect my boy there."

Hayley smiled. "I will," she said, giving Tyler a squeeze.

Closing the door behind Charlie and Joni, Tyler looked at Hayley. They smiled meekly at each other. Without saying a word, they sat on the bed and held each other. In silence, they stared at the wall. Tyler noticed the gun was still sitting on top of his dresser where Charlie had set it. A shiver ran down his spine. He jumped up and using a golf glove, slipped it back into the plastic sack. He then shoved it into his top drawer and covered it with socks and boxers.

He flipped the light switch off and crawled back into the bed with Hayley. She fell asleep after a while, but Tyler couldn't sleep. His mind was racing. He was trying to figure out what would happen next and what they should do. He was trying to think like Charlie, and to his surprise, he thought he might be doing just that.

At Charlie's house, Joni fell asleep on the couch, so Charlie took a spare blanket out of his closet and draped it over her. He brushed the hair out of her face.

"I love you, Joni," he said to her.

She didn't respond, but she didn't have to. Charlie knew; and he also knew, though he didn't want to accept it, that if Officer Jones was the murderer, exposing him would keep Joni safe.

Charlie didn't feel like sleeping, so he grabbed a cigar and a jacket. He went out onto the porch and lit the cigar.

As the smoke curled up toward the moonlit sky, Charlie thought about what had happened that evening. He was struggling to accept that fact that Officer Jones could be the killer while he simultaneously fought denial because, as had been pointed out, the gun could have been stolen by the true killer.

There were so many questions to be answered, and it pissed Charlie off. All he'd done was answer questions about the murder, and now there was at least one more, undoubtedly the biggest yet.

It had to be played just right, though. If Laureth was the killer, Charlie could ruin what little friendship he had with Officer Jones. However, if Laureth was innocent and Officer Jones had pulled the trigger, he couldn't let him off too easily because he felt closer to him.

"Fuck," Charlie said before spitting a wad of phlegm over the porch railing.

Several hours and three cigars later, the sun began to peek over the horizon. Charlie squinted his eyes against the light and flicked his cigar onto the lawn. He stood and stretched his stiff legs. Peeing off the front steps, he let out a moan.

"It's Wednesday," he said to the crisp morning air. "Great. One day until production."

He zipped his pants back up and went inside. Joni wasn't on the couch. He looked around and found her sitting at the small kitchen table sipping a cup of steaming coffee.

"You didn't sleep at all, did you?" she asked over her cup when he walked into the room.

He shook his head. "No. Couldn't. This is some heavy shit, Joni."

With sad eyes she said, "I know, babe."

Charlie sat down at the table across from her and grabbed her hands. "This sucks."

"I know."

"What should I do? I always have the answers, but this time I just don't know."

Joni smiled thinly. "Charlie Harrison, I will never believe you don't know what to do. You know. You just have to believe. You're a damned good journalist. Everyone thinks so. Even your dad. You always talk about wanting to make it big. This is your shot, baby."

Charlie nodded. "I guess. But I'm scared, Joni."

Joni smiled sweetly. "I know you are. But you can do it. Stop being a pussy."

Caught so off guard, Charlie burst out in laughter. Soon Joni joined him. When they regained their composure, Joni refilled her cup of coffee and brought Charlie one. She sat back down.

"So after a sleepless night of cigars, what kind of plan did you come up with?" Joni asked.

"Not a whole hell of a lot, actually," Charlie said, taking a drink of coffee.

"You've got nothing?" Joni asked skeptically.

Charlie grinned. "I've got a little more than nothing."

Joni stood up. "I bet you do. Now we better get ready for school. I'm going to go shower."

Charlie raised his coffee cup to her departure. "Have fun."

After getting ready, Charlie and Joni drove to campus. As they pulled into the parking lot, Officer Jones drove past them. Charlie waved as they met. Then he and Joni looked at other.

"Creepy," Joni said.

"Yeah. Very," Charlie said he pulled into a parking spot.

They walked to the *Clarion* offices hand in hand. Inside, Joni went to her desk, and Charlie went into his office, closing the door behind him. He sat down in his chair and took a deep breath. He knew what he needed to do. It wasn't something he wanted to, but this was a murder case. It had to be done.

Charlie picked up the phone and dialed the phone number of Deputy Bonner.

"Hello?" came the deputy's voice.

"Deputy Bonner. This is Charlie Harrison," Charlie began.

"Harrison. Great," Deputy Bonner said, cutting Charlie off. "What have I been telling you? You call every fucking day. Nothing has changed. The press conference is still taking place Friday. Jesus."

Charlie flipped on the digital recorder wired into the phone line. "I know. I know. This is about something else."

"Well, tough shit, Harrison. I'm not answering any more of your questions. You can wait until the press conference. It's only two days away."

"True, but . . ."

"No, Charlie. I don't care if you have to put out the paper tomorrow night. You'll just have to include what we announce at the presser in the next issue. Sorry."

Charlie sighed. "Please, Deputy Bonner. Listen to me."

"No."

"I don't have a goddamned question," Charlie said through gritted teeth. "I have something you need to know. Something you need to see."

"Bullshit, Charlie. You've pulled that kind of crap on me before. You make claims, but it always ends the same—you asking me a bunch of fucking questions. I'm not dealing with it. Not now. We're too close."

"But I think you could be closer. Like if you had the murder weapon."

"Listen, you little shit!" Deputy Bonner said loudly as he began to get angry. "We're the fucking cops. We'll worry about that. It's called routine police work. It's what we do. You just be a good little reporter and jot down what we tell you Friday. Got it?"

Charlie shook his head and pinched the bridge of his nose. "Fine. Fuck it. I'll just wait until the press conference. You win for now. Just know that you'll be sorry you didn't let me talk today. And I'm going to put that fact in my story."

"Shut the fuck up, Charlie. You ain't got shit."

"Whatever. You and the rest of the gang from Mayberry are going to be sorry."

"Go fuck yourself!" Deputy Bonner said before slamming the receiver down.

Charlie jerked the phone away from his ear. "Asshole."

He hung up and shut off the recorder. Leaning back in his chair, Charlie put his hands on top of his head. He looked at the wall across from him. He wasn't pleased with the way the call had went, but while playing it in his mind last night on his porch, he wasn't surprised either. He knew Deputy Bonner would react that way. That's why he had called him instead of Sheriff Giles. The sheriff might have let Charlie get a word in, and then Charlie would have had to tell them.

Instead, though, Charlie was now on the record as trying to tell the police they had found the gun that had to be the murder weapon. This kept them all a little safer with the law, Charlie figured. At least, he hoped.

Charlie slid up to his computer and turned it on. He hit the play button on the recorder and began to transcribe his conversation with Deputy Bonner. As far as Charlie was concerned, part one of his plan was finished, but there was still more to do. He had to start writing the story that was going to run in Friday's paper. He had to stay ahead of it because he planned to get Officer Jones on the record, but not until the last possible moment so nothing could interrupt the publishing of the *Clarion*.

He began to write the story. It was a shameless piece that painted him and his staff as heroes, but it told all the facts. And the fact was they had become a big part of the story because they had found the gun.

Charlie left places in the story for what Officer Jones would say, if anything. He also included a recap of everything they had reported before, including a preview of the upcoming press conference and the new quotes from Deputy Bonner, which clearly showed the sheriff's department had ignored an attempt by the *Clarion* to assist in the solving of the case. Charlie was careful not to say either Officer Jones or Dr. Laureth had committed the crime. He merely said how the gun, which appeared to be the murder weapon, belonged to Officer Jones, and how Dr. Laureth had a history of violence and was being held in custody as a prime suspect.

As Charlie saved the story, he knew it was solid, and he knew it would get even better once he talked to Officer Jones. That had to wait until right before they sent the pages to the printer, just in case Officer Jones really did it and tried to stop them from publishing the issue.

Looking at the clock on the wall, Charlie began to wonder where Tyler was. As he waited, he went about rearranging his desk and organizing his papers. He found the name of Dylan Parker.

"That little faggot," he said to himself. "I need to do a story about him. Next week, maybe. I'm winning an award this week."

As Charlie finished putting things in some semblance of order, Tyler and Hayley came into the office.

Charlie stood up and walked out of his office. "Where the hell have you two been?"

Tyler shrugged. "We were working. Then we got distracted."

Hayley giggled and blushed. "But we got almost all the stories for the next issue done," she said pulling a jump drive out of her jeans pocket and tossing it to Charlie.

Charlie sneered. "Good. Must not have been too long of a distraction then. You should work on that, Tyler."

Tyler stammered, trying to come up with something to say in response.

Charlie waved a hand at him. "Don't hurt yourself trying to insult me back. Besides, Ty, as long as you got yours, who cares?"

Joni came around the corner. "That's how Charlie does it. Trust me. I know."

Everyone laughed at Charlie's expense until he quieted them down. "Okay. Okay," Charlie said. "Enough. We've got to talk. I've got a story to show you."

He went back to his computer and printed off the story he had been working on. He handed copies to the other three and stood watching as they read it.

Hayley was the first one to finish reading it, and she looked at Charlie. "This is good. Really good."

Charlie nodded with a slight smile. "Thanks, Ginger."

"I agree," Tyler said. "We're going to look like heroes."

"Especially because we found the gun," Joni said.

"Yep," Charlie said proudly. "We'll have helped bring a murderer to justice, and the *Clarion* will finally be recognized by the Texas Intercollegiate Press Association."

"Thanks for saying I found the gun," Hayley said.

Charlie shrugged. "You did. I only report the facts," he said with a wink.

Studying the story, Tyler said, "You have these places where you plan to put quotes from Officer Jones. You think you know what he'll say?"

"No," Charlie said with a slight shake of his head. "I just put the quotes where it works if he says what I hope he does. I will probably have to do a little reworking once I talk to him."

"When are you going to do that?" Joni asked, since Charlie hadn't told her any of this earlier that morning.

Charlie looked at Joni with steady eyes. "Tomorrow night. I'm going to call his cell phone and get him to answer a few questions. We'll see what he says. I'll add it to the story quick, and we'll send it to the press."

Everyone nodded.

"Until then," Charlie said, "we go home and wait. We'll do production like normal tomorrow night."

"So then it is time to do some editing," Tyler said, pointing at the jump drive in his friend's hand.

"I guess so," Charlie said.

By 7:00 p.m. that night, everything was ready for the next day's production. All that remained was paginating the issue and finishing the final story. Everyone left and agreed to meet back at the offices by noon Thursday.

When they did, the air in the newsroom was electric with nervous excitement. The twins showed up at their prescribed time to do the layout. Charlie brought them up to speed about what was happening, and with grave faces, they went to work, trying to make the issue the best looking one yet.

By eight that night, the paper was nearly laid out. Joni went into Hooks to get food for everyone. When she got back, they ate with little talking. Everyone was too preoccupied about what Officer Jones would say. At 9:00 p.m., Charlie said he was going to call Officer Jones. He went into his office, and everyone else followed to listen in on the conversation.

Taking a deep breath, Charlie turned on his digital recorder, put the phone on speakerphone and called Officer Jones' cell phone.

"Hello?" Officer Jones answered groggily.

"Nick. It's Charlie. Did I wake you?" Charlie asked.

"No. No. I was just resting my eyes and watching a little TV. What's up, Charlie?"

Charlie swallowed hard. "Well, tomorrow's that press conference, and I've got a few questions about the murder. Bonner won't help me, so I was hoping you could."

Officer Jones was silent for a moment. "I don't know much, Charlie. No more than you really. I don't want to be involved in this."

"Well, that's okay. It's more of a question about guns. I don't know much, but I wanted to learned a little, uh, background so I can ask good questions tomorrow. You know about guns, right? Could you help?"

"Well," Officer Jones said slowly. "I don't know a lot, but I guess I could try to help you out."

"Great," Charlie said, taking a ragged breath. "The gun that killed Alison. What kind was it again?"

"I don't know, Charlie. It could have been any kind of gun that fired the right bullets."

"Right. What kind of bullets were they, though?"

"It was a .45-caliber. Probably a handgun, according to Sheriff Giles."

"Oh. Okay. And a bullet that size, how many would it take to kill someone?"

Officer Jones thought for a moment. "That depends on where a person is shot."

"Okay. But Alison was shot four times. Why do you think that is?"

Officer Jones sighed. "I don't know, Charlie. Alison was shot in all the right places. Any one of the shots would have been enough. Sheriff Giles said it looked like the shooter wanted to make sure she was dead."

Charlie looked at the others but said nothing to them. Then to Officer Jones, he said, "Why would the shooter want to make sure she was dead?"

"Why did the guy shoot her in the first place?"

"True, but how much knowledge would a person have to have to know where to shoot a person?"

"Not a lot. Any murder-mystery movie would have it spelled out."

"Okay. But the gun. Would it need anything special to do it?"

"What do you mean?"

Charlie's mind raced to quickly come up with an explanation. When he came up with one a few seconds later, he said, "Well, in the movies the bad guy usually has a silencer or a pillow to help keep the noise down. You think this gun had anything like that?"

Officer Jones said nothing for a moment.

"Nick? You still there?" Charlie asked.

"Yeah. I'm here."

"So you think there was a silencer or something on the killer's gun?"

"Maybe," Officer Jones said slowly. "No one reported hearing a gunshot that night. What are you getting at, Charlie?"

"Well," Charlie said, again scrambling for words. "I'm just curious about this gun. I just think it might be the missing link in the case. And I want to ask Sheriff Giles about it, since the gun's never been found."

Officer Jones said nothing.

"So," Charlie said, hurriedly continuing. "I just want to see a .45-caliber gun. To get a better idea of what we're dealing with. Do you have one I could see?"

"Uh, well . . . ," Officer Jones stammered. "I do. Did. But . . ."

"What do you mean, Nick?"

"I have a .45, but I don't know where it is."

"What do you mean? Was it stolen or something?"

"No. No. I always keep it in the house. Never take it out, and if I'm not here, I keep the house locked up."

"So where is it?" Charlie asked, leaning closer to the phone with excitement.

"I don't know. I-I must have just misplaced it."

"Oh. Okay. That sucks. You sure someone didn't steal it?" Charlie asked again.

"No. It wasn't stolen."

"You think you'll ever find it?"

"I don't know. It doesn't matter. You have any other questions?"

Charlie leaned back and stared at the phone. He couldn't believe what Officer Jones was saying. He clearly had no idea the group had found his gun, and his answers weren't painting a good picture for himself.

"Uh, yeah," Charlie finally said. "Do you think Dr. Laureth did it? Because that's probably what they're going to say in the morning."

"Like I told you before, Charlie. I don't know."

"But do you think he might have had reason to do it?"

"People do things for different reasons. I don't know."

Charlie sighed. "Okay. But assuming Sheriff Giles is going to announce charges against Dr. Laureth in the morning, you think he's doing it just because he's up for re-election and wants to use a conviction as a reason he should be reelected?"

"Jesus Christ, Charlie!" Officer Jones shouted into the phone. "The sheriff's a better man than that! Enough! If you're going to ask such stupid questions, we're done talking!"

"Okay. Okay," Charlie said loudly. "I'm done. Just calm down. Thanks for your time, Nick."

"Yeah. Sure," Officer Jones said before hanging up.

Charlie shut off the recorder and turned off the speakerphone. He looked at the crowd gathered around him with raised eyebrows. "So? What does anyone think?"

"He still might not have done it," Joni said. "Maybe the gun was stolen, and he just doesn't realize it. Maybe he truly thinks he just misplaced it."

Charlie shook his head. "I don't think so," he said sadly. "My gut says he did it. He was too dodgy on those questions."

"Yeah, but he never gave a reason he would have done it," Joni said.

"He did ask," Tyler said. "I hate to say it, but I think he did it too."

Hayley nodded. "It sure sounds like it."

"Yep," Charlie said, turning to his computer. "And now I've got a story to write."

"But we can't say he did it," Tyler said urgently.

"I know," Charlie said. "I'll hedge around it. Whatever I write might flush him out. At least I hope it does. This campus needs closure."

"And we need that award, right?" Tyler said dryly.

Charlie managed a weak smile. "Why not? We've earned it."

Charlie began typing in everything Officer Jones had said, using the recording as a reference. It took a little reworking to make it flow, but soon it was done and the twins stripped the story across the top of the front page.

Charlie looked over the issue one last time before sending it to the press. Everyone agreed to stay at the office all night to wait for the edition.

They played cards all night, drinking Coke to help stay awake. When they heard the paper being dropped off at the front door, they all rushed to get them and bring them into the office. No one said a word to Drew, which struck the pressman as odd, but he didn't care. He had to get back to the news office to ready for a special issue. The *Bowie County News* was planning a special, extra edition to cover the expected announcement of charges being filed in the murder case.

Inside the *Clarion*, the staffers looked over the paper. The images of Officer Jones and Dr. Laureth helped really draw attention to Charlie's story at the top of the page.

"This looks good, everyone," Charlie said.

"So should we deliver it?" Hayley asked.

"No," Tyler said before Charlie could answer. "We need to wait. Deliver it right before the press conference. That way nothing can happen to the copies, and we can hand out copies at the conference."

Charlie smiled. "I like it."

Chapter Thirty-one

Thirty minutes before the press conference began, the six *Clarion* staffers split up the newspapers and spread out across campus. They quickly distributed the copies at the various newsstands, handing out copies to students they passed. Along the way, Tyler swung by his dorm room and put the gun, still in it its plastic sack, into a backpack, which he slung over his shoulders.

With just a couple minutes to spare, the group rendez-voused back at the golf course clubhouse. The patio was packed with reporters and cameras, easily three times as many than were there during the last press conference. Most were wearing jackets or long-sleeved shirts to cut against the cool breeze.

Charlie had a bundle of newspapers tucked under his arm. When he met the other five, the twins, Joni, and Hayley grabbed the bundle from Charlie. They split it and entered the crowd of reporters. They handed a copy to everyone there while Charlie and Tyler pushed their way to the front of the crowd.

Just as the other reporters were finishing Charlie's story, Sheriff Giles and Deputy Bonner stepped out of the club-house and up to the lectern. St. Alfanus President Alcott, wiping his eyes with a handkerchief, and Director of Marketing and Public Information Paula Garcia were with them, as well as County Attorney Leslie Black, who was smiling devilishly, and Officer Jones.

Charlie looked at Tyler. "Oh shit. He's here."

With wide eyes, Tyler nodded his head. "Yep. Holy shit."

Behind them, the other reporters were beginning to talk in a moderate murmur among themselves. Sheriff Giles stepped up to the many microphones and tapped on them loudly. This time no television reporter or camera operator scolded him. They were busy reading the *Clarion*.

"Hello, everyone," Sheriff Giles said in his typical drawl. "I'm so glad you could make it."

The crowd turned a portion of its attention to the sheriff, though they continued to talk to each other.

"We have some important news to briefly share with you today," Sheriff Giles continued. "Recently Dr. Arthur Laureth was arrested for attacking one of his students here on campus, where he is an English professor. It then came to our attention, due to a history of violence in his past, he could be behind the murder of Alison Alcott. County Attorney Leslie Black, who is with us here today, did not hesitate in issuing a search warrant of the home of Laureth. There we found something very important. We found four spent rounds fired from a .45-caliber gun. This matched the method Alison was killed. The evidence is damning, folks. Therefore, Ms. Black has filed charges of first-degree murder against Laureth. I'm proud to say, with President Alcott here, we got the sorry son of a gun who did this to the beautiful Alison Alcott. People of Hooks and Bowie County can once again rest easy. The Bowie County Sheriff's Department has taken this murderer off the streets. Everything is safe once again."

Everyone standing behind Sheriff Giles began clapping, though the gallery of reporters stayed silent and had confused looks on their faces. Sheriff Giles embraced President Alcott and shook hands with Deputy Bonner, Leslie Black, and Officer Jones.

He then stepped back up to the microphones. "Now, I will take a few questions."

A newspaper reporter from Dallas shot his hand into the air. Sheriff Giles recognized him.

"Sheriff, what about the gun? If the student newspaper reporters found it, why didn't your department listen to them? How can you be sure Laureth did this?" the reporter asked.

Sheriff Giles' face flushed. "What are you talking about?"

Hayley strode to the front and handed the sheriff a copy of the paper. He quickly read it and growled, "Sonofabitch!"

"That's right," Charlie said suddenly as he stepped forward. "Deputy Bonner wouldn't listen to me when I called him and told him we found what we believed to be the murder weapon."

"What?" Deputy Bonner shouted before snatching the paper from Sheriff Giles.

"Tyler, the gun," Charlie said, motioning for the bag.

Tyler handed Charlie his backpack, and Charlie unzipped it and pulled the gun, still in the plastic sack, out. He held it up for everyone to see. "We at the *Clarion* decided the murder weapon had to be out there somewhere since nothing had turned up yet. We figured the Bowie County Sheriff's Department hadn't looked in the pond behind the fourteenth green. We were right. We found this. It is a Colt .45. It has a silencer on it, and it has a tiny bag tied to it to catch all the spent shells, as you all read in the story. That bag has four spent rounds in it. The exact number used to take the life of Alison. The shells found at Dr. Laureth's house can't be the right shells."

The crowd of reporters began to talk loudly, some shouting questions at Sheriff Giles. He looked like he was about to faint. Deputy Bonner had passed the paper to Leslie Black and Officer Jones. They were reading the story.

Tyler looked at Charlie and was impressed. He was showing a lot of guts doing this, but he was just repeating what had been reported in the *Clarion*, for the most part. Even so, Tyler felt pride rise up inside of him. He was proud to be a journalist, a reporter for the *Clarion* and most of all, Charlie's friend. He hoped he could be as good of a journalist as Charlie.

Charlie shouted over the roar of the crowd, "Also! The gun doesn't belong to Dr. Laureth! It belongs to Officer Jones! Nick Jones!"

Sheriff Giles spun to face Officer Jones, and Deputy Bonner put a hand on Officer Jones' shoulder as he began to reach for his handcuffs. Officer Jones' face turned red.

"You motherfucker!" Officer Jones yelled, pointing at Charlie.

Deputy Bonner tried to grab Officer Jones by the wrist, but Officer Jones swung and connected with a punch to the deputy's jaw. He staggered back, and Officer Jones grabbed the gun from the deputy's holster. President Alcott and Paula Garcia ran back into the clubhouse, and Leslie Black jumped off the patio. The crowd of reporters all ducked down, but cameras continued to roll and pictures continually snapped.

Sheriff Giles spun around and reached for his own gun. "Put it down, Nick!" he shouted, pointing his gun at Officer Jones.

"Fuck you, Bill! This little asshole doesn't know what he's doing! He's just a dumb kid!" Officer Jones shouted at Charlie, who hadn't ducked because he was frozen with fear.

Tyler was crouched on the patio, covering the heads of Joni and Hayley with his arms. As he watched the scene unfold, he saw Officer Jones tighten his grip on the trigger of Deputy Bonner's gun.

"Just calm down, Nick! It isn't too late!"

"Yes it is!" Officer Jones screamed with an anguished face as tears began to seep from his pained eyes. "It's way too late!"

"You don't want to do this!" Sheriff Giles shouted back.

"Why not?" Officer Jones said with desperation. "Alison's already dead. I'll go to jail a long damn time. This all could have been avoided if Gerry had just started treating me like I deserved. I've been working here a long fucking time, Bill. He could have given me a raise. Given me more time off. Instead, he treated me like his nigger bitch."

"I understand, Nick," Sheriff Giles said as he inched closer to Officer Jones. "Just put the gun down."

Tears were streaming down Officer Jones' face. "No. I won't. I could have gotten away with it. No one would have known. I would have felt better about things because Gerry would be hurting as much as I am. All I wanted was a little respect. I thought he was my friend, but he just wouldn't act like it. Then you and Randall came up with a way to pin it on Laureth. It was perfect, but Charlie here fucked it all up!" he exclaimed with venomous hatred.

Sheriff Giles was stunned beyond words. He said nothing but continued to inch closer.

"Stop! Don't move anymore!" Officer Jones shouted, turning the gun toward Sheriff Giles.

He froze in place but still pointed his gun at the security guard. "Okay, okay, Nick. Don't do anything hasty."

"Fuck you," Officer Jones said in a barely audible whisper.

He turned the gun back toward Charlie, who was still frozen in place with his eyes wide and hands shaking. The sacked gun had fallen to the patio long ago.

"What do you have to say, Charlie?" Officer Jones asked, the gun trained on his chest.

Charlie shook his head and mouth in a "sorry," but no words came through his teeth.

Officer Jones sneered through his tears. "Sucks knowing your life's about to end, doesn't it? Alison pissed herself. At least you and I haven't stained our shorts yet."

Charlie's eyes widened even more. Officer Jones squeezed the trigger. The crack of the gun echoed off the clubhouse. The reporters screamed and hit the ground. The bullet flew from the end of the barrel. It struck Charlie in the center of the chest. Blood sprayed out around him. He let out a groan and stumbled backward until he fell to the ground in a pool of his own blood.

Sheriff Giles yelled and fired his gun three times. Officer Jones's body jerked as each bullet slammed into him. Deputy Bonner's gun slipped from his fingers, and as he fell over the lectern, a strange smile crossed his face.

Joni began screaming hysterically and scrambled to Charlie's side. She pressed her hands to his chest, trying to stop the flow of blood gushing from the wound. Tyler and Hayley joined her, both crying and talking to Charlie. They told him to hang on and that he'd be okay.

The reporters in the crowd began standing up. Some shot pictures of the scene, while others stood staring at what was before them, cameras and note pads dangling limply at their sides. All of them had tears running down their faces.

Sheriff Giles went to Officer Jones and checked for a pulse. Then he looked at the group huddled over Charlie. He grabbed his radio and called for an ambulance.

When the paramedics arrived, Tyler had to help pull Joni away so they could work on Charlie. They quickly lifted him on a stretcher and loaded him into the back of an ambulance. Joni, who was crying so hard she was dry heaving, forced her way onto the ambulance. The paramedics gave up fighting her and raced away toward the Hooks Hospital.

As the ambulance left, Tyler held Hayley as they both cried and watched it leave. The other reporters began to attempt to ask Sheriff Giles questions, but he refused to answer them.

The reporters began to leave, but Tyler and Hayley didn't move. They stood on the putting green crying. A couple times Hayley had to pull away to vomit, but every time she did, she came back up to Tyler's arms.

Tyler tried to sooth her, but he was trying to cope with what had just happened himself.

PART FOUR

Chapter Thirty-two

The hot May sun beat down on Tyler's bare shoulders as he arrived at the gate. He carried his shirt in his hand, and he made sure it was still rolled tight. Carrying it with him, he pushed open the gate. It squeaked loudly in the still air.

As he stepped through the threshold of the gateway, Tyler's nostrils were bombarded by the smell of fragrant flowers. The sound of mosquitoes and honeybees buzzing in flight filled his ears.

Tyler looked around. Headstones of varying colors filled the fenced-in cemetery. Sprinkled around nearly every tombstone were flowers of different colors. Several had American flags and wreaths stuck in the ground near them. People hadn't come back to pick up their Memorial Day decorations yet, though the sign at the gate said they only had a couple days to do so before the cemetery sexton threw them away so he could mow.

Seeing so many gravesites made Tyler sad. Not for himself, but for the families of the deceased. In his year at St. Alfanus, he had experienced more death than he ever cared to. Even though this cemetery was miles from Hooks and on the outskirts of a Dallas suburb, Tyler knew that the deaths in Hooks reached far beyond its city limits.

He slowly made his way through the cemetery, looking at each gravestone. Seeing the names with dates marking births and deaths, made him realize how short life was.

At the far corner of the cemetery, Tyler could see a black marble headstone glittering in the sun. The dirt stretching out from the tombstone had little grass growing on it. Tyler cut across the cemetery toward it.

When Tyler got to the tombstone, he knelt at the base and looked at the name engraved. It read: Charlie Douglas Harrison.

"Hey, Charlie," Tyler said, his eyes misting up with tears. "How are ya, buddy?"

Tyler ran a hand over Charlie's name.

"I've been good," Tyler said. "Thanks for asking."

Tyler smiled and chuckled quietly.

"I just wanted to stop by and say hello. You know, catch you up to speed on what you've missed."

Tyler sat down on the dirt and faced Charlie's tombstone. Sitting cross-legged, he rested his elbows on his knees and folded his hands under his chin.

"First, I guess you should know Joni misses the shit out of you. God knows why. She graduated. Your parents took her in and are helping her out. She's finally started to get a handle on what happened. When I talked to her yesterday, she told me she was going to be moving out here with your folks and going to work for them. She's doing okay. Don't worry about it. I'll help keep an eye on her as much as I can, but you know that won't be an easy task."

Tyler wiped his eyes.

"They put up a special plaque for you in Cormac Hall. President Alcott told me several times how grateful he was you were around and helped find his daughter's killer. Too bad you weren't there to hear it. You wouldn't have believed the nice crap he was saying about you. Guess if he really knew you, he'd have thought twice about most of it. As for the case itself, that got kind of interesting after . . . well, you know."

Tyler took a breath.

"Anyway, Nick died the next day. I don't know if you saw it or not, but Sheriff Giles shot him after he, uh, shot you. I'm pretty sure I told you that at the funeral, but even if I didn't, I figure you need to know. And it's just as well. Better than him just sitting in a prison with free room and board, right?

"Well, after that and going by some of what Nick said, an investigation took place. Looks like Sheriff Giles was as crooked as you thought. He was going to pin the murder on Dr. Laureth. Deputy Bonner was in on it. So was that attorney lady, Leslie Black. A district attorney came in and fired them all before he arrested them for a bunch of stuff I can't even remember. They'll be locked up for a good while, and they'll never wear a badge again. When Dr. Laureth caught wind of it, he sued the shit out of Bowie County. He got a nice settlement. He left St. Alfanus. Last I heard, he was moving to Montana. His girl, Bethany, transferred to the University of Alabama. He told me he had no hard feelings toward you. He said he knew you were just doing what you thought you needed to. So that's good, I guess."

Tyler stopped talking for a moment and looked up at the sky. A single sparrow flew overhead. In his mind, Tyler believed it was Charlie swinging by to say hello.

He looked back at the headstone. "Oh, and your buddy Graham is about finished with his book. He's been busting his ass to get it finished. He caught me at the funeral and told me what was going on. He seems like a good guy. He really liked, likes you. I've been helping him with the book as much as possible.

"Speaking of the funeral, it was beautiful, man. Sorry I couldn't give a better speech. I was just . . . it was too . . . I guess I'm a pussy. But I miss you, man. You're my best friend."

Tyler dropped his face into his hands. Sobs wracked his body. He sat there crying for some time before he was able to regain his composure.

"Sorry," he said, wiping his nose on the back of his hand. "Sorry. I guess what you're probably really wanting to know is how the newspaper went. We finished the year at the *Clarion*. Me, Joni, and Hayley. I think we would have done you proud. I handled the coverage of everything that happened with you and the case after that day. I did my best to channel my inner Charlie. I didn't realize how much I'd learned from you until I had to do it without you.

"Oh, and you know how you were so worried about winning an award? Well, you did."

Tyler unrolled his shirt and pulled out a laminated copy of a certificate. Holding it up to the tombstone, Tyler said, "This is the award for Texas Intercollegiate Press Association Journalist of the Year. They presented it to you posthumously. You got a standing ovation, man. Going up to accept it for you was almost as hard as being at the funeral. The *Clarion* also won Best Newspaper of the Year, and you and I won awards for our reporting on the murder. It was a great day at the awards. I wish you could have been there."

Tyler laid the certificate on the ground and pulled a couple of railroad spikes out of his shirt. He drove the spikes through two edges of the certificate to hold it in place so it wouldn't blow away.

"I do have something else to tell you about the paper, Charlie. I'm not going back next year. I'm not going to be the editor like everyone thought. And neither is Hayley. Neither of us is going to work there. We just can't take it. It's too tough. Too many memories. They have hired someone else to be the editor, and it's a friend of yours, I think. His name is Dylan Parker. You two are close, right?"

At this joke, Tyler burst out in laughter, and for a moment it felt like Charlie was right next to him laughing too.

"I know," Tyler said. "It's a bad joke. But he really is. The *Clarion*'s going to go to shit, which sucks, but you left your mark. No one will ever be able to deny that. Hell, you marked that entire campus. You're a legend now, buddy. Isn't that great? I guess I kind of made my mark too. I won the

NAIA Championship. By two strokes. Coach Grower was so excited I think he might have come in his pants."

Tyler was smiling, but he wasn't happy. He didn't want to tell Charlie his next bit of news, but he knew he had to.

"There's one other thing, Charlie. I'm leaving St. Alfanus. I'm transferring schools. After I won the championship, I got offers from D-one and D-two schools. I chose Wichita State up in Kansas. It's close to home. I thought it would be a hard decision, but with you gone and knowing I couldn't stand to work at the paper without you, I decided pretty quick. Hayley was pissed at first, but she's okay with it now. We're going to try the long distance thing. I think it'll work. She graduates next year anyway. Who knows? Maybe she'll be able to move up to Wichita with me then.

"And don't worry, I'm going to work on the paper there. It's called *The Scribe*. I know, it sounds pretty gay, but it's a good paper. Hopefully it will be nice and quiet. At least nothing as exciting as the shit we went through here. Really, though, I've been looking at it. They've got a website, just like we talked about setting up. I'm going to try to learn more web stuff. I want to be a journalist. A good one. I want to make you proud.

"I'm actually on my way back home now. I rented a car to drive home. I've got it loaded down. I'll be back in Kansas sooner than I think, I guess. But don't worry, I'm still going to keep an eye on Joni. Like I promised. And I'm going to come down from time to time to say hello and check on you too."

Tyler stood up and brushed his shorts off. He pulled his shirt over his head and stood looking down at Charlie's grave. He placed a hand on the top of the stone. It was warm from the sun.

"I love you, Charlie," he said. "See you soon."

Tyler turned and walked away. He left the cemetery and climbed into his car. Starting the engine, he took one more look across the cemetery toward Charlie's grave. Then he shifted into drive and pointed the car north. Toward Kansas. Toward home.

Chapter Thirty-three

Mary Thomas walked across the campus of Wichita State University as birds chirped and a light breeze rustled the trees. She had a tall cup of coffee in her hand and the latest copy of *The Wichita Eagle* tucked under her arm.

Entering Elliott Hall, she took a sip of her coffee and took the flight of stairs to the basement. She fished her keys out of her pocket and unlocked the door to the offices of the *Scribe*. She went inside and unlocked her own office before sitting down at her desk.

Mary was the business manager at the student newspaper serving Wichita State. She was a permanent staff member in her fifties. The position she held used to be a student position, but the paper's budget had gotten out of hand. So several years ago, the position became a job for someone hired by the university. The rest of the staff positions were held by students, though, so the paper stayed independent of the school.

Mary enjoyed her job. Working with the college students made her feel younger, and she loved seeing what they produced. Publishing three times per week while maintaining a full course load was no small feat, and Mary was proud to be a part of the *Scribe*.

She turned on her computer and unfolded the *Eagle*. She flipped to the sports section and saw the story she was looking for at the top of the page. The headline read: Shockers sign golf phenom.

"There he is," Mary said with a smile as she looked at the picture of Tyler Fox.

She wasn't interested in his golfing ability. Instead, she was interested in the second half of the story, which talked about Tyler's work at the *St. Alfanus Clarion*. He had helped uncover a murderer, winning several journalism awards for the effort, and now he was going to come to work for the *Scribe*.

"He's going to help a lot," Mary said to herself.

Someone came in the front door. Mary looked up. It was the *Scribe*'s editor, Cory Johnson. Cory was a mousey man. He was short and walked with a strange, bouncing step. His hands were always moving, his fingers seeming to be stuck onto his hands at odd angles.

"Hi, Mary," he said in his scratchy voice as he walked in past the receptionist desk and gave an awkward wave.

"Morning, Cory," Mary said as he went and unlocked his own office, which was next to Mary's.

Mary rolled her eyes. Cory was destroying the *Scribe*. He didn't understand how to work with people, and his judgment of what was news and what wasn't had made the *Scribe* less reputable than it had ever been. Mary's eyes drifted back to the picture of Tyler.

"I hope you can save us," she said, patting the story with her hand.

Another person came through the door. It was the *Scribe*'s old advertising manager who was now the marketing director, Lisa Wilson.

Lisa made a beeline for Mary's office and sat down in a chair across from Mary. "How you doing, Mary?" she asked brightly as she ran a hand through her shoulder-length blonde hair.

"Better," Mary said.

"What? Why?" Lisa asked with confusion.

Mary turned the paper so Lisa could see the story. "Read this," she said.

Lisa picked up the paper and quickly read the story. "He's a stud, eh?"

"Yeah," Mary said proudly. "And he's coming to work for us. We'll finally have a real journalist. Maybe we can get

him to be editor when Tweedledee next door finally graduates and leaves."

Lisa smiled. "That would be nice. And he's a junior? So
he'll be in my class. Cool. He's cute," she said, leaning closer
to Mary and smiling.

Mary smiled. "I thought you might like him. It took some
convincing, but I got him hired."

Lisa's eyes widened. "Cory didn't hire him? That little
egomaniac is going to flip."

"Who cares?" Mary said with a wave of the hand. "We
need him. You saw how Cory messed up that story about
the campus stabbing. This Tyler boy would have done better.
Maybe he can help."

"True," Lisa said with a nod, "but how often does that
kind of stuff happen?"

"Stabbings? Not too often anymore. Things have gotten
safer around here, you know that, but think about this. Our
readership is dropping. The students think the *Scribe* is a
joke. A real journalist like him might be able to help turn us
around and get us back to actually turning a profit."

Lisa nodded. "That would be nice. I love working here. I'd
hate to see it close down."

Mary nodded slowly. "Yep."

"But how?" Lisa asked. "How could this new guy actually
help? Corey has sunk this paper in deep."

"I know he has, and I don't know how Tyler can help,"
Mary said. "Maybe he can't. But maybe he can. Taking a
chance with him is a lot better than just letting the *Scribe* dry
up and die."

"Sorry, but that was funny," Lisa smiled broadly. "You're
right. He could help, but Tyler's going to be worrying about
golf too. He probably won't have a lot of time for the paper."

"I know. And I feel bad for him. He seems like a nice
kid, but Lisa, he could save this paper. You know it's in bad
shape. You've seen the sales numbers. And the Student Fees
Committee is getting colder and colder toward us. We need a
boost. Tyler could be that boost."

Lisa thought about this a moment and nodded. "True. If he's as good as this story makes him out to be, he might be able to save us."

"Exactly," Mary said. "He's a journalist. A really good one. He could be our savior."

CPSIA information can be obtained at www.ICGtesting.com
Printed in the USA
LVOW040249220312

274258LV00001B/114/P